Other books by James Hanna

The Siege: A Prison Uprising Redefines Justice
Call Me Pomeroy: A Novel of Satire and Political Dissent
A Second, Less Capable, Head: And Other Rogue Stories

I0540813

Forthcoming….. *The Ping-Pong Champion of Chinatown*

Awards received by James Hanna...

The 2017 Readers' Favorite International Awards gave James Hanna's novel, *Call Me Pomeroy*, the gold medal in the humor category.

The 2017 Readers' Favorite International Awards gave James Hanna's novel, *The Siege*, the bronze medal in the literary fiction category.

The 2017 Independent Press Awards gave James Hanna's short story collection, *A Second, Less Capable Head and Other Rogue Stories*, a silver medal in the anthology category.

The 2018 Readers' Favorite International Awards gave James Hanna's short story collection, *A Second, Less Capable Head and Other Rogue Stories*, the gold medal in the anthology category.

Shackles and More Gripping Tales

By James Hanna

Shackles and More Gripping Tales

By James Hanna

Published by Sand Hill Review Press www.sandhillreviewpress.com,
1 Baldwin Ave, #304, San Mateo, CA 94401
(415) 297-3571

Library of Congress Control Number: 2018951954
ISBN: 978-1-949534-030 Case Laminate
ISBN: 978-1-949534-023 Paperback
ISBN: 978-1-949534-047 Ebook

Art Direction by Tory Hartmann, Sand Hill Review Press
Graphics by Backspace Ink.

SHRP
Sand Hill Review Press
1 BALDWIN AVE, #304, SAN MATEO, CA 94401

To Clyde James Hanna

SHACKLES AND MORE GRIPPING TALES

The following stories have previously appeared in these literary magazines and anthologies:

Title	First Published
Tower Duty	*Sixfold /Trampset*
The Sugar Shack Dress Company	*Red Savina Review*
The Hangings	*A Lonely Riot/Literally Stories*
The Time My Dad Chewed Out a Cop	*JokesReview/Literally Stories*
I'm Going to Kick Some Ass	*The Flagler Review*
Hayley's Picnic	*Fear of Monkeys*
Summer of Love	No prior publication
USA	*The Broke Bohemian/Fear of Monkeys*
Deceptive	*BioStories/Literally Stories*
Spooks Alive	No prior publication
I am Not a Crook	No prior publication
The Phoenix Climbs	*Red Savina Review*
The World Baseball League	*A Lonely Riot*
Little Darling	*Trampset/Curious Things*
Sam the Poontang Man	*Empty Sink Publishing/Fear of Monkeys*
Like a Motherfucker	*Trampset*
Bull Croc	*Fault Zone*
Busting Willie Sherman	*Literally Stories*
The Time Dad Took Me to a Whorehouse	*The Hunger*
Busting Yu Yan	No prior publication
Shackles	*Sandhills Review* (Under the title "The Holding Cell")

Contents

Introduction

James Hanna has been a regular contributor to the short fiction site, *Literally Stories*, for several years now. His diverse work is always popular and his story, "The Time My Dad Chewed Out a Cop," was chosen as a reader's favorite. His work is entertaining and accessible even though he most often uses his stories to examine the darker side of life with characters who are damaged by their reality.

Whatever the subject matter, James displays an acute perception of the world we live in. He explores the issues of exploitation, boundaries, temptation, social acceptability, the law, and corruption often through the actions of unsavory characters with their own selfish agendas.

James' social commentary is clear throughout his work. Whether it is from the passivity of the old couple in "The Hangings," with their strange acceptance of their pending execution, the innocence of the hustler in "Sam the Poontang Man," who learns that everything depends on who you take money from, or the hubris of the Cop in "Busting Yu Yan," who is willing to use entrapment as a means to an end. All these characters are well-observed and therefore recognizable to the reader.

There is a wryness in all of James Hanna's work and therefore a touch of devilment. He also balances his stories perfectly with a subtle counterpoint. James uses the hidden, unsavory side of our character to fuel the issues in this very colorful and immensely entertaining collection. The stories are multilayered and each one, in its own way, requires some contemplation from the reader. This means that you never truly remove yourself from a James Hanna story. We at *Literally Stories* believe that this is a great collection of short fiction.

Diane Dickson, Nik Eveleigh & Hugh Cron
Editors at *Literally Stories*

Tower Duty

WHEN CANCER TOOK MURRAY, I was such an ingrate. Weren't my forty years of marriage to him enough? Weren't the two daughters God gave us enough? He lived almost a year after Doctor Diver diagnosed his brain tumor—wasn't that enough? Why must we set our hearts on things that must be limited? The Lord gives, the Lord takes—we should let it go at that.

How I wish I could follow my own advice. When that dark shadow fell across Murray's bed, I bawled like a calf. "Not yet, Bunny," I said. "Not yet." But he slipped away from me without saying so much as a word. My God, I'd have given my very soul for another day with him. But souls like mine are a penny a dozen. Why on earth would God make an exemption for a dumpy little housewife from Newcastle? A bailiff's daughter who'd lived her whole life in a podunk Indiana town?

Yet, the Lord wanted *Murray's* soul—why I can't imagine. A TV hound, a sloppy drunk, and an absentee father, he was in *no way* remarkable. The Lord might have just as well left him with me for all the good he was. Goodness, was he really worth all my tears? I think some women are criers, and that's all that needs to be said about it.

Still, I was such a wreck at the funeral that Billie and Sarah Jean, our daughters, had to hold me up. Afterwards, I went to see Father Mulligan at The Holy Family Cathedral. Father Mulligan is such a well-meaning man—I wish I had treated him better. "We cannot understand God's ways," he told me in a voice that could butter pancakes. "But know that he loves you, Loretta."

I wanted to scratch his eyes out, I wanted to slap his face. "If you *ever* want me back in your parish," I snapped, "you will have to say more than 'God loves you.'"

After Murray was laid to rest, I volunteered at the Newcastle Food Pantry. I had to keep myself busy so as not to lose my mind. So every day, for three hours a day, I handed out Spam and boxes of cornflakes to people down on their luck. It helped to not be so selfish, it helped to think about others for a while. Sometimes, I even held hands with them and we said a little prayer.

But each afternoon, after working in the pantry, I visited Murray's grave. The small things were what I remembered most: how he hogged the covers at night, how he always drove five miles under the speed limit, how he liked his morning coffee black with four teaspoons of sugar. One afternoon as I stood by his grave, his voice popped into my head. It gave me such a fright that I dropped my memorial roses. *Stop wasting your time, Loretta*, he said. *Go back to the church, I'm not here.* How sanctimonious he sounded—is that what death does to a soul? If he wants to nag me like a bill collector, I'd rather he just move on. He was a whole lot nicer before God took him—I guess because he was soused half the time.

One afternoon, as I stood by Murray's grave, I noticed two trees on a hill. One of the trees was lush and flowering, the other was leafless and gnarled. And I realized my life was just like those two trees. My youthful bloom was gone—I was pretty when I was young. But now I was like the second tree—twisted, old, and droopy, but still of some use to the birds. Thank God, I was learning to look up.

•

MURRAY NEVER EARNED much money as a representative for Universal Windows. He was mostly paid in commissions, and he wasn't that good a salesman. But although I know how to make do with little, I still needed to find a job. That isn't so easy for a woman of sixty who hobbles like a goose. Thirty years ago, I broke my knee when I fell off a step ladder. Doctor Diver said I needed surgery, but who has time for that? With two daughters to raise and a husband to feed, I had to stay on my feet. "Don't tell me how to run my life," I said to Doctor Diver. That was the last time he ever spoke to me about surgery.

A month after Murray passed, I went to Walmart and asked for a job. The manager said they weren't hiring. I also applied at Target, but they didn't want me either. I even went to the local college and asked for a job in the cafeteria. "I make a real mean pot roast," I told the personnel director. He was a pleasant man with a comb-over and a little pot belly like Murray's. Well, he put me on a waiting list, but never called me back.

I finally got a job as a guard at the Indiana Penal Farm—a factory farm correctional facility five miles out of town. Imagine me wearing a blue uniform and telling grown men what to do. But they're always hiring at the Penal Farm, I should have gone there first. They have to staff three shifts, so they hire any warm body.

Major Bundy, who interviewed me, asked so many questions. "Can you say no to inmates?" "Could you shoot a man from a tower?" "Do rapists and thieves disgust you?" I guess he was trying to frighten me, but he didn't scare me one whit. We're all God's children under the skin. We all need the love of the Lord. And since the job was mostly sitting, it wouldn't be hard on my knee.

They sent me to a two-week training academy at the Westville Correctional Facility—this enormous fenced-in complex beside Lake Michigan. I learned how to search a bunk; I learned how to fire a Mini-14, which is a lot like a squirrel gun. I also learned how to keep my mouth shut when the instructors were trying to talk. Lieutenant Brady, who ran most of our classes, took me aside on my first day of training. Such a serious little man he was, and he scowled like Old Man Winter. "Loretta," he said, his voice sharper than a tack. "You've told me, 'God bless you' six times today. *Nobody* needs that much blessing."

•

WHEN I SHOWED UP at the Farm for my first morning roll call, Major Bundy summoned me into his office. "Can you say no to inmates?" he repeated—my, what a tiresome question. I told him he needed to say no to doughnuts—that man must weigh four hundred pounds. He said, "Honey, we don't need wise apples here."

"Apples for you would be wise," I said.

Major Bundy laughed like a donkey—I guess the man has a good heart. "Be careful here, Loretta," he said as he rubbed his heavy jowls. "This work's not for everyone."

They paired me up with Officer Whitley who worked in the intake and processing unit. It's a long narrow building with unwaxed floors where newly arrived prisoners are housed. Our job was to assign the new inmates to cells when they got off the prison bus. We also marched them to the dining hall for meals.

Officer Whitley, a silver-haired gentleman in his seventies, gave me a piece of advice. "Let 'em know when you're walking the range," he said. "Rattle your keys, shuffle your feet, whistle a tune real loud. You catch 'em doing drugs or something, you'll have to write 'em up. If you write up too many of these scumbags, you may end up getting jumped."

But the inmates didn't seem mean to me—not as mean as Officer Whitley. They nodded politely and called me ma'am and asked me for something to read. The fish—that's what they call new inmates—are not allowed to have books. They just sit in cramped cells day after day while they wait to be assigned jobs. My God, even robbers and thieves don't deserve to be that bored.

On Sundays, we marched the fish to the prison chapel where they listened to Chaplain Clayton. The man is half saint and half banty rooster—he's always quarreling with someone then apologizing for his temper. But that man can belt out a sermon much better than Father Mulligan. I guess it takes a congregation of felons to bring out the fire in a preacher. He's a handsome man too—his shock of white hair makes him look like Martin Sheen.

Each day, Chaplain Clayton left the chapel, laden with Bibles and pamphlets. And he handed them out to the fish. He said the prison can't stop the men from receiving religious material. Even a fish is allowed to have literature that might bring him closer to God. So I went to the Christian bookstore in Newcastle and got the seller to donate a bunch of books. Books about criminals and heretics who turned their lives over to Jesus. And I gave these books to the men on the fish range, and they all said, "Thank you, Missus Yoakum." The book they liked best was the one about the Manson Family.

Well, Major Bundy stopped me in the parking lot and scolded me like a parrot. "You can't run a lending library, Loretta," he said in his big gruff voice.

"I'm not lending those books," I snapped. "I'm giving them away."

"You're bending the rules, Loretta," he said.

I said, "Jesus bent 'em too."

Major Bundy shook his head and said, "You gotta learn to tell inmates no. If you try to be friends with these bojacks, you're going to end up in their trick bag."

The next day at roll call, the Major announced that I was being reassigned. I was going to go to the school dorm, and I'd be on the afternoon shift. "Be careful of the cons in that dormitory," Major Bundy advised me. "All that education is making them smarter crooks."

This time they paired me up with a female officer. Her name was Officer Collins, and her shoulders were as broad as a man's. She also wore her hair short like Ellen DeGeneres. I can't say I approve of that kind of lifestyle, but she was nice enough to the inmates and liked to crack a joke. I suppose the love of the Lord can even be spread by sinners.

Officer Collins was very patient as she coached me through the job. Not that I needed a whole lot of coaching—there wasn't that much to do. Three times a shift, we counted the inmates while they sat upon their bunks. We then compared our totals to make sure the numbers matched. We also searched footlockers at random to check for weapons and drugs. If an inmate had any contraband, we put him on report. And, once every hour, we phoned the key room and gave a status report. I think they made us do this so we wouldn't fall asleep.

Most of the inmates in the school dorm were boys around twenty years old. And a few of them liked to hang around the officers' desk and chat with me. Like all boys, they were a little bit mischievous, and they started to pull my leg. "Ain't choo scared to work here, Missus Yoakum?" one of them said.

"Why, are you going to murder me?" I asked. They got a big laugh out of that.

One of the boys, whose name was Bubba, started calling me Mother Yoakum. "Hippity hop!" he'd call out to the dorm whenever I announced count. "If yer butt ain't on yer bed, Mother Yoakum gonna cut a switch."

Bubba and I had some lively chats, which helped pass the time. He was a skinny boy with crooked teeth and tattoos of women on his forearms. He always had a foolish smirk on his face, and he seemed a little bit simple. My goodness, the things he told me would have made a sailor blush. "Didja know," he said, "that I dropped out of high school 'cause it interfered with my jacking off?"

"Too much of that, Bubba," I said, "will *keep* you simple-minded."

"Yer right," Bubba said, "'cause I did a dumb thing. I robbed a 7-Eleven to get money to buy myself porn."

"Bubba, that's so silly," I said. "Why didn't you go to church?"

Bubba said he now went to church to listen to Chaplain Clayton. He said he was going to get baptized and spread the word of the Lord. He also told me that in a couple of months he would have his GED. When I told him I was proud of him, he snorted like a colt. "I gotta serve four more years, Missus Yoakum. What can I do with that kind of time once I got my GED?" I assured him I would pray for him, and I hoped the time passed quickly.

After I'd been in the school dorm three weeks, Major Bundy gave me a lecture. He told me I was being much too friendly with inmates, and I needed to cut that out. "You can't be buddies with them, Loretta. I explained that once already." When I told him those poor boys needed to talk, he said, "Let 'em talk to the chaplain. If a con spends too much time with an officer, it makes him look like a snitch."

Major Bundy said I was being reassigned—he was pulling me out of the school dorm. He said I'd be going to the northeast tower to work the midnight shift.

•

THE FOLLOWING EVENING at midnight, I started my new assignment. They put me in the guard tower at the remotest corner of the prison. The tower shack was a concrete room atop a fifty foot pillar. It was empty except for a desk, a chair, and a toilet that needed cleaning. The room was surrounded by windows, which gave me a bird's-eye view of the grounds and the dormitories behind the double wire fence. A rack by the desk held a Mini-14 to shoot escaping inmates.

The shift supervisor, Captain Hodgkins, was a lean little man with the face of a weasel and a temperament to match. He told me to keep my eyes open and to report anything suspicious. He said I could take a snack with me if I put it in a paper bag. He said, "Don't be taking no lunch box up there. I searched an officer's lunch box last week and found a television in it."

"I'll bet he got good reception," I said; Captain Hodgkins didn't laugh.

"If I catch you sleepin' on duty," he said, "I'll fire you on the spot. If you let an inmate climb over the fence, I'll fire you on the spot. If you show up one minute late for roll call…"

"You'll fire me on the spot," I said. Goodness, what a tiresome man. I wanted to box his ears.

It was quiet as a morgue in the tower, but I didn't feel lonely at all. Sitting fifty feet above the prison made me feel so much closer to God. Each hour on the hour, I punch-dialed the intercom phone to check in with the key room officer. "All's well here, hon," was all I ever said. Since the inmates were all sound asleep in their bunks, I had nothing else to report.

Of course, Captain Hodgkins did what he could to catch me nodding off. I never knew when that silly man would sneak up the spiral staircase. I think it was a bit of a game to him, so I decided to play along. Every time he appeared at the doorway, I offered him cookies and coffee.

•

ON MY THIRD NIGHT in the tower, I saw movement inside the fence. Two shadowy figures were dawdling behind it like lovers out for a stroll. At first, I thought they were guards; a perimeter light wasn't working too well, and I could barely make them out. But when they started to climb the inner fence, I knew an escape was happening. I punch-dialed the key room officer. This time, I got no response.

I slid open a window and gave them a shout; they had already scaled the inner fence and dropped to the ground below. They looked brighter now because they had taken their shirts off to cover the razor wire. Their shirts hung down from the wire like flags.

I racked the slide of the Mini-14. "I can see you both real plain," I called out.

"How ya doin', Missus Yoakum?" one of them answered. I recognized Bubba's voice.

"I was doing just fine 'til you got here," I said. "Bubba, you need to stay put."

"Why? You gonna murder me?" Their laughter fluttered like moths.

Well, duty is duty but oh my God, my hands were shaking like Jell-O. "Bubba, you're going to miss breakfast," I said. What a silly thing to say.

"Can't talk with you no more," Bubba said. "What church do you go to, Missus Yoakum? I'll meet you there on Sunday and buy you a *pancake breakfast.*"

As they started to climb the outer fence, I could feel Murray lurking beside me. *Loretta, stop your chatter,* he said. How annoying that man had become.

Bubba was the first to reach the top of the fence, so I pointed the rifle at him. When I released the safety, I felt more alone than I had ever felt in my life. It must have been just like Jesus felt the day he was nailed to the cross. The day they marched him to Calvary and hung him between two thieves. *Why, Lord?* I prayed. *Why this test? Why did you give me this test?*

As my finger found the trigger, a shadow fell over Bubba. It was the same dark shadow that fell over Murray before he left me behind. I squeezed the trigger gently, as though I was milking a cow. The report sounded hollow, the gun had no kick—so it startled me when Bubba froze before climbing over the top of the fence.

"*Damn,* Missus Yoakum, I'm sorry," he said then he didn't say anything more. He just swayed like a bough struck by lightning then fell to the ground with a thump. Even when his friend started shaking him, Bubba lay as still as a log.

"Don't shoot no more, please!" his friend shouted, and he kept on shaking Bubba. "Bubba," he cried. "You sack of shit! Just look what you made her do!"

The prison alarm was now wailing so loud it could have awakened the dead. But Bubba lay still as a mannequin, and a puddle grew around him. I can only hope the good Lord heard me when I said a prayer for him.

•

THINGS ARE TOPSY-TURVY—they don't add up anymore. Do you know they gave me an assembly for shooting that wretched boy? I received a color guard salute, and a bagpiper played a march. And the superintendent made this speech about how well I'd done my duty. Goodness, from all the fuss they made, you'd have thought I had won the lottery.

After the ceremony, Major Bundy called me into his office. "Those boys profiled you, Loretta," he said. "They knew you were in that tower. The only reason they climbed that fence was because they didn't think you would shoot."

A month later, I went on medical leave—Major Bundy signed off on it. A plum-size lump had shown up in my lung, and I couldn't catch my breath. Doctor Diver ordered a bunch of tests, and he looked like he was concerned. But I can't really say that I dwelled on it much. Winter comes to all.

I don't want to go to heaven though—not if it's full of Father Mulligans. My God, I would be bored to death there. I don't want to see too much of Murray either—he's turned into such an ass. I guess forty years of marriage to him really were enough. No, I want to be where that poor boy is—wherever the Lord chose to put him. I want to spend more time with him. I want to box his ears.

○ ○ ○

The Sugar Shack Dress Company

HI, MY NAME IS GERTIE MCDOWELL. I was born in Butler County, Kentucky, and I suppose I'll spend my life here. I live on the family farm Ma gave me when she went into a nursing home. That happened last year after Pa took off for Branson, Missouri. He went there to join a country band, and he's busy getting famous. I don't hardly hear from Pa no more.

I live near a town called Turkey Roost, and it really ain't nothing too special. It's got half a dozen streets, a whole bunch of bars, and a McDonald's whose arches used to be powdered with coal dust. Just a typical strip-mining town is all. On Saturday night, a girl can't do much except stroll up and down the main drag. Or maybe gather her girlfriends up for a slumber party and watch movies on the Turner channel. I watch a lot of movies, and I like the old musicals best. My favorite is *West Side Story*—Natalie Wood sure could sing. But I'm kinda gettin' off the subject.

Turkey Roost is pretty depressing 'cause the mines have all closed down. Donald Trump said he would keep the mines open, so the whole town voted for him. But I don't see a whole lot of evidence that that's ever gonna happen. The union headquarters are all boarded up and most everyone's on the dole. Of course, that ain't the Donald's fault—the man is a living saint. 'Cept for maybe his pussy grabbing and all them Twitter rants. Anyway, the air's a whole lot cleaner, and that's gotta count for something.

I got married straight outta high school, and that weren't such a good idea. I got wed to Benny Pearman who was in my graduating class. Benny he got a job at a Sam's Club down in Nashville. He don't work there no more though 'cause he broke his hip moving boxes. So what he does now is play Fantasy Baseball and draw a disability pension. I ain't exactly sure why I married Benny—he just kinda proposed a year ago, and I didn't see much reason to say no. But I kinda wish I'd held out for a dude named Tommy Lee Weaver. Tommy Lee starred alongside me when I was in our high school production of *Annie*. He played Daddy Warbucks, and he hadda wear a swimming cap so he could look like he was bald. His hair is thick and redder 'an a chestnut, and I saw it peeking out of his swimming cap when we were singin' together on stage. Tommy Lee also wrote a poem that got published in the school newspaper. And he gave me a buncha black-eyed Susans after the final performance of *Annie*. I don't hear from Tommy Lee no more 'cause he went to Eastern Kentucky University in Richmond. He said he was gonna further his education so he can be a pharmacist.

Well, after Benny and I got married, I went to work at a Walmart in Bowling Green. My job was to stand at the entrance and greet folks comin' in. I'm real good at that 'cause I got a nice smile and my hair is dyed platinum blonde. I don't work there no more though 'cause Walmart shut itself down. That happened after the United Auto Workers tried to start up a union there. So what I do now is buy lottery tickets and find reasons to get out of the house. I kinda wish I had never married Benny—he just parks himself in our Barcalounger, sips beer, and plays made-up baseball. I kinda wish I had gone to Richmond and moved in with Tommy Lee.

Well, you can only buy so many lottery tickets, and you can only do so much pining. So I decided that maybe it was time that I started up my own business. I'm real good at making dresses—I sewed all the costumes for *Annie*. So I set up a shop in this ol' barn that sits behind our house. I bought a dozen bolts of fabric and a Singer sewing machine and one of them torso dummies to fit the dresses on. After I made me a buncha dresses, I took pictures of 'em with my cell phone. And I put the pictures on a website that read *Frocks by Gertie McDowell*.

Well, even though I'm a real good dressmaker, I only got one dress order. Patty Bill Willis, who runs an egg farm near Coon Creek, asked me to make an Easter dress for her ten-year-old granddaughter. I ain't never made no Easter Dress so I went on the internet, checked a few of 'em out, and printed out one of the pictures. Easter dresses have real high waists and they don't have no bust at all, and they got so many ruffles that they're practically Christmas tree shaped. Well, I made a cute little Easter dress, and it fit Patty Bill's granddaughter perfect. Patty Bill said her granddaughter was gonna be the best-dressed girl at the egg hunt.

I charged Patty Bill forty dollars, which I thought was pretty reasonable, but Patty Bill just looked at me like I was trying to pick her pocket. She didn't pay me no money, but she gave me about six dozen eggs. So every night for a week, I fixed omelets with hominy grits.

•

THERE AIN'T MUCH POINT in having a business if it don't bring you no money. Heck, I checked my website every day for a month, but I didn't get no more dress orders. Benny Pearman said it's probably 'cause I ain't found my demographic. He said I ain't gonna get no orders unless I do more reachin' out. So I put together an email pitch and linked it to my website, and I sent it to all the women's wear distributors I could find on the internet. I didn't get no replies 'cept one from Coldwater Creek. All they wanted to do was send me a catalogue.

Well, a coupla months later, I'd pretty much decided to close my business down. That's when opportunity came knockin' like a sinner at heaven's door. This email popped up in my mailbox from a retailer called Sugar Shack Trends. I ain't never heard of that company, but I think it has foreign roots. It was sent by a gentleman named Jean Valjean who musta been a Frenchman.

Dear Miss McDowell, the letter read. *Your daring hemlines and use of lace have come to our attention. Would you consider joining our distributorship and enhancing the Sugar Shack Brand? We are a rapidly growing company with outlets all over the world, and we would be honored it if you would consider becoming one of our designers. Congratulations on being invited to join the Sugar Shack family.*

Well, I read the email a coupla times and my heart started to pound like a mallet. Shucks, I ain't never been invited to join no family. The only family I got now is Ma, and she's in a nursing home. And she don't do nothing but sit in her room and watch *Frasier* reruns on TV. So I sent an email to Jean Valjean, and I thanked him for the offer. And I said that as long as it didn't cost me no money, I'd be proud to promote his brand.

It weren't but fifteen minutes before that gentleman emailed me back. He said I had made a wise move that was going to change my life. He said his company only hired the most promising designers, and then he went on to explain to me how things were going to work. He said I would be responsible for making the dresses and taking them to the customers, and his company would be responsible for quality control. He also said my work was so beautiful that I needed to keep a low profile. He said there were plenty of imitators out there that would steal my designs if they could.

There was a contract attached to the email, which was kinda hard to read, so I showed the contract to Benny Pearman 'cause I wanted a second opinion. Benny said he knows nothin' 'bout contracts, and I oughta proceed with caution. He suggested I test the waters before dipping in my toes.

Well, I emailed that fella named Jean Valjean and asked if I could have a trial run. He said that would be no problem, and he admired my business savvy. He instructed me to make a red cocktail dress for a woman in Beaver

Creek, and he sent me the woman's measurements and told me to do my best work.

Since I wanted to make a good impression, I ordered this real neat fabric. The fabric was stretch satin and it shimmered like a ruby, and the texture was so smooth and silky that it electrified my palm. Well, I made a cocktail dress using an example I found on the internet. 'Cept I gave it a plunging neckline and I kept the hemline low, and I put a slit in the side of the dress that rode up past the knee. When I was done, it was all I could do not to bawl like a week-old calf. The dress was so beautiful it looked like an angel oughta wear it.

I mailed the dress to Jean Valjean's post office box for its quality inspection. A few days later the dress came back looking more beautiful than ever. The company had added some lace to the neck and put in some fancy pleats, and the Sugar Shack label, featuring a picture of a cottage, was sewn into the neckline. A note was pinned to the dress, and it said that I did a wonderful job. The note also listed the address of the woman who was gonna buy my dress.

Well, I put the dress in a garment bag and I hung it in the back of my Jeep, and I drove an hour to Beaver Creek to make my delivery. Beaver Creek is a gutted farm town that only has one street, so it took me only a minute to find my customer's house.

The woman who answered my knock on the door was kinda dried-up and old, so I ain't sure what she wanted with a brand new cocktail dress. But I gave her the dress in the garment bag and she gave me a weary smile, and she handed me an envelope and told me to count the money.

I counted out five hundred dollars in fifty-dollar bills, and I told the woman I wasn't expectin' to get paid quite so much. She told me she'd seen my site on the internet and admired the work I'd done. She said she didn't mind paying top dollar for such beautiful designs.

Before she went back into the house, the woman patted my cheek. She told me to have a wonderful day, and it was an honor to make my acquaintance. And she assured me it wouldn't be long until I became a famous dress designer.

Well, with all that cash in my wallet, I felt richer 'an Bill Gates. And that woman, she sure made my day when she said I was gonna be famous. But it seemed sorta odd that she paid for the dress without even trying it on.

•

WHEN I GOT HOME and checked my email, there was another message from Jean Valjean. He said the customer who bought my dress had told all her friends about me. He said my reputation was spreading, and he had another dress order. He said a woman from Rocky Mound—a town in Tennessee—wanted me to make her a black maxi dress with a split. He also said it was the thrill of his life to be representing me, and that he was gonna reduce his commission to only forty percent.

Well, I sent an email to Jean Valjean, telling him what the cocktail dress fetched, and he told me to put two hundred dollars in an envelope and send it to his post office box. He said the rest of the money was mine 'cause I'd done such a marvelous job. He also advised me to keep things hush-hush—at least until he secured a patent for everything I designed.

Shucks, I felt kinda sad that I couldn't go out and celebrate my success. But if you're gonna stay successful, you can't be slacking off. So I went online and found a picture of a real cool maxi dress, and I ordered a bolt of duchess satin 'cause I wanted the dress to shine. When the satin arrived, I gasped like a faucet—it practically blinded me. I couldn't believe how light hit the fabric and bounced right offa it.

I followed the basic design of the dress then I made a couple of changes. I cut the back away, and I left one shoulder bare then I shortened the hemline a bit so the customer could show off her ankles. I worked all through the night on the dress 'cause I completely lost track of time. By the time I was done, the fingers of dawn were creepin' through the window. The way the fabric glowed in the first light of day made me feel kinda weak in the knees. It truly looked like the dress had been touched by the hand of God.

Well, I mailed the dress to that Sugar Shack company for its quality inspection, and a few days later the dress came back with a note from Jean Valjean. He wrote that the dress was a masterpiece—a garment fit for a queen—and that an angel musta guided my hands when I put the dress together. He also said that inspecting my work was like worshipping at a shrine, so he was gonna cut his commission down to just thirty percent.

•

I KINDA WISH the hand of God would do something 'bout Benny Pearman. 'Cause Benny he started lecturing me about all the time I spent makin' dresses. He said a marriage is gonna suffer if a couple don't spend time together. Well, since Benny has nothing to offer me but beer and Fantasy Baseball, I told him our marriage was already suffering as much as it needed to. I said if I gave up making dresses, it would suffer a whole lot worse. So I bought Benny a super-wide Flat-Screen TV and I got him a case of Budweiser, and I told him to enjoy himself 'cause I had a delivery to make.

I drove two hours to Rocky Mound, another boarded-up mining town, and I delivered the dress to a square-jawed woman who mighta been a transvestite. Her arms were kinda muscular and her chest was kinda sunken, so for a moment I was worried that I made the bust too large. But the woman she just smiled at me and called me a lovely child. And she handed me an envelope fulla hundred dollar bills.

The woman she asked me to count the money before she accepted the dress, so I counted the hundred dollar bills and there was ten of them. I felt my knees start to buckle and I felt real light in the head, and if the woman hadn't caught me I'd have toppled off her porch. When I told her she'd paid too much for the dress, she winked and shook her head. She said my reputation precedes me and not to sell myself short.

As I drove back to Kentucky, I was shaking like a drunk; it was all I could do to keep the Jeep from driftin' off the highway. So I parked the Jeep in Opryland, which is just outside of Nashville, and I treated myself to a fancy dinner of pork chops and collard greens. By the time I got back to Turkey Roost, it was ten o'clock at night, but I stopped at the post office anyhow and I stretched 'til I heard my neck crack. After that, I mailed three of them hundred dollar bills to that Sugar Shack company.

•

WELL, I SIGNED that Sugar Shack contract and dress orders kept pourin' in, and I spent every waking minute making dresses and delivering them. I didn't deliver the dresses 'til I first sent 'em to Jean Valjean 'cause he told me he was havin' 'em professionally photographed to show in a catalogue. I never saw the catalogue, but he said it looked real great.

Benny he got in my face one day and gave me an ultimatum. He told me I hadda choose—it was either them dresses or him. I told him that weren't no contest at all and to not let the door hit his ass when he left. So Benny moved in with his mother and sent me some divorce papers, and after I had a good cry I sent a text message to Tommy Lee Weaver. I asked Tommy Lee how he was doin' and I asked if he still wrote poems, and I told him he looked really silly when he was wearin' that bathing cap. Tommy Lee he called me back on my cell phone and said he was doin' fine. He said he was in a relationship now and a baby was on the way, and he said he remembered the fun we had when both of us starred in *Annie*. I wished Tommy Lee the best of luck, and I'm sure I meant it too. You can't begrudge no happiness to a man who played Daddy Warbucks.

Well, I kept on making dresses and I banked almost all of my profits, and it weren't too long before I had thirty thousand dollars stashed away. But makin' dresses is lonely work, so I phoned Ma every night. Ma she told me not to fret 'cause you just can't hurry love. She said one day my prince will come, and I gotta be patient 'til then.

I thanked Ma for her advice even though it was pretty corny. Just 'cause a fella's prince don't mean that I'll wanna take up with him. What if he's as bald as a billiard ball or has ears like England's Prince Charles? But maybe he'll be like Jean Valjean who sounds real suave in his emails. Mr. Valjean sounds like a Latin gentleman with frost around his temples, and I'll bet he's been all over the world and made love to a whole lotta women. So I send an email to Jean Valjean, and I thanked him for all his support. And I said he oughta give me a knock if he's ever in Turkey Roost. I said maybe we could go to a Cracker Barrel and have us some chicken and dumplings.

Well, Jean Valjean he emailed me back. He said he'd be honored to meet me, but we can't be seen dining together. He said there's fashion spies everywhere and we gotta watch out for them, 'cause one of them moles might follow me home and steal all my designs. But he promised to send me a bracelet with the Sugar Shack logo on it. And he said when he got all my patents secured, we might have us a meal together. He said he's real fond of chicken and dumplings and likes to eat collard greens too.

•

MONTHS WENT BY and I never got no visit from Jean Valjean. But I made and delivered a whole lotta dresses, and the money kept rollin' in. I made dirndl dresses and tunic dresses and baby doll dresses with lace. I made slip-on dresses and granny dresses and even a coupla caftans. And I delivered them dresses all over Kentucky and most of Tennessee. I delivered 'em to quaint little towns that looked like they seen better days. Places with names like Possum Hollow, Goose Valley, and Gopher Hill. Places with shutdown union halls and stores with empty window fronts. But although the towns weren't that inviting, my clients all welcomed me. A lot of 'em gave me a hug and called me a lovely child. The way they looked at me, you have thought all their Christmases had come.

Well, my partnership with that Sugar Shack company ended a little abruptly. But you probably already guessed that this was gonna happen. One day, I was making a corset dress—a dress with tight lace around the middle—when I heard this knockin' on the barn door. The knocking was kinda rapid, like a woodpecker was makin' a nest, so I was kinda surprised when I opened the door and saw a gentleman standing there. The gentleman was dressed in a business suit and his hair was brown with white flecks in it, and he looked so dapper and sexy that my heart leapt like a frog.

"Would you like some supper?" I said to him. "I could make you some chicken and dumplings."

The gentleman blushed redder 'an a cherry tomato—he seemed to be kinda embarrassed. But his manners were so elegant that he reminded me of George Clooney. He said "please" when he told me to turn around and place my hands behind my back, and he put the handcuffs on me so careful it felt like he was slipping on bracelets. He even asked me to watch my step when he walked me to his car, and he said that he hoped them cuffs weren't gripping my wrists too tight.

The gentleman drove me to Bowling Green, where they got a federal courthouse, and all the way there we chatted like we were a couple of old friends. I asked him if he was married, and he told me he was divorced—he said that being a DEA agent was kind of hard on a marriage. I asked him if he had children and he said he had two girls, and he saw them every weekend and took them to their soccer games. He asked me how come I got involved in dealing powdered meth, and when I said I didn't know nothin' 'bout that, he patted me on the shoulder. He told me I shoulda checked the hems before I delivered them dresses.

When he dropped me off at the Warren County Jail, we were as close as two pups in a litter. He shook my hand after removing the cuffs, and he said he hoped things worked out for me. So I asked him to look me up once I was out of jail. I told him I'd never fault him for being a federal agent. I told him I thought I would make him a real devoted wife.

•

WELL, I'M STUCK in the Federal Prison Camp in Alderson, West Virginia. The trial it didn't go too well, so I'm gonna be here awhile. When I told the judge what happened, he thought I was pulling his leg. He said Jean Valjean is a character in a Victor Hugo novel. He said Sugar Shack ain't no company, it's the name of a popular song. He told me that court ain't no place to be telling whoppers that bad, and if I thought I was getting away with them, I was dumber than broccoli. So he gave me five years for trafficking drugs and he sent me to Alderson, and he said he hoped I'd use the time to ponder my crooked ways.

They call this place Camp Cupcake 'cause Martha Stewart once stayed here. And I gotta admit the inmates are nice and the guards are real polite. I'm sharing a two-bunk cell with a woman named Bertha Jean, and she let me join a gang of woman that she calls her family. My job is in the sewing shop where they make clothes for federal inmates. I kinda like this assignment 'cause it helps me pass the time. I also like strolling the grounds 'cause the place looks like a college campus.

On Christmas, I got a card from that agent that busted me. He said he hopes I'm doing well, and we'll have coffee when I get out. He said he thinks I'm a really nice girl that just got led astray. I also got a letter from Pa who's still in Branson, Missouri. Pa said I'm real trustin' of strangers, and that ain't always a good thing. He said he was gonna hire a lawyer to help me with an appeal.

Well, I thanked Pa for his concern, but I ain't sure I got duped all that bad. I shoulda known that Sugar Shack ain't no name for a dress company. I shoulda known that Frenchmen eat frog legs and don't like chicken and dumplings. And I shoulda known there's no market for satin in towns named Beaver Creek. Maybe I'm dumber than broccoli, but dern it I shoulda known.

o o o

The Hangings

1

MAGGIE AND I sit on our front porch at dusk. We drink ice tea and watch the sun sink. In our fifty-five years of marriage, we have rarely missed a sunset.

Today, the sun bleeds through the haze, and the horizon is apple red. Maggie rocks in her rocker, knitting a shawl. I smoke a pipe filled with Captain Black tobacco.

Maggie sings a fragment of a song while she knits. *"Give us any chance, we'll take it."* She pauses, shakes her head, and keeps on knitting. "That's all I remember, Poppy," she says. She still calls me Poppy after all these years. Sometimes, it gets on my nerves.

"It's from *Laverne and Shirley*," I say. "We watched it on ABC back in the seventies—it came on the year we got married." I sing the next bar to help Maggie recall the song. *"Read us any rule, we'll break it."*

Maggie drops a stitch. "I rather liked that show, Poppy," she says.

"I liked it too, Maggie," I say. "Especially that episode where the girls got into a tizzy."

"They got into a tizzy every week, Poppy. I *wish* you could be more specific."

"They got into a really big tizzy that week. I think they were wearing space suits."

"Were they, Poppy? I don't remember them in space suits."

"I liked them on *Happy Days* too. The girls were even funnier on *Happy Days*."

Maggie sighs. "I never liked *Happy Days* much. That Jewish boy was such a braggart."

She recovers the stitch and keeps knitting. Despite her comment, she sings two bars from the *Happy Days* theme. *"Sunday, Monday, Happy*

Days. Tuesday, Wednesday, Happy Days." She puts down her knitting, "It's Wednesday," she remembers. "We have to attend the hangings."

The hangings now happen twice a week. Every Wednesday and Saturday, in towns across the country, fanatics are hanged in the courthouse squares. It is considered poor etiquette not to attend the hangings.

"It's disgraceful," says Maggie, "the way they drag those things out. The noisy bands, the endless speeches. Just hang them and be done with it, I say. Let's be Christian about it."

"'First they came for the socialists,'" I quote. "'Then they came for the unionists.'"

Maggie does not like me to be trite. "They came for you a few days ago."

"Yes, but they let me go."

"Wasn't that because you turned in Doctor Beckman? Didn't you tell them he was a writer?"

"He might have been one."

"That's true," Maggie says. "If I started a journal, would you turn me in also?"

"I would never turn you in, Maggie."

"What if they put you back in that jail? What if they beat you again?"

I have always been honest with Maggie. "They would have to beat me twice. I owe you that much, Maggie."

Maggie looks amused—my answer must have pleased her. "Thank you, Poppy," she coos. "You know how to make me feel better."

I puff my tobacco and sing a Dylan song I remember. *"People don't live or die, people just float. She went with the man with the long black coat."*

"Be careful whose music you sing," Maggie cautions. "That's such a socialist song."

I shrug. "They're going to come back for me anyhow. I may as well sing that song."

Maggie shrugs too. "When they've picked you up once, they always arrest you again. You told me this never could happen, Poppy."

"That was before the bombings."

"Those dreadful bombings. Will they ever stop?"

"He promised to stop the bombings."

"Yes," Maggie says. "He promised that, didn't he?"

The shawl she is knitting is blue—blue is a primary color. It is not smart to knit in non-primary colors. When Mabel Leibman was arrested last week, she was knitting a beige sweater.

Maggie finishes a row. "He's so much like Lincoln. I never knew how much."

"Lincoln shut down the courts," I say. "He shut down newspapers too."

"I'm glad he's a lot like Lincoln."

My pipe is cold, but I do not fill it again. Captain Black tobacco is scarce. You can no longer find it in stores.

"I love you, Maggie," I say.

She takes a sip of ice tea and sighs. The evening is dry and hot, as though someone left an oven door open. Maggie does not like heat.

I pat Maggie's wrist. "Let's go into the house. Let's turn on *Happy Days*."

Maggie taps her foot. "You never listen, Poppy. We have to attend the hangings."

"If they hang them quickly, we can still catch *Happy Days*."

"They won't hang them quickly," Maggie snaps. "They never do anymore."

I don't like to make Maggie angry; she has a tongue like a thorn. "After they cut down the bodies," I say, "lets buy some frozen yogurts."

Maggie swirls the ice tea in her glass, and the ice cubes rattle like bones. "Every time I get cross with you, Poppy, you want to buy frozen yogurts."

I change the subject. "Will the Boy Scouts be there, do you think?"

Maggie strokes her neck. "The Boy Scouts are always there, don't you remember? It's the Boy Scouts who fit the nooses. It's the Boy Scouts who cut down the bodies."

"I hope they cut them down right away. Before their tongues turn blue."

"They cut Doctor Beckman down right away, and his tongue was as blue as a Smurf."

"They would have hanged him sooner or later. He never attended the hangings."

"No," Maggie says. "It was rude of him to never go to the hangings. I don't know where that man picked up his manners."

"I'm glad they let me turn him in. It gave us this evening together."

"This evening is hot," Maggie says. She presses the glass of ice tea to her brow then takes another sip.

Our anniversary is today, and I have a surprise for her. "We are going to fly to Hawaii," I say. We flew to Hawaii fifty-five years ago to spend our honeymoon. Maggie liked the rainforests and waterfalls. She did not like the dormant volcanoes.

Maggie rolls her eyes. "You promise that every year, Poppy. How quickly you forget."

"This year I'll book a flight early."

"I don't do well on planes," Maggie says.

"We'll sit on the beach and drink Mai Tais"

"That wouldn't be much of a change."

Maggie returns to her knitting. The shawl is getting thick. "I'm glad you're so quick to forget," she says.

"Why is that, Maggie? Tell me again."

She coughs and continues her knitting. "We have to attend the hangings."

2

MAGGIE AND I sit on our front porch. She rocks in her rocker, knitting a scarf. I sit on a stool with my pipe in my hand. We drink ice tea as we watch the sunset.

The haze is heavier, and it is hard to make out colors. It traps the heat so we sweat a great deal. Maggie always corrects me when I complain about our sweating. She says, "Poppy, women don't sweat, they glow. How many times must I remind you?"

Maggie likes to remind me of things. Sometimes, I pretend to forget so that Maggie can remind me. I don't know what I would do without Maggie.

I am smoking my last pouch of Captain Black tobacco. Maggie is glad that I will soon be out of Captain Black tobacco. She says it smells like dead roaches.

"Would you rather it smelled like live roaches?" I ask. I take another puff.

Maggie titters and keeps on knitting. "Poppy," she says, "you can still make me laugh."

"I'm glad I still make you laugh," I say.

She frowns like a judge. "I do wish you'd stop it. Laughing is illegal now."

I'm glad that Maggie reminds me of this. Sometimes, I forget that laughing can get you hanged.

The hangings take place every day now. In hundreds of towns across the country, turncoats are strung up in droves. They do not laugh when the nooses are put around their necks. They stand like statues and wait for the ropes to tighten.

I am glad that the hangings take place every day. Maggie no longer has to remind me on what days the hangings are scheduled.

We attend the hangings six days a week. We no longer attend the hangings on Wednesday. On Wednesdays, we stay home and watch *Laverne and Shirley*. It is risky not to attend the hangings, but we like to watch *Laverne and Shirley*.

We do not watch *Happy Days* anymore. Maggie does not like the Jewish boy. She says it is scandalous to watch a show that has a Jewish boy in it.

We don't watch television as much as we used to. We watch the televised speeches, we also watch the marches, but we don't watch the football or the porn. Most of the time, the television watches us.

He promised to stop the bombings, but bombings have increased. Buildings are bombed all over the country every single day. Still, he appears on television each night and says he will stop the bombings. Some say he orders the bombings himself. It is not funny to joke about the bombings.

Maggie is knitting a bright red scarf. She no longer knits in blue. He told us that traitors wear blue. He says the bombers wear blue. He says you cannot hide from him if you ever dressed in blue. I remember when Maggie knitted in blue, but she likes to correct me about this. She says blue is worn only by murderers, and she never knitted in blue.

I suspect they will hang me today. They arrested me several weeks ago and then they let me go. That was because I turned in Doctor Beckman—I told them he was a writer. That gave me a few more evenings with Maggie. I like to spend time with Maggie. But they always come back and hang you after they let you go. This happens within a month.

I look at Maggie. I think I will miss her even though she gets on my nerves. "Today is the day," I tell her. "We may as well say goodbye."

"We've been saying goodbye for years," Maggie says. "One more time won't make any difference."

"Does that mean you won't come to my hanging?" I say.

Maggie rolls her eyes so I know I am making her cross. "If they hang you on Wednesday—no," she says. "I'll miss *Laverne and Shirley*."

I am glad that today is Monday. I don't want her to miss *Laverne and Shirley*.

"If they hang me today, will you come?" I say. "I'll buy you a frozen yogurt."

Maggie does not look at me. She stares at her knitting instead.

"Poppy," she says to me after a while, "you may as well save your money. In all the years we have been married, I've never liked frozen yogurt."

I am surprised to hear that Maggie does not like frozen yogurt. Every Sunday, after church, I buy her a frozen yogurt. I also buy her a frozen yogurt on the days we attend the hangings. What else don't I know about Maggie?

I speak to her gently—I don't want her upset. Not on the day of my hanging. "Why did you tell me you liked frozen yogurt?"

"Why did you believe me, Poppy?"

A van is parking in front of our house. Men are sitting in the van. It should be no more than an hour until the rope bites into my neck.

"Do you remember when we went to Hawaii?" I ask.

"That was fifty-five years ago, Poppy."

"It seems like yesterday, doesn't it Maggie?"

Maggie groans and puts down her knitting. "You don't *remember* yesterday, Poppy. You only remember Hawaii."

"I remember you liked the waterfalls, but not the dormant volcanoes."

"No," Maggie says. She rubs her eyes. "I did not like the dormant volcanoes."

"Would you rather the volcanoes were active?" I ask.

She chuckles and picks up her knitting. "Poppy," she says, "you still make me laugh."

"I'm sorry," I reply.

I hear the van doors slam. Men are walking towards our house. I can practically trace out my name in the haze, and they look like a mirage.

"They're here, Maggie."

She keeps on knitting. Her eyes do not stray from the scarf. "Are they wearing red or blue?" she asks. The needles leap in her hands.

I look at the men, but I don't answer Maggie. I can't tell what color they're wearing.

3

A WEEK AGO, they hanged Poppy. And I did attend that man's hanging. My, what a fuss he made. Standing beside the gallows, he begged the hangman to wait. All so he could hand me a dollar to buy myself a frozen yogurt. Poppy believed every problem in the world could be solved with a frozen yogurt. Not that his hanging was much of a problem. He dropped like a sack of potatoes, and his neck snapped like a whip.

Why on earth did I go to his hanging? Was I really hoping for closure? I still feel his absence when I sit alone on our porch. But I felt his absence when he was alive, so it's really not much of a change.

He comes to me in my dreams, you know—my, what a tiresome man. He used to snore like a trumpet, which kept me awake half the night, and now he has the temerity to bother me in my dreams. I truly wish he would just move on and let me enjoy my sleep. Doesn't he have anything better to do than to come around pestering me? No, he probably doesn't—that man did like our bed.

I go to the hangings alone now, and I'm finding them rather tiresome. Do you know they're hanging women and children? First, they hang the women and then they do the children. The women grow rigid the instant they're hanged; the children squirm like eels. That's because children are lighter, and it's harder to break their necks. Their little legs pummel the air as though they're riding invisible bikes.

He appeared on television last night to explain why he's hanging the children. He said the children come from bad seed. He said if the children are not eliminated, they will grow up to bomb our cities. He explained that he hangs the mothers first so they won't see their children swing. I'm glad he's such a thoughtful man. I'm glad he's destroying bad seed.

The smog has grown much thicker; I can no longer see the sunsets. But it's bad for your eyes to look into the sun so that's probably for the best. Poppy often gazed at the sunsets, and it's a wonder he didn't go blind. I do think he lost his sense of smell though—his tobacco stank like dead roaches. "Would you rather it stank like live roaches?" he asked me the day they took him away. Up until the moment they hanged him, that man could make me laugh.

I sit on our porch, hand-stitching a sunset quilt, and it's hard on my arthritic fingers. The quilt has yellow, red, and blue so I use three colors of yarn. I no longer knit shawls and scarves with blue yarn, but I still stitch blue into my quilts. A sunset wouldn't look authentic without a bit of blue.

The patrols are much more frequent now. Black vans, the kind they took Poppy away in, glide up and down our street. They took away Gertrude Edelman and ten-year-old Aaron, her son. They took away Precious Jackson; they took away Marquis Jones. They did not take away Margaret Sullivan; she came to see me yesterday. She said she admired my quilt. She said blue is a telling color. That's high praise coming from Margaret, she's the prefect of our block.

Any day, they will hang me for putting blue into my quilt. So I always have my makeup kit on me and I always wear freshly-ironed dresses. Before they hang me, they just might allow me to freshen up my face. A dab of rouge would look nice on my cheeks when the color drains away. I must ask Margaret to speak to the hangman before he stretches my neck. It would be very disrespectful if I did not leave a pretty corpse.

He appeared on television yesterday, interrupting *Laverne and Shirley*. It was one of my favorite episodes, the one where the girls have a séance to get rid of a household ghost. He told us it's his painful duty to hang the Boy

Scouts too. He said the Boy Scouts are planting bombs. He promised the bombings will stop once the Boy Scouts are hanged.

I do believe his speeches have awoken the trollop in me. Yesterday, when I heard his brave words, my nipples grew harder than bullets. That's a fine howdy-do for a woman near eighty who stopped menstruating decades ago. If they're going to hang me for impure thoughts, I hope they do it quickly.

I pray there is no afterlife; I don't want my thoughts to go on. And I certainly don't want to meet the souls of traitors and murderers. Imagine spending eternity hearing their wretched laments. No, I don't want to go to an afterlife; I might be compromised there.

The quilt is nearly completed. A bit more blaze in the yellow, some ripple in the red, a tad more nuance in the blue, and I think it will be done. I rather wish Poppy were here to see it before I put it away. But Poppy liked everything I stitched, so his compliments didn't mean much. My god, I hope there is no world to come; I don't want him back in my hair.

I stitch a little faster as the van pulls into our driveway. I do not look up as I hear the doors slam. I do not watch the men as they tromp to the house. I do not even offer them a glass of ice tea when they're standing on the porch.

I pluck a loose thread and I keep on stitching. "Wait 'til I'm finished," I say.

∘ ∘ ∘

The Time My Dad Chewed Out a Cop

DAD AND I are shooting brown rats at the Putnam County Dump. I've got me a .22 Long Rifle while Dad has a Winchester 70 with a scope. We keep a tally of the rats we shoot 'cause that makes it a bonding experience. So far, I've plastered six of them while Dad's shot seventeen. We're shooting good 'cause there's a harvest moon out and we can see them like it was daylight. And Dad's been swigging Johnny Walker to keep his hands from shaking. A couple belts of Johnny Walker turns Dad into Daniel Boone.

Well, Dad, he sets his rifle down and folds his pudgy arms. 'Cause Dad, he don't like showing me up—that's just the way he is. He's a gentleman, my father.

"Toby," says Dad—he still calls me Toby even though I just turned sixteen. "Toby," he says. "I ever told you about the time I chewed out a cop?"

I slip a fresh clip into my .22 and keep on spotting rats. "Tell me about it, Pa," I say. I've heard the story a coupla dozen times, but I want to hear it again. You can't tell a good story too often is how I look at it.

Dad guides the bottle to his lips and takes a real long pull. His Adam's apple bobs like a float on a fishing line. Then he belches louder 'an a bazooka and starts telling me the story.

"Happened a coupla years ago out on Route 36. It was ten o'clock on a Saturday night—drunk drivers were everywhere. And your ma and I was driving home from Big Jeb Bowen's wedding. Big Jeb had him a pitch-in wedding where all the guests hadda bring a dish. And Ma, she brought some Swedish meatballs that nobody wanted to eat.

"Well, Ma said the SPCA oughta investigate Big Jeb. She said, 'That man pinches nickels so hard he makes the buffaloes squeal.' I said to Ma, 'Ya can't fault a man for knowing the value of a dollar.' Ma said, 'You can when his bride is barefoot and don't have no wedding dress.' I said, 'Woman, that proves my point. Why spend a hundred dollars on a dress that's only gonna be worn once?' Ma said, 'Once is too many times if it's Big Jeb Bowen you're marrying.' I said, 'Woman, shut your mouth—you got no call to complain. You put way too much pepper in those goddamn Swedish meatballs.'

"Well, Ma said Big Jeb Bowen is the one who oughta be ashamed. 'Didja see what he put on the dining room table?' she said in a voice dry as lint. 'Half of a watermelon, and he called it a salad bar.' By now the pickup was starting to stray like a slut on roller skates. And Ma said, 'Pa, watch your driving.' And I said to her, 'Watch your mouth.' But before I could straighten out the truck, I heard the chirp of a siren. And lights started flashing blue and red just like on the Fourth of July.

"'Now what?' I said as I eased the pickup onto the shoulder of the road. 'You tripped on your pecker is what,' said Ma. She likes to use that expression a lot, but it don't insult me none. When you got a beauty the size of your Pa's, you can't *help* but step on it.

"Soon, this cop the size of a hippo waddled up to the side of the truck. He had eyes as mean as a fighting cock and jowls like a stud hog. He said, 'Lemme see your license and registration, bub.' I said, 'Is somethin' wrong, officer?' He said, 'You crossed the dividing line, pardner.' 'That ain't *all* he done,' shouted Ma 'cause she can't keep her piehole shut. 'He said I gotta wear my wedding dress 'til it's nothing but a rag.'

"The cop he stuck his chest out and said, 'Is that how you treat your wife?' 'It's a hundred dollar dress,' I told him, an' the woman only wore it once.' 'You penny-pinching sonuvabitch,' said the cop. 'You oughta be ashamed.' I said, 'Why don't you make a big deal out of it and put my butt in jail?'

"'Maybe I *will* put you in jail,' said the cop. 'I still got my quota to fill.' And he slipped the handcuffs offa his belt and clicked the strands into place.

"Ma she just kept talking 'cause the woman can't plug her yap. 'He insulted my Swedish meatballs,' she said. 'He told me I used too much pepper.' The cop said, 'Meatballs ain't tasty unless they got pepper in 'em.'

"I said to the cop, 'Get outta my face. I ain't eating no meatballs with pepper.' And the cop said, 'Pardner, get outta the truck and put your hands on the hood.'

"Well, I farted loud as thunder before getting outta the truck. I said to the cop, 'That's what happens when you're eating meatballs with pepper in 'em.' As the cop put the bracelets on me, he said, 'Don't you worry none about that. You're gonna eat nothing but chitlins when you're booked in the greybar hotel.'

"The cop drove me to the county lockup, which is on Griffin Boulevard. And before I knew it, I was sitting in a cell surrounded by rapists and robbers. Big hairy men with tattoos on their arms and names like Bubba and Spike. They all had dongs like horses, and they hung 'em in my face.

"'You don't look like no jailbird,' said one, the biggest of them all.

"'I ain't,' I said. 'Unless it's a crime not to buy your wife a dress shop.'

"The dude he got all thoughtful and started scratching his head. He said, 'A woman don't need more 'an two or three dresses. She can only wear one at a time.'

"'This cop told me different,' I said. 'He told me to buy her a dress. And that's when I tore him an asshole the size of a Thunderbird.'

"The thugs, they got all respectful and nodded like bobbleheads. And they stuffed their dongs back into their pants like they were hogging buffalo catfish. All of 'em agreed that ya can't fault a man for tearing a cop a new asshole. Not when the cop tried to force him to buy his wife a dress.

"The thugs decided I was a hero, and they took up a collection for me. They said I deserved the best damn lawyer that eighty-five cents could buy. And they served up this wine made from raisins, and we all got louder 'an sailors on shore leave. And when the jailer told us to shut our mouths, I told him to jack me off. Hell, I ain't gonna obey no pissant jailer after chewing out a cop."

•

BY NOW, I've shot me eleven more rats and Dad and I are tied. But Dad don't pick up his rifle 'cause the story is only half-told. "Tell me what happened next," I say 'cause I ain't heard the good part yet. Dad takes a long swig of whiskey to loosen up his throat then he belches like a blasting cap, which scares off all the rats.

"Monday morning," he says, "the cop drove me to the Putnam County Courthouse. And he told me he ate all them leftover meatballs 'cause Ma didn't want 'em no more. He said he ate 'em with Ketchup and a pint of Boston beans. I said, 'Don't be lighting no cigarettes 'til you've had yourself a shit.'

"The cop frog-marched me into the courtroom and sat me in the jury box. The place was so damn crowded there weren't no room left in the pews. That's 'cause the courtroom was fulla drunks that got busted over the weekend.

"I spotted Ma in the gallery; she was wearing her wedding dress. The dress was fulla moth holes and was yellower 'an a corpse. It looked like she had slept in it then dragged it through a barn.

"When the court reporter took her seat, I stopped looking at Ma. That reporter had tits like a dairy heifer and legs that could strangle a mule. Hell, I already had a hard-on when the bailiff shouted, 'All rise!'

"This cross-eyed judge with a face like a bullfrog took his seat on the bench. And I sat there for three damn hours while the bailiff kept calling cases. And this public defender came up to me, and said she could cut me a deal. She said if I entered a guilty plea, she could get me off with probation. Well, I told her she'd have to do better 'an that if she wanted to get me off. I told her I wasn't taking no deal—not if it meant that I hadda eat meatballs that even Big Jeb won't touch. And not if it meant I'd end up in the poorhouse to keep your ma in dresses.

"After three hours, the bailiff called my name, and I stood in front of the judge. 'Mr. Dawes,' the judge boomed, as he held up some papers. 'I've got an arrest report on ya and a statement from your wife. You've been charged with drunk driving, farting too loud, and neglecting a mighty fine woman. How do you plead to them charges?' Well, I wanted a swig of whiskey after spending the weekend in jail. So I said to him, 'Yer honah, I wanna take the fifth.'

"The judge said, 'That's not funny, Mr. Dawes. How you wanna plead to them charges?'

"I looked around the court and cleared my throat and puffed myself up like a toadfish. And I gave a speech so bitchin' the whole damn building shook.

"I said, 'Yer honah, what are things coming to when a man's gotta eat foreign meatballs? Next thing you know, he's gonna be drowndin' in bird's nest soup and borsht. And how's he gonna keep a woman in dresses when she only wears 'em once? He'll have to move to China, so he can buy 'em on the cheap.'

"The judge, he put down his gavel 'cause he knew I had a point. He said, 'I don't like dresses from China, and I don't like beets in my soup.' He looked at the cop all suspicious-like, and the cop started pissing his pants. The judge asked, 'You been selling us out to the Chinks and fucking Mr. Dawes wife?'

"The cop couldn't do nothing but stutter, so I kept on addressin' the court. 'Where's it gonna end, yer honah?' I said. 'Where is it gonna end? When we're riding around in rickshaws and calling each other comrade?'

"I heard someone shout, 'Here, here!' And someone else yelled, 'USA!' And everyone started cheerin' like I'd just been elected pope.

"The judge thought for a moment then said to the cop, 'I'm tossing out this case. And I'm tossing you into the slammer for endangering public safety. Don't you know riding in rickshaws puts splinters in your ass?' The bailiff double-cuffed the cop and walked him to the holding tank. The cop screamed, 'I only fucked her once' but judge just said, 'Next case.'

"Before I knowed it, the crowd hoisted me up and carried me outta the courtroom. And Ma hurried along behind us 'cause my speech had her hot for my pecker. And people pounded my shoulders and said I should run for Congress. But I told 'em I'd rather go fishing and catch me some largemouth bass."

•

A MONTH LATER, Dad and I are sitting out on our back porch. That was after Ma poured his booze into the sink then threw him outta the house. Dad kept shoutin' that whiskey don't spoil, but Ma wasn't havin' none of that.

Dad sits there sipping a fifth of scotch that Ma ain't discovered yet: a bottle he hid in the woodpile where Ma wasn't likely to look. And I sit there munching watermelon and spitting out the seeds. I can't spit 'em very far, which is kinda disappointing. I'll bet if Dad gave me a Heimlich pop, I could spit 'em twenty feet.

Dad says to me, "Toby, I ever told you about the time I chewed out a cop?"

I've heard the story about two dozen times, but I said, "Tell me about it, Dad." You can't tell a good story too often, and that's just how it is.

∘ ∘ ∘

I'm Going to Kick Some Ass

I STUDIED HER MUG SHOT, memorizing her face. She was a boney woman in her early twenties. Her forehead was broad, her nostrils flared, her cheek bore a menacing scar. Her eyes were perturbed as though stung by the flash of the booking camera.

Since she had struck her ex-boyfriend with a hammer, the photo seemed grimly prophetic. The victim had even phoned me to say he was still being harassed by her. So I braced myself when the front desk clerk buzzed my office, telling me that she had reported for her intake interview.

Pocketing my handcuffs, I stepped out of my office and walked to the reception area. The room was packed with other probationers, but I recognized her from her mug shot. She was sitting alone at the back of the room, texting on a cell phone.

As I strode towards her, she eyed me suspiciously. Her gaze was like that of an animal poised for flight or fight.

"Lorena Jefferson?" I said.

She nodded her head like a cobra.

"Tom Hemmings," I said. "Come with me, please. I'm going to be your probation officer."

Rising from the chair, she accompanied me back down the hallway. She did not look at me nor attempt conversation. As she shuffled into my office, I closed the door behind us. I fished the handcuffs from my pocket.

"Put your hands behind your back," I said.

She obeyed me immediately, as a soldier might obey a superior officer, and I slipped the cuffs onto her wrists. She did not speak until I had set the teeth and fastened the safety locks.

"Awwww, Mr. Hemmings," she drawled. "Whyja have to do that?"

"Anything sharp in your pockets?" I said.

"Naw, Mr. Hemmings. I ain't never done no drugs."

33

I patted her down then emptied the pockets of her jeans. She had nothing on her but her cell phone, a bus pass, and a couple of dollars in loose change. She slumped in a chair by my desk while I filled out a booking card.

"Whyja have to do that?" she repeated.

"Why did you violate the stay away order?" I said. "Didn't you think he would file a complaint?"

"I guess," she muttered. "He done about everything else to me."

"Did he cheat on you?"

"Yeh."

"Beat you?"

"Yeh."

"Spend your money on crack?"

"Course he did."

Her answers did not surprise me. Women charged with domestic battery were almost always victims themselves. Those brave enough to strike back were usually put on probation. The irony was irresistible.

"So why did you go to his house?"

She raised her eyebrows. "I wanted to see my son, sir. He won't let me see my son no more."

"So you told him you'd kick his ass again. That's a terrorist threat, Lorena."

She dropped her gaze as though searching for dimes and drew a shallow breath. "He beat *me* up a hundred times, sir. I beat him up only once. As I see it, I got some ass kickin' comin'."

I placed the booking card aside and inventoried her property. "Do you want to make a phone call?" I said.

"Naw, sir."

"You need to blow your nose?"

"Naw, sir."

I dropped her property into an envelope and sealed it with a piece of Scotch tape. "Are you ready?" I said.

She looked at me and shrugged. "What I gotta do to be ready?"

"Do you need to compose yourself?"

She turned her head sideways, scratching her nose on her shoulder. When she finished this maneuver, she smiled. "For a cop you ain't having much fun, Mr. Hemmings. How come you're askin' me all them questions?"

"I'm only doing my job."

She snorted. "Your job is to put me in jail, sir. Ya don't gotta bug me with silly-ass questions."

"It was silly of *you* to threaten him," I said.

"S'ppose it was," she replied. "But why do I gotta be sensible while the law gets to play the fool?"

"You'll see a judge tomorrow," I mumbled. "Maybe he'll let you post bail."

"Ain't that up to *you*, Mr. Hemmings. Whatcha gonna tell him?"

I made no reply as I helped her to her feet. The probation department had a zero tolerance policy when violent probationers reoffended. If I were to comply with departmental policy, I would ask that she be sent to state prison.

I held her by her elbow and walked her to the jail elevator. As I glanced at her face, her proud stoic face, I knew I would disobey the department. "How are those cuffs?" I asked her. "Not too tight, I hope."

•

THE FOLLOWING MORNING, having read her presentence report, I went into the courtroom where I had put her on calendar. According to the presentence report, she had been born in South San Francisco and raised in the foster care system. She had worked a series of food service jobs, never for very long, and was last employed as a night watchman for a pet store, a job from which she was fired after quarreling with the manager. She was now living in a subsidized hotel in the Tenderloin District and drawing a General Assistance pension. She had no prior arrests, which I found a little surprising. The jail psychiatrist had diagnosed her as binary thinker with an explosive disorder.

I entered the holding tank, a bare brick room crowded with women in jumpsuits. She was sitting alone in a far corner of the room. She looked like an outcast.

"Mawning, Mr. Hemmings," she murmured.

Suppressing a pang of pity, I sat beside her on the bench. *She's dangerous*, I reminded myself. *She almost killed a man. There's a reason the probation department takes a hard line when violent felons reoffend.*

"I 'pologize for my appearance," she said. "Guess orange don't suit me too well."

"How did you sleep?" I said.

She yawned. "That why ya come to see me, sir? To be askin' me how I slept?"

"I'm only doing my job," I said.

She cracked her knuckles and groaned. "How many times ya gonna say that, sir? It ain't like I'm faultin' you for it."

"I didn't come here to be lectured," I snapped.

"Naw, ya come here to make me a deal. Maybe ya shouldn't do that, sir— ya might get yourself in some trouble."

I had received that same caution at the training academy fifteen years ago. *Don't get emotionally involved with them. Keep a professional distance.* I reminded myself that collusion could result if I got too close to a client.

She stroked my shoulder with the palm of her hand. "Ya got dust on your jacket, Mr. Hemmings," she said. "Don'tcha wanna look good for the judge?"

I removed her hand from my jacket and placed it onto her lap. "If your ex starts annoying you, call me. If you want to kick his ass again, call me. In fact, any time you get pissed off, I want you to give me a call."

She wiped her hand on her jump suit and winked. "If you wanna be a hard-ass, sir, you oughta make better deals."

"Don't you think you can handle it?"

She folded her arms. "I ain't sure *you* can, sir. Not if you just wanna do your job. If I call you every time I'm pissed off, you won't have no time for that."

•

THE NEXT MORNING, she came to my office. The judge had released her on her own recognizance, pending a bench hearing for violating her probation. She was wearing dark-blue eyeshadow that made her look like a bandit.

She wrinkled her nose as though hit by an odor then sat on the chair by my desk. "I s'ppose you want me to thank you," she murmured.

"Thank me for what?" I said.

"For askin' the judge to let me out of jail. The women in there are crazy—they thought I was some kinda snitch."

"Did you give them a reason?"

"Naw, you did, sir. When you came into that cell by the courtroom and tried to hold my hand. Didja forget you're a cop, Mr. Hemmings?"

I shrugged. "We still have a deal, Lorena."

She locked her ankles under the chair and shook her head vigorously. "Not when I'm wearing orange, we don't. If one of them bitches had jumped me, I'd 'a' knocked her flat on her ass."

I recited her terms of probation to her: a year of counseling, some community service, and a fifty dollar monthly probation fee. She rolled her eyes as she signed and initialed the grant. "I gotta *pay* to come see you?" she said.

"If you put it that way—yes."

"Sir, I ain't sure you're worth fifty dollars a month. Ya act like ya don't want me around."

"Now why would you think that?" I said.

She folded her hands neatly onto her lap. "Can't ya see? Mr. Hemmings, I'm ugly as sin. I got scars on my head where he beat me, sir. I can't wear my hair in no permanent."

"Why didn't you call the cops on him before he set them on you?"

"I s'ppose I shoulda," she said. "But I *never* been no snitch. He beat my ass a hundred times, and I never snitched him out once."

"Why would you want to protect him?" I said.

She looked at me with haunted eyes then tilted her head to one side. "That's just the kinda woman I am, Mr. Hemmings. I'll also be standin' by you. Even though you put me in handcuffs, even though you took me to jail. Even though you might send my ass to the pen, I'm gonna stand by you."

•

I REFERRED HER to a group counseling program at Center for Special Problems, a low-budget city project for residents with mental health issues. I also gave her a list of centers where she could receive supervised child visitations. And I dropped by her hotel in the Tenderloin to confirm her living arrangements. Her room contained only a bed and a dresser. It looked as though nobody lived there.

She was perched on her bed, hunched over her cell phone and playing *Angry Birds.*

"You need a television, Lorena," I said.

She cocked her head like a spaniel. "There wouldn't be no point in that, sir. The residents here steal from the rooms to get money to buy 'emselves crack."

"At least you can lock your door," I said lamely.

"They'll only pick the lock. I can't even brew a cup of tea 'cause this whore ran off with my hotplate."

Feeling overmatched, I placed my hands on my hips. Since I wasn't Dirty Harry, I would have to feign being a hard-ass. "If you have evidence of that," I said, "I want you to tell the management."

She put down her cell phone and rubbed her eyes. "Management ain't gonna care, Mr. Hemmings, so there ain't no point in snitchin'. I'll just have to do what a bitch gotta do."

"I suppose that means kicking her ass."

"I'm gonna do more 'an that, Mr. Hemmings. That missy won't mess with my Kool-Aid no more after I scratch out her eyes."

"You know what *I'll* have to do if you do that?"

"Whatcha gotta do, Mr. Hemmings."

"I'll have to lock you back up. And that's going to break my heart. You want to break my heart, Lorena?"

"Naw, sir, naw."

"You going to scratch someone's eyes out?"

"Naw, sir, naw," she muttered. "But don't be expectin' no cup of tea when you come to pay me a visit."

A day before her hearing, she called me on my office phone.

"Mr. Hemmings," she said in a panicky voice. "I ain't gonna look good for the judge."

"I know that," I said. I had read her progress report from Center for Special Problems. The report described her behavior in class as hostile and withdrawn.

"You need to open up," I said.

"That ain't no way to put it, sir. That class is fulla transexuals that wanna get into my pants."

"Be glad you're not that attractive," I joked.

She snorted over the phone. "That don't make no difference, Mr. Hemmings—I come from South San Francisco. A bitch got no use for gender benders when she comes from that part of town."

"Lorena," I said, "if you pick a fight, you know where I'll have to put you."

"Where ya gonna put me, Mr. Hemmings?"

"The Hotel California. And that's going to break my heart. You want to break my heart, Lorena?"

"Naw, sir, naw."

"Are you going to beat up a transexual?"

"Naw, sir—I ain't going to do that. But if one of 'em grabs my pussy, I'm gonna be angry at *you*."

•

HER REVOCATION HEARING went smoothly in spite of her behavior in class. Over the objection of an irate assistant DA, the judge cut her some slack. She was sentenced to two days in jail, time she had already served, and was ordered to come back to court in a month with a better progress report.

A day later, she dropped by my office. She was wearing a leopard skin jacket and had dyed her hair coral pink.

"Are you trying to scare off the trannies?" I said.

She rolled her eyes impatiently and sat down in the chair by my desk. "Whyja tell the judge I'm a special needs client. I don't need nothin' special."

"You need to finish your counseling," I said.

"I *know* that, Mr. Hemmings. But the instructor he gave me some time out from class. I'm doin' art therapy now."

"I'm glad that works for you."

She sighed like a dog in a cage. "I'm sittin' around drawin' pictures, sir. How come that makes you glad?"

"Just fake it until you make it. That's all you have to do."

She pulled a loose thread from her jacket. "Like you been fakin' it, sir?"

"What do you mean by that?"

"You're s'ppose to be a cop, Mr. Hemmings. But you ain't been kickin' my ass. I'm gonna lose my respect for you unless you start kickin' my ass."

"When would you like me to start?" I said.

She dug her cell phone from the pocket of her jacket and started playing *Angry Birds*. "I ain't listenin' to you, Mr. Hemmings—see? I ain't showin' you no respect."

We sat for several minutes while she played her video game. "Damn," she said. "This level is fucked up. It's hard to bomb them pigs."

"Keep that up, Lorena," I said, "and I'll do what I have to do."

"Whatcha gonna do to me, Mr. Hemmings?"

Holding my cuffs in a pistol grip, I clicked the strands into place. "I'll march your butt to jail."

"And that's gonna break your heart, I s'ppose."

"Yes, it will break my heart."

She played the game for another minute then offered me her cell phone. "Ya wanna try an' improve on my score?"

"I want you to put that away."

"All right, Mr. Hemmings, I'll put it away." She slipped her cell phone back into her pocket then patted me on the wrist. "But I don't want you forgettin' you're s'ppose to be a cop."

•

I RESIGNED MYSELF to her calling my cell phone almost every day. Her calls usually came around four p.m. as I was riding home on the Caltrain. I had given her my schedule and told her when best to phone me. And, apparently, she considered it poor etiquette to bother me at work.

Our conversations grew as predictable as an *I Love Lucy* rerun. First she would inquire if I'd had a pleasant day. Then she would announce her chagrin with somebody in her building or counseling program. Her solutions to these provocations were patently the same. "If somebody fucks with my Kool-Aid, sir, I'm gonna kick his crotch."

When I promised to slap her in leg irons, she came to my office unannounced. "Why do I gotta be in a program that's only making me madder?"

"It's supposed to teach you patience," I said.

"I know how to be patient already. I was patient for five whole years. Never raised my voice to him, always bowed my head. Don't be preachin' to me 'bout patience, sir, 'cause you don't know what patience is."

Her outburst was so unscripted that I labored to respond. "That's enablement, not patience," I said. "Braining him with a claw hammer wasn't too smart either."

"Well, it got me out of the house. It got him offa my back. And now I'm having me some fun by messin' with your head. The best thing I ever done, Mr. Hemmings, was to kick his motherfuckin' ass."

"You still have to finish that program."

She shrugged "'Cause ya don't wanna put me in jail? What kinda reason is that, Mr. Hemmings."

"A bad one," I admitted. "But it's all the reason I've got."

"Well, go ahead and *put* me in jail. That really ain't much of a threat."

"Consider it a promise," I said, removing the cuffs from my pocket.

She shook her head and stared at the floor. She looked like a jilted bride.

"Is that all you got to promise me when I toldja I'd stand by you? I been patient enough already, sir. An' I got the scars to prove it."

•

SHE STOPPED CALLING me each afternoon, an interruption I rather missed. But I had anticipated being on her shit list and was ready for the snub. When her program sent me a letter of termination, my indignity only increased. Was it to get back at me that she had threatened her instructor and stormed out of the classroom? Had she decided to break my heart as dramatically as I broke hers? An incoming call woke my cellphone, and I pressed it to my ear.

At first I did not recognize the voice: the tone was too smooth, the timbre too sunny, the pitch too disembodied. It was a voice as honeyed as treacle, a voice to be poured over crepes. It was the voice a recording gives you when you phone your congressman.

Having hoped to speak first with Lorena, I almost shut off the phone. I wanted to hear a less syrupy voice than the one that assailed me now. And her voice was bold not solicitious, like that of a warrior queen.

The probation chief repeated his questions. "When are you locking her up?"

It took only that whiff of temerity to tighten my grip on the phone. "How carefully did you read that report?" I said. "She told the instructor, 'You just bought your ticket.' That's not a specific threat."

"I know what she meant by it, Hemmings. When are you locking her up?"

I gripped the phone as though clutching an eel. "Maybe next Tuesday," I said. "Unless she turns herself in."

"Would a three-day suspension change your mind?"

"Make it a week," I answered. "I've got some artwork to do."

I shut off the the phone, unduly sustained by the thought of a disciplinary suspension. I was starting to plan my vacation when I heard the rap on my office door. I opened the door and let her in. She had a can of pop in her hand and a sketchpad under her arm.

"What choo hollarin' about, Mr. Hemmings?" she said. "I heardja clear out in the hallway."

"Did you come here to break my heart?" I said.

She tossed the can into my wastebasket and sat down in the chair by my desk. "Sheeit, Mr. Hemmings. Locking me up won't break your pissant heart."

"If it doesn't, I don't know what will," I said.

"Your bossman wants me in jail, don't he, sir? And you don't wanna be no cop."

She rose to her feet and faced the wall, her hands tucked behind her back. "Quit talking your bullshit, Mr. Hemmings. Do what you gotta do."

"Do you want to take your sketchpad?" I said.

"You do what you gotta do."

I slipped the cuffs on her as though they were bracelets then set the safety locks. "Anything sharp in your pockets?"

"Naw, sir, there ain't," she said.

She did not break stride as I grasped her arm and marched her butt to jail. She did not speak again until the gate shut behind us and we stood in the booking bay. As I ran a wand alongside her body, she gave me a wary glance.

"Mr. Hemmings, I swear. If I don't take care of you, I don't know who else will."

° ° °

Hayley's Picnic

HAYLEY ROSE CONNOLLY, a dark-eyed girl of seventeen, was a new student at Putnamville High—a seedy little school downwind from a hog farm. Accustomed to fancy private schools, she found Putnamville High to be utterly disagreeable. Still, she would have to make the most of it; her father, a big shot at IBM, had lost his job when the local plant relocated to India. Now he was managing a dreadful little gas station in the boonies and earning Walmart wages. And Hayley, who had once had her own private bedroom and bathroom, was crammed into a three-room trailer with her parents and six noisy sisters. How horrid it was to be suddenly poor. How she missed her tennis club friends.

Hayley despised the pupils at her new school: oafish farm boys, pimpled nerds, and gossipy small-minded girls with way too much eye shadow. But, still, she wanted the students to like her. An accomplished socialite, she was used to being the center of attention at country club dances and debutante balls.

And she wanted to *stay* the center of attention, even if it meant mingling with the great unwashed. But the Putnamville students showed no interest in her. The boys took one look at her underdeveloped breasts and did not initiate conversations. And the girls glanced incuriously at her before resuming their mindless chatter with one another. *Whatever is a girl to do?* Haley wondered. *Will I ever be popular again?* As she sat by herself in the school cafeteria, nibbling a bologna and cheese sandwich, Hayley felt cheated and depressed.

One afternoon, while riding home on the school bus, Hayley had an idea. *I'll have a picnic*, she thought. *I'll invite the entire senior class. We'll play lots of games and have wonderful refreshments. And then I'll be popular once again.* But where would she find money for a picnic? Her family now qualified for food stamps, and her miserly father had cut her allowance to fifty cents a week.

Another idea popped into her head. *What if I went to the local merchants—the butcher, the grocer, the fruit vendor at the farmers mart—and offered them some of the refreshments in exchange for a little help? If the butcher provides the ground meat, I'll make him some scrumptious burgers. If the grocer gives me some flour, I'll bake him a heavenly cake. If the fruit seller gives me some lemons, I'll make him a mouth-watering punch. After the merchants have had their share, there will be plenty left over for the kids.*

Hayley went to her mother and told her about her idea. Her mother kissed her daughter and said it was a wonderful plan. And she promised to help host the party, which would take place in the town park behind the trailer.

Her heart thumping wildly, Hayley hopped into her father's Ford and visited the local merchants. At first, they looked at her skeptically and solemnly shook their heads. But when she flashed a hundred watt smile and told them they could sponsor the picnic, they changed their minds. The butcher gave her ten pounds of ground chuck. The grocer gave her a sack of flour, a packet of cocoa, and a box of baking soda. And the fruit vender provided her with a whole crate of freshly picked lemons.

The next day at school, Hayley passed out invitations to everybody in the senior class—invitations she had printed on cream colored paper.

Come frolic in the summer breeze
Beneath the sheltering boughs
Where robins chirp and flowers please
And lovers make their vows.
The fun will commence 1:00 p.m., Saturday,
at Turkey Trot Park.
Refreshments supplied by Mercantile Meats,
Gus's Groceries, and Fabio Fruit & Vegetables.

When she had delivered the last invitation, Hayley hurried to the local Dairy Queen. There, she toasted her enterprise with a Rocky Road ice cream float.

•

A DOZEN KIDS showed up on the day of the picnic, almost half of the senior class. Hayley greeted each one of them at the entrance to the park. She shook their hands as though working a pump handle. "How marvelous of you to come," she gushed. Her smile was as bright as a beacon and never left her face.

While the kids pitched horseshoes and played volleyball, Hayley slapped the hamburger patties onto an outdoor grill. And then she squeezed the lemons and made a spicy punch.

After the kids were done with their games, Hayley poured each one of them a teacup full of punch. The rest of the punch she emptied into a cooler full of ice packs. She had promised the fruit vendor plenty of punch for his daughter's birthday party, and she didn't want to disappoint him. He had been so generous with her, after all.

"All you can drink," Hayley said to her guests as she passed the teacups around. When the kids gulped their punch down and asked for more, Hayley chirped, "No, that's *all* you can drink." The kids looked disappointed and still a little parched, but all of them agreed that it was the finest punch they had ever drunk.

The aroma of burgers now ripened the air—burgers sizzled to perfection. Of course, she would have to give them to the butcher; he was hosting a Fourth of July celebration and expected lots of hungry guests. But the grill was coated with plenty of grease—pungent, meaty grease. Opening a sack of buns, Hayley smeared each one with a generous mopping of grease. She then filled the buns with onions, pickle relish, and a squirt of Poupon Mustard.

"May I Poupon you?" Hayley joked, and the kids had a hearty laugh. They did seem perplexed that their buns had no meat, but all of them agreed that the buns were the freshest they had ever tasted.

Once the kids had devoured their buns, Hayley clapped her hands. "Time for a little cake," she trilled. Opening a cardboard box, Hayley removed a huge chocolate cake. It was four layers high, heart-shaped, and made with farm-fresh eggs. On top of the cake was an inspiring message written in pink piping gel. *I will always serve my friends*, the looping letters announced.

Seizing a knife and spatula, Hayley cut out a sliver of cake. The rest of the cake she put back in the cardboard box. Naturally, it would have to go to the grocer; such a wonderful man. He was hosting his fiftieth high school reunion, and he only deserved the best.

Slowly, meticulously, Hayley doled out crumbs from the single sliver of cake. She piled the crumbs onto paper plates then covered each pile with a dollop of frosting. "Let them eat cake," she tittered as she passed around the plates.

The kids poked tentatively at the crumbs, eager to make them last. How delicious they were, how spongy and moist, how heavenly they smelled.

A treat like this could not be rushed, all of them agreed. Only a shameless glutton would hurry such a delight. When the kids had eaten the last of the crumbs and licked the paper plates clean, they declared Hayley's cake to be among the tastiest in the land.

A brilliant sunset lit up the park as the picnic came to an end. The gloaming was captured in Hayley's eyes, which sparkled like cubic zirconia. As she watched the last ray of sun disappear, Hayley chuckled with delight. "At last, at last," she said to herself, "I'm popular once again."

•

NOW THAT SHE was back in demand, Hayley kept her image intact. She wore only the brightest of Dollar Store jewelry; she dyed her hair platinum blonde. She even ran for senior class president and lost by just twenty-two votes. The cheerleader who won must have stuffed the ballot box, just like she stuffed her bra.

When her senior year was over, Hayley received a proposal of marriage. The dear old gent who owned Mercantile Meats asked her to be his wife. Delighted, Hayley accepted at once. What a joy it would be to move out of that ratty old trailer.

To celebrate the nuptials, Haley planned a potluck reception. She rented the county fairground, she bought a white chiffon dress, and she made sure the whole town of Putnamville would share the glorious day. *Cash and gift cards equally welcome*, the engraved invitations read. There must have been rain in the forecast because this time nobody came.

o o o

Summer of Love

"TURN ON, TUNE IN, DROP OUT." Catalyzed by this catchphrase, a wave of youthful pilgrims descended on the congested sidewalks and tenements of Haight-Ashbury—an oasis of perpetual partying, interchangeable sex, and mind-altering drugs. *"People in motion,"* crooned Scott McKenzie in his famous ballad, "San Francisco." But the affect was more one of paralysis: a state not dissimilar to that of the lotus-eaters of Greek mythology.

The hippie culture was, of course, unsustainable: a benign yet exhausting pose destined to collapse from overextension. Visit the Haight today and you will find only vestiges of that famous summer of '67: a poster shop, a vinyl record store, the abandoned home of the Grateful Dead. A few old hippies still sit in the parks, and they will not be offended if you offer them five dollars to pose for a picture. After all, they are much like statues: effigies of a vitality long spent.

The Summer of Love was forty years old when I became a San Francisco probation officer. I was placed in a domestic violence unit, so it seemed unlikely that a former flower child would ever come my way. But I had been on the job for only a month when one was assigned to my caseload: a rail-thin woman in her mid-fifties. She was wearing a caftan, love beads, and a headband with several drooping feathers. Although she had bruised the scalp of her former boyfriend, she did not impress me as a batterer. With her Roman nose, jingling bracelets, and long stringy mane, she better resembled somebody's eccentric maiden aunt. And her lack of body weight suggested that she was in delicate health.

I held out my hand as she entered my office. "Tom Hemmings," I said. "I'll be your probation officer."

She pinched my fingers as though testing a melon then sat on the chair by my desk. "Cynthia Majik," she said. "I guess I'll be your probationer." She studied me as though I were a painting. "Well," she said. "You seem harmless enough. I was expecting you to slam me against the wall and tie me up with flex cuffs."

"I'm a bookworm who carries a badge," I said. "I'm not into slamming bodies."

"How quaint," she laughed. "A cop that reads. Have you read Lobsang Rampa, Thomas?"

"Wasn't he a plumber who claimed to be a lama?"

"He was," she said. "But he wrote like a poet. Isn't that enough for you, sir?"

"It might be," I said, "if he wasn't insane. I read somewhere that he gave his cat credit for dictating one of his books."

She folded her arms and sighed like a faucet. "My dear, the cat's name was Fifi Greywhiskers. Please have the manners to use her name."

"That's way too much etiquette for a cat."

She frowned. "If you don't think cats have souls, you're more of a pig than you think. My cat has been with me for twenty years. Next month, he'll be old enough to vote."

"You didn't tell me his name," I teased.

"His name is Winston Churchill. I call him Winnie for short."

"That's not too original."

She tapped her foot. "I'm not at all original, Thomas. I read Rod McKuen poetry, I listen to The Doors, I even belong to the Cannabis Club. I'm really a bit of a cliché."

"A hippie who brained her boyfriend? That sounds original to me."

She patted my wrist as though calming a child. "If a misdemeanor makes me original, you're much too easily impressed."

"I'm more impressed by your rap sheet," I said. "Half a dozen arrests by the DEA. Not a single conviction."

"Do you actually think I'm a drug dealer, sir?"

"I doubt that."

"I dispense marijuana to the sick and infirm. People with cancer, people in hospice care, people in chronic pain."

I shrugged. "Only the feds would criminalize that."

"Did you protest the Vietnam War?" she asked.

"Of course."

"My goodness. A cop with a conscience. I guess that makes *you* original."

She told me her personal history as I filled out her background form. She was born in a small town in North Dakota, her mother was half Sioux, her parents died in a car crash in the spring of '67. Abandoning a foster home several weeks later, she hitchhiked to San Francisco and worked as a volunteer in the free medical clinic on Clayton Street. While attending the Monterey Pop Festival, where she helped manage the stage, she fell under the spell of a man whom she called her spiritual husband. That the relationship lasted four decades was no compliment to her "husband." She described him as the "guru type": a self-declared sage who brought home runaways and had sex with them. Tiring of his philanthropy, she brained him with a meat tenderizer, an incident that resulted in her immediate arrest and her placement on probation.

"I barely grazed him, Thomas," she said. "The only reason he called the police is that he wanted me out of the house."

"If you ask me, it's kind of surprising that you didn't clock him sooner."

"I *didn't* ask you, Thomas."

"Why did you even put up with him? You should have left long ago."

She fingered her love beads fastidiously as though she were counting pearls. "Are you judging me, Thomas? I'd rather you didn't. A woman can't be a prude when she lives in the Tenderloin."

"Forgive me for being appalled," I said.

"Forgive you?" she said. "No, I don't think I will. But I'm still going to bake you some brownies."

"Are you hoping to expand my consciousness?"

She chuckled then shook her head. "I'm not *that* starry-eyed, dear. But I do offer help where it's needed. Aren't you getting a little tired of being correct all the time?"

"Would you rather I went to pot?"

She yawned while patting her mouth. "You're beginning to bore me—let's finish this meeting. Please give me my instructions and let me be on my way."

Her terms of probation were standard, so it didn't take long to explain them to her: a stay away order from her guru boyfriend, a hundred hours of community service, and a one-year anger management program. "It's the judge who thinks you need counseling," I said when she looked at me accusingly.

I handed her the probation grant and asked her to review it. She lingered over the contract as though checking a shopping list. "My judge presumes too much," she said finally, "if he thinks it's counseling I need."

"You need it to get off probation. I'll send you to a program."

She signed the grant with a flourish then initialed each of the terms. When she was finished, she tore off her copy and tucked it into her purse.

"Winston Churchill may die soon," she said. "What I *need* is another cat."

•

I SENT HER to the Tenderloin Mental Health Clinic for treatment and assessment. She was diagnosed as a manic-depressive who suffered from

PTSD, a condition she had long been alleviating with medical marijuana. Her psych report also stated that she was selfless to a fault, exhausting herself by working in soup kitchens seven days a week. She was also in the habit of giving money to the homeless at Saint Anthony's Church, a practice that did not seem compatible with her meager General Assistance checks. The report stressed that during her manic phases she was in danger of collapse, and suggested that she take alprazolam so as to better pace herself.

Unimpressed, I chose to ignore the report. I did not wish to challenge her maverick spirit with antiseptic advice. Not when she embodied the very best of the hippie phenomenon.

I visited her in the Dalt Hotel where she lived in a city-subsidized apartment. The apartment was cramped and depressing, and smelled of cat litter and incense. The bed was unmade, the dresser messy, dirty dishes filled the sink. And a poster of Timothy Leary hung over the stove like a specter.

She was sitting at a small table, arranging some Tarot cards. "Can you handle clutter?" she asked me as I walked into the room. A huge mangy tabby slunk out of my way and hopped upon her lap.

"Winnie doesn't like you," she said. "I rather thought he would."

"I'm not here for his approval," I replied.

She shrugged and kept laying down cards. "I hoped you two would hit it off. You're both irredeemable snobs."

"I'm used to snubs," I said as I sat on a hardback chair.

She swept up the cards and shuffled them. "So what brings you here, Thomas?"

"A home visit."

"How civil. Or is that part of your job?"

"It is."

She cut the deck. "Did you hear that Winnie? He's not here because he likes us."

"No need for tea and brownies," I joked.

"I've already *baked* you the brownies," she snapped. "At least, you can take them with you."

She spread out the cards in the shape of a fan and turned three of them face-up. "If you're not here socially, how about a reading? I'll even charge you for it."

Sheepishly, I looked at the cards. "Will you think better of me if I took the reading for free?"

She stroked the cat. "You're a cop, Mr. Hemmings. A little more polished than most, but you *are* a cop on my back. No, I will not think better of you, but I'll give you a free reading anyway."

She arranged the three cards in a pyramid shape and studied them thoughtfully. "The Hanged Man, the Hermit, the King of Swords. The Hanged Man means you are stuck, the Hermit means you're a skeptic, the King of Swords means you're obsessed with control—that's probably why you became a cop."

I judged her remarks to be over-rehearsed, a set of pat phrases she probably used to get suckers to pay for more readings. No matter that cops are role players too; I had certainly had purer moments. I had cheered when Richard Nixon resigned, I had protested a colonial war, I had even sampled a hit of acid during a peace march on Washington. That I was now a peace officer did not really mean I had wholly abandoned the faith. At least, the oppressions I championed were milder than those that once stood in their place.

"Thomas," she said, "what do you hold *sacred*?"

"Will law and order suffice?"

She reshuffled the cards. "The law is an ass—am I not proof of that? You must be rather desperate if the law is the best you can do."

"And yet you are giving me brownies," I said.

"My dear, that's because I have standards."

She dropped Winston Churchill onto the floor and fetched a plate from the kitchen counter. A dozen brownies, each wrapped in cellophane, lay upon the plate. I accepted them out of courtesy; I did not plan to sample them.

Sensing my disinclination, she patted me on the arm. "Thomas, my dear, *do* make sure that you return the dish."

•

I GOT RID of the brownies by handing them to a band of homeless people. When she reported to my office the following week, I gave her back her plate. She slipped it into her purse and smiled without conviction. "What did you do with them, Thomas? I know you didn't eat them."

I confessed to my act of charity. "Will *that* redeem me a little?"

"What do you want with redemption?" she asked. "You seem happy enough as a cop."

"It was the act of a kindred spirit."

"It was the act of a charlatan. Kindred spirits are benevolent, Thomas—they don't flash badges and guns."

"If I were that forgiving, I couldn't do my job."

She folded her hands in her lap and yawned. "When I told you you were original, that wasn't a compliment. I would find you far less annoying if you behaved like a typical cop."

"You'd prefer me to be a cliché?"

"I would—I can handle typical cops. I guess that comes from being arrested half a dozen times."

"You handled the feds pretty well. They let you off every time."

"Do you really think they are done with me, Thomas? They have me in their database, and they're always looking for snitches. It's only a matter of time until they arrest me again."

"Give up your cannabis card. Stop dealing pot."

"Do you think that will make a difference?" She waved her hand impatiently: the subject of drug busts and federal overkill was boring her to distraction. "My dear, shall I tell you about *real* kindred spirits?"

I felt myself blush. "Yes," I said, "if you think I have more to learn."

She told me about a Grateful Dead concert she had attended twenty years ago. The concert was delayed when it started to rain, but she had sat in the downpour with thousands of Dead Heads as though she had no mind of her own. The rain finally stopped and a rainbow emerged, and the Grateful Dead took the stage. "It was as though the rainbow united us, Thomas. It was as though we had one soul. I was never less lonely than I was at that moment. I was glad to be a cliché."

"Sounds like heaven," I said, unconvinced.

"Don't be condescending," she said. "It's bad enough that you pity me— you don't have to fib as well."

"All right, I'll say it. Those were fair-weather friendships. You're worth much more than that."

She looked at me curiously then shook her head. "Are you planning to lecture me, Thomas, for holding a memory dear. I'm a silly old woman who lives with a cat. How much am I really worth?"

•

WITH THEIR BASEBALL CAPS, blue jeans, and polo shirts, they did not look like federal agents. They looked like three kids on a fishing trip who had wandered into my office. I expected them to start talking about baseball or the kegger they had attended last night. I did not expect them to show me a warrant for her arrest.

Two months ago, they had caught her on film peddling weed in Grandview Park. She had sold an ounce of Acapulco gold to an undercover buyer—enough pot for a felony conviction if the matter went to trial. Of course, it was not her they wanted—she was worth more as a witness. If she agreed to testify against her supplier, they would ask that her charge be dropped.

Having learned that she was scheduled for an office visit, they wanted me to talk to her. They hoped I might convince her to give up the name of her source. I asked them to wait in the reception area while I prepared her for the bust.

"Some kids plan to lock you up," I said, after escorting her to my office.

She eased herself into the chair by my desk then rummaged through her purse. "Yes, I spotted them in the hallway," she said. "They've bothered me before." Removing a brush from her purse, she began to stroke her hair. "Will you ask them to wait a few minutes? I want to look presentable for my mug shot."

"They should pick on someone their own damn size."

"That *someone* would be hard to find, my dear? They're a bunch of silly boys."

"They ought to be tossing a frisbee somewhere or trying to pick up girls."

"Well, at least, it's nice to be wanted," she said.

"It isn't you that they want. They want you to drop a dime."

She checked her face in a hand mirror then pinched color into her cheeks. "I'm not really sure I can spare a dime, Thomas. I spent the last of my assistance check on a catnip mouse for Winnie."

"I forgot that you have standards," I said.

"It seems that you do too."

"Ask your public defender to subpoena me. I'll testify on your behalf."

"That won't be necessary, dear." She reached back into her purse. "There's something far more important that I'd rather have you do."

"Yes, I'll feed Winston Churchill," I said.

"And try not to show him your badge." She patted me on the elbow and gave me the key to her apartment.

•

A FEDERAL PUBLIC DEFENDER phoned me. Her voice was youthful, fruity, and hinted of sorority rushes. She told me the case had been filed in District Court and the offer had been made. Cynthia had simply shaken her head and offered the court some brownies.

"Why didn't the judge cut her loose?" I asked. "She was busted by the Backstreet Boys."

The attorney laughed. "I kinda got that impression, hon. She said those kids would be much better off if they found something useful to do."

"Not everybody has standards," I said.

The attorney fell silent. I clutched the phone, wondering if we had been cut off. "They have the law," she said, finally.

"Does the law really need to have them?"

The fruity voice grew caustic as the lawyer continued to speak. "No one wants her in federal prison, not even those dorky boys. If she would help herself just a teensy bit, the judge will throw out her case. A single name— that's all it will take to get her back on the street."

"I doubt that the streets hold her dear enough for her to make a deal. She lives in a dump in the Tenderloin."

"Maybe you could convince her, hon. She speaks very highly of you."

Feeling a flush of undeserved pride, I defused the compliment. "That isn't because I'm her mentor," I said. "It's because I'm feeding her cat."

The attorney again fell silent. I waited for her to speak. "If you ask me," she said after several long seconds, "she's cuckoo for Cocoa Puffs."

"I didn't ask you," I said.

She laughed. "It seems you're the one holding her dear. But *I* need to know more about her before I pitch her case. Like, isn't she kinda crazy? Are there problems with her probation?"

"Only one," I blurted. "Her standards are higher than mine."

•

HER CASE was scheduled in the federal building on Golden Gate Avenue. Flashing my badge, I bypassed the checkpoint and entered a museum-like foyer. Some Chinese dancers were performing a number, and a bake sale was taking place.

I located her court and pushed past the portals. Her attorney was not in the courtroom. I showed my badge to the bailiff and ducked into the holding tank.

She was alone in the tank, perched on one of the benches. Her legs were tucked in a lotus position, and her eyes were closed in meditation. Her jump suit was much too large for her; it made her look like a child.

Opening her eyes, she scowled at me. "What are you doing here, Thomas?" she said. "I *hope* you're feeding my cat."

I sat beside her and held out my palm. "I hope you can spare a dime."

"If that's your idea of a joke," she replied, "I'd rather you spared me your wit."

"How much were you paid to sell that ounce?"

"I didn't receive a cent. I sold it for a friend."

"The same friend you brained with a hammer?"

"Yes."

"You've already taken a fall for him. You don't really owe him another."

53

She took my hand in hers and smiled thinly. "You're such a lecturer, Thomas," she said. "I ought to be taking notes."

"I'm here to back you up."

"How gallant. And what do you know about loyalty?"

"I know you should drop that dime."

Releasing my hands, she bowed her head as though she were sitting in church. "A dime for a memory—*really*, Thomas? When we joined our hands on the Golden Gate Bridge, when I wore a wreath of white roses? Goodness, the fog was so silvery we could barely see Alcatraz."

"He didn't deserve you."

She arched her eyebrows. "Deserving has nothing to do with it."

"It will in prison."

"A vow is a vow. Didn't you make one yourself when you let them give you that badge?"

"That's different," I said.

"Is it?" she answered. "The law is an ass and you know it."

"Give them his name, they'll forget about you."

"And allow them to wipe the slate clean? Not when I took his hands in mine and became his other half."

"You pledged yourself to a child abductor."

"That makes no difference, Thomas. My totem is the eagle—a bird that mates for life."

The door to the holding tank opened, and the bailiff called out her name.

"If you're not going to fly the coop," I said, "there's nothing I can do."

She looked at me sternly and rose to her feet. "Thomas," she said, "just feed Winston Churchill. I don't want him wasting away."

●

HER PUBLIC DEFENDER was standing at the podium when I walked into the courtroom. She was pretty young woman in a pink skirt suit and high heels that looked like stilts. The DEA agents had also arrived and were sitting at the District Attorney table. Still dressed in jeans and polo shirts, they were texting on their cell phones.

The young attorney was making a pitch to a justice that resembled Judge Judy: a sixtyish woman who looked as though she was impatient to leave the courtroom. In a voice that could sweeten coffee, the attorney kept dissing the drug buy, claiming that the agents had paid more than street value and were guilty of entrapment. "Are you serious?" the judge kept repeating as the lawyer presented her case. An assistant district attorney sat quietly, content to let the lawyer talk. Hunched in front of a tablet, he was playing *Words with Friends.*

When the public defender finished her spiel, the judge looked in my direction. "Would the probation officer care to weigh in?" she asked.

My pitch was equally impotent: I stressed that the defendant kept all her appointments, that she was too self-denying for crime, and that if she ended up in federal prison I would have to feed her cat.

Ignoring my stab at humor, the judge fixed her eyes on Cynthia. "Miss Majick," she said, "please take the offer. I won't be able to sleep tonight if I'm forced to send you to prison."

Stepping up to the podium, Cynthia cleared her throat. "I did charge too much for that ounce, your honor. I usually make very fair deals."

"Then please make another, Miss Majik."

Cynthia folded her arms. "Goodness, your honor!" she exclaimed. "How much more is that silly ounce worth?"

"You'll find out tomorrow," the judge said. "Tonight, I want to sleep."

As the judge breezed out of the courtroom, Cynthia patted my arm.

"Make the deal," I insisted.

"Don't be so dramatic," she said.

"I'm being benevolent."

"No you're not, dear. You're determined to play the hero, and that's not what I want from you."

"Would you rather rely on karma? Or maybe the King of Swords?"

"Why *not* karma?" she said. "I've been busted six times for possession, and the curtain hasn't fallen on me yet."

"You talk as though we're in a theatre."

She laughed and poked my side. "Court *is* theatre, Thomas. I should think you would know that by now."

"All I know is it's time you grew up."

"Is it?" she said. She squeezed my hand. "So why are you trying to diminish me, dear? Do I trouble you all that much?"

The courtroom was now almost empty, her attorney was nowhere in sight. She let go of my hand and allowed the bailiff to walk her back to the tank.

•

A KNOCK on my office door awoke me from a nap. I opened the door, and she entered my office. Sitting on the chair by my desk, she gave me a vinegary smile—the same smile she gave me yesterday when we sat in the holding tank.

"Thomas, please don't look so surprised. You make me feel like a ghost."

"You caught me unawares," I said.

"Were you sleeping on the job?"

"No," I lied.

"Don't fib to me, dear. I don't like it when you fib."

"I take it that judge will be sleeping tonight."

"She threw out the charge this morning. She told those boys they would have to find some other way to make their cases. Goodness, they looked so annoyed I almost felt sorry for them."

"Fuck them," I said.

"Don't be so self-righteous. They did what they thought was right."

Opening her purse, she removed a paper and handed it to me. It was a federal court order dismissing the drug charge. "You meant well, Thomas," she said, "and I love you. I know you don't want to hear that."

I shook my head self-consciously. "You loved those fair-weather hippies, you love that child abductor. And now you love the cop on your case. You deserve far better than that."

"Deserving has nothing to do with it, dear. I told you that once already." She rose to her feet. "May I hug you?" she said. "Or will that violate my probation?"

Pushing my chair away from the desk, I stiffly returned her embrace. Her body felt so fragile it was almost like holding a bird.

•

SHE COMPLETED her counseling and community service without getting busted again, and I filed a motion asking the court to terminate her grant early. She patted my cheek in the courtroom after her sentencing judge granted the motion. "How nice to be successful, Thomas. You must be so proud of me."

"Be proud of yourself," I answered. "You won't have to come see me again."

"Thomas," she said. "What a stickler you are. Will you take me to jail if I do?"

After I closed her case, she dropped by my office weekly. Each time, she turned up three Tarot cards and gave me a cursory reading. Her shtick was always the same: I had nothing whatever to fear. "I see no redemption *for* you, dear. *You* will always be a cop."

Her tight observation afforded me a hermetic satisfaction. But I did buy a Tarot deck and used it to probe her conceits. Was it true that cats had souls? Was there depth to Rod McKuen? Did a nerd with a badge have alternatives other than being correct all the time? The Tarot cards glittered on my desk, leaving my questions unanswered.

When her visits stopped, I grew concerned and dropped by her residence. No one came to the door, so I opened it with the key she had given me. Only Winston was in the apartment, and he brushed against my leg. The cat was half-starved, so I filled up his bowl and patted him on the head. Unlocking my cellphone, I then made a call to the Medical Examiner.

An irritable clerk made me wait for ten minutes before reading me the report. The cause was pulmonary failure, she had passed in Grandview Park. Her body lay unclaimed in the San Francisco Morgue.

○ ○ ○

USA

WHENEVER my shit catches up with me, I know just what to do. I brace like I got a stick up my ass and shout out, "USA." Those three fucking letters are all it takes to keep me out of trouble. Hell, people will cut you all kinds of slack if they think you're a patriot.

I never served in the Army, but I have done some soldiering. Five years ago, when I turned sixteen, my parents packed me off to military school. I learned how to target shoot, spit shine shoes, and perform the manual of arms. And I hadda do a whole lot of pushups because they kept finding porn in my bunk.

Well, I lasted a whole year in military school before they booted me out. They expelled me because I exposed myself to a girl in the local movie theater. She was famous for jerking off cadets, so I didn't think she would mind. But all she did was squeal like a sow when I gave her a bologna salute. Next thing I know, I was on probation and my soldiering days were over. I went to stay with my parents in Santa Clara—that's where I'm living today.

Yes, I'm a pervert, but don't put me down. I'm a pervert in the baddest sense of the word: a guy whose appreciation for snatch prevents him from being too perfect. I'm a pervert like Bill Cosby; a pervert like Bill Clinton. I'm a perve like Professor Humbert, the scholar in that book *Lolita*. It don't matter that I quit community college because it interfered with my masturbation. I still have lots of knowledge from all the reading I've done. I read like a fiend, up to three books a year, and I have a library of Marvel comics.

I've been put on probation a couple more times, but only for petty shit. Like jollying my Roger in adult movie theaters and peeping into windows. That kept me from becoming a CIA agent even though I majored in criminal justice. That and the fact that I'm kind of underweight: I tip the scales at a hundred and thirty pounds and I'm almost six feet tall. So I work as a clerk in a motor lodge on El Camino Real. It's a pretty cool job all things considered.

They have me on the midnight shift, which means I can smoke pot in the breezeway and read all the cock books I want.

I kinda admire Donald Trump: the way he avoids getting busted and all. Man, he's groped all kinds of women and the cops never lay a finger on him. So I went to a Donald Trump rally when his presidential campaign came to San Jose. I was hoping I could maybe learn a little something from the Groppenführer.

I must have been the only one in the convention center who wasn't a raving suck-up. Me, I don't give a shit about anything but marijuana and porn. But when the crowd chanted *"USA,"* my heart pounded like Paul Revere's horse. *"Lock her up"* kinda sucked and *"Build that Wall"* blew chunks. But *"USA"* was so awesome, I almost jizzed my pants. There's no way you can put a dude down when he's shoutin' "USA." Not unless you want people thinkin' you're a goddamn communist.

Riding home on the Caltrain, I cracked some heavy wood. I was still hopped up from the Trump rally, and the train was packed with women. And I was pressed up against this Mexican chick who looked like Penelope Cruz.

Not thinking that she would notice it, I started to dry hump her. But she turned around and glared at me then slapped me in the face. So I pinched her hard on the tit and said, "Bitch, get out of my country!"

Now I've got nothing against Mexicans, man; we need 'em to pick our fruit. But I swear I could hear Texas crying, "Remember the Alamo!" Even so, I knew I would be up shit creek if I didn't get off that train quick.

By the time the train pulled into Santa Clara, I had managed to squeeze down the aisle. But that Mexican chick was chasing behind me, jabbering away in Spanish. She followed me as I jumped onto the platform where a couple of transit cops were standing. *"Es un pervetido,"* she shouted. *"That boy, he grab my breast."* She pointed at me and stamped her feet, and the cops had to hold her away from me. Meanwhile, the train remained in the station while passengers watched through the windows.

After the cops put the bracelets on me, I decided I'd give it a try. I stuck out my chest like Nathan Hale and shouted, *"USA."* The cops looked at each other warily—they must have been Trump supporters. So I shouted, *"Build that wall"* for good measure. The cops just shuffled their feet.

When they asked the chick if she wanted to press charges, she said, *"Please just cut off his huevos."* I guess she was an illegal and was scared to go to court. The woman hopped back on the train, and the cops had a little discussion. Once the train was out of the station, they laughed and turned me loose.

•

I HAVE THIS great collection of sexy women's shoes. Slingbacks, sandals, flats, you name it, they're all in my collection. I only have one of each pair because I snatch them off women's feet. It's kind of a hobby of mine, and I've gotten real good at it. That's because I studied evidence law before dropping out of community college.

I always make my grabs in towns that are at least twenty miles from my home. First, I pick the place where I'm gonna grab the shoe. Usually, it's a restaurant because women are sittin' down there. The next thing I do is plan my escape. I do that by parking no more than a block from where I plan to strike. I also put a stolen plate on my car in case some do-gooder writes down the number. For good measure, I put on a Guy Fawkes mask right before I snatch the shoe. That way people are likely to think some nut job made the heist.

After I shuffle into the restaurant, I seat myself at a table. Nobody ever takes notice of me because I look like a computer geek. I take my time picking my target: I always pick a woman sittin' alone, never one with a man beside her. And while I'm choosing my target, I order a burger and fries and leave a ten dollar bill on the table. Man, just because I'm a pervert doesn't mean I'm a deadbeat too.

Once I've picked my target, I create a little distraction. I do this by rolling a smoke bomb across the restaurant floor. And while everyone's blinded by smoke, that's when I make my move. I hold my breath, put my Guy Fawkes mask on, and snatch myself the shoe. And then I walk out of the restaurant as though I'm late for a date.

Now no one ever follows me because they're coughing from the smoke. So I'm really good at keeping my cool when I walk back to my car. I take off my Guy Fawkes mask in one quick motion and toss it into the street. Then I whistle a little tune as though I'm out for a stroll.

Once I'm behind the wheel of my car, I slowly drive away. I never run a red light or a stop sign because that'll attract attention. And, first chance I get, I park my car and switch my license plate.

Now all that planning is a pain in the ass, but I've only been caught one time. That was about a month ago when I made this stupid grab. It was a doofus move, and I should have known better. But after attending that Donald Trump rally, I felt badder than Doctor Doom.

I got caught when I was taking BART home from Berkeley—I go to night school there. I'm earning myself an associates degree in hotel management. And the University of California has an off-campus program that doesn't take up all your time.

Well, the moment I got to the train platform, I noticed this Asian chick. She was wearing a dress with a slit down the side and spike heels that looked like weapons. Her legs were longer 'an a gazelle's, her mouth was as red as a plum. So I decided, come hell or high water, that I had to have one of her shoes.

As the train came shrieking into the station, I shoved her onto her ass. And I grabbed me one of those spike heel pumps as though I was snatching a diamond. As I hustled back up the escalator, taking three steps at a time, I heard her screaming, *"Pervert, pervert."*

I walked through the concourse cool as you please, tucking the shoe under my jacket. But a couple of BART guards spotted me as I made my way through the turnstile. Man, those assholes were on my butt like I was Jeffrey Dahmer. And it was gonna be a bitch to outrun them because I don't have a whole lotta wind.

With BART's finest behind me, I raced down the street, and my lungs felt like they were on fire. To make matters worse, some demonstrators were blocking the whole damn street. Trump had just been elected president, so protesters were everywhere. They were carrying signs that said *Pussy Grabs Back* and *Not Our President*. Well, I couldn't squeeze past those marchers, so that donut squad tackled me.

As those goons cuffed me up, I took a big breath even though I was gasping for air. And then I threw my head back and bellowed, *"USA."* And damn if this gang of Trump supporters didn't crowd around them guards. One of 'em said, "Let him go. You guys are just wannabe cops." Another said, "Watcha think you're doin' busting a patriot?"

While all that ruckus was going on, I slipped out of the handcuffs. Shit, that was kinda easy: my wrists are as thin as beanpoles. Then I picked up the shoe, which had dropped to the sidewalk, and ran like a greyhound on crack.

Later, when I got home to my bedroom, I sat down and stroked the shoe. It was a Bella Vita Dress Pump, one of those Italian brands. It looked great in my collection.

•

DID I TELL YOU I do some peeping at the motel where I work? I have this special room that I only rent out to couples, and I've drilled a spy hole high up on the wall of the room right next to it. I've watched lots of couples through the hole while they're busy having sex. Sometimes, I film the sex with my cell phone, so I can watch it again and again. Man, I've even filmed kinky stuff like bondage and golden showers.

I've watched hundreds of couples fornicate, and I only slipped up once. That happened a few weeks after Trump was elected president. What happened was this guy and his girlfriend checked into the motel around midnight. The guy was wearing a *MAKE AMERICA GREAT AGAIN* cap, the kind they manufacture in China. And the girl was wearing this T-shirt that said, *DRAIN THE SWAMP*. The words *DRAIN* and *SWAMP* were sticking right out because her tits were the size of pumpkins.

Well, I booked the couple into my special suite—I even gave them a discount. Then I snuck into the room next door to them, so I could watch them through the hole. I could hear the woman squealing because the walls are cardboard-thin. But I couldn't see a goddamn thing—he was doing her in the bathroom. Panicked, I ran to the tool closet and came back with my drill. Then I bored a hole through the part of the wall that was opposite the bathroom.

Now I don't know how they heard the drill as loud as that woman was squealing. But, the next thing I know, they were standing in the room where I was keeping watch. They both looked ready to kick my ass even though they were draped in towels. I couldn't even say I was hanging a picture because my willy was still in my hand.

The guy said, "What are you? The king of the perves?" The woman said, "Hit him, Judd." So I hummed a few bars of "Made in America" then I hollered, *"USA."*

The guy said, "Honey, I'd knock him flat if he wasn't a real American."

The woman kinda giggled and hitched the towel higher on her breasts. "We do have to stick together," she said. "And he's such a sweet-looking boy."

Well, we ended up having a threesome, and I waived the charge for the room. And before they left the next morning, both of them shook my hand. They even gave me a mug that read, *Deplorables for Trump.*

•

SOMETIMES, when I'm done jacking off for the day, I think about my life. I coulda been a Green Beret or maybe a Navy Seal. Except that I don't have a whole lotta wind and I don't like pushups much. And I've got some pretty bad habits that I've wrapped up in the flag. But there's no point in gettin' down on myself—I'm havin' too much fun. And America, real America, has taken me into its heart.

∘ ∘ ∘

Deceptive

THOSE WHO SAY the truth will set you free have probably never been polygraphed. I had the experience in my early thirties during a campaign of self-renewal, leading inevitably to the West Coast. After spending a decade as a counselor at the Indiana Penal Farm, a provincial Midwest prison, I felt like a bastard at a family reunion. Was it because I built on my education instead of boozing with good ol' boy guards? I had attended a nearby state university under a blind assumption: the patented belief that a master's degree would open the door to promotions. Sadly, the reverse proved true. Organizations will stigmatize overachievers as surely as they flag the fuckups. (If you doubt this, watch any season of *Survivor*.) And so I was deemed overqualified when I faced the promotion boards. One of the inmates summed it up well when I told him I was leaving. "Sounds like a plan," he said. "Do it soon. You don't need to be hanging around Podunk, Indiana."

I relocated to the Golden State and submitted a job application to the Santa Clara Department of Corrections. California has always been an innovator in the field of criminal justice, so I was more than confident I would soon take my place among the learned elite. I applied for the position of deputy jailor, a menial job, but one from which I intended to soar like a butterfly shedding its cocoon. Before long, I would be devising programs, publishing in correctional journals, and initiating critical reforms.

I reported to the Santa Clara Government Center to take the written test. The questions struck me as wholly redundant, and I scored in the high nineties. The oral interview, which took place at the Santa Clara County Jail, was also an effortless challenge. One of the board members, a plump correctional lieutenant with a goatee, simply shook his head. "Ten years as a counselor," he said. "A master's in criminology. And you want to work as a deputy jailor?" I told him I needed a change, and he laughed. "I see," he snorted. "Are ya gonna take up surfing?" The board gave me a ringing endorsement, which left me with one final obstacle. To wear the uniform of a deputy jailor, I would have to pass a polygraph examination.

I received a letter from the Santa Clara Human Resources Department, instructing me to report to the Government Center, Room 101, to take the polygraph test. I was advised to allow three hours for the test and to bring a number two pencil. I chuckled at the irony of the location. Room 101—wasn't that the chamber of horrors in Orwell's *1984*? The place where aberrant Winston Smith was reduced to a quivering pulp? Convinced I would fare better than poor Winston, I showed up early on the day of the test.

Armed with my number two pencil, I entered Room 101. The room was utterly barren except for a desk and a chair. No carpet cushioned the floor, no flowered plants scented the air, not even a requisite landscape painting hung from the drab green walls. Behind a second door, in what must have been the testing chamber, I could hear a couple of voices. Voices so strained and muffled that they seemed to belong to ghosts.

I sat by the desk and waited, my pencil as sharp as a tack. After ten minutes, the second door opened and I felt my muscles tense. The man who entered the room was so fleshless that he appeared to be carved from bone. His nose was sharp and hawkish, his smile was frozen in place, and a thick pair of horn-rimmed glasses expanded his muddy brown eyes. He looked at me incuriously and handed me a booklet. He smelled of cheap aftershave.

"Answer these questions, pardner," he muttered. "Answer 'em truthfully."

He vanished back into the testing room in a lingering wave of Old Spice.

I broke the seal to the booklet and began to read the questions. There were approximately two hundred of them and they made me feel like a freak. *Have you ever exposed your anus or genitals for sexual gratification? Have you ever been married to two persons at the same time? Have you ever had sex with animals?*

Indignant, I cruised through the questions and marked almost all of them no. Only a few gave me pause. *Have you ever engaged in drug use?* Well I smoked pot a few times in college. And once I sampled a dab of meth. *Better check yes*, I decided. *I don't want to make the scrolls flutter.*

Have you ever been referred to a collection agency? another question read. *Once*, I remembered. When I didn't pay a medical bill because I had been overcharged. *Do they really need to know that?* I wondered. I gritted my teeth and marked the yes box.

Have you ever abused, struck, or injured any person under fifteen? I remembered spanking my toddler brother after he crapped on the living room rug. Did I have to put *that* down? I shrugged and checked the yes box once again.

You'll be given a chance to explain your answers, the last section of the booklet advised. I signed and printed my name in this section, acknowledging the terms of the test. I then pocketed my pencil and waited for Ichabod Crane.

An hour passed. No one came. *Has he forgotten me?* I wondered. Eventually, the voices grew louder—they seemed to be at odds. "If you've stolen a car we'll find out!" boomed Ichabod when the inner door finally opened.

The woman who dashed across the room looked angry and harassed. "Do I look like a car thief?" she shouted back as she opened the door to the hallway. Glancing at me, she held her nose then hurried from the room.

A practical soul may have seen this incident as a portent of pending doom. But my instincts were akin to Don Quixote, not savvy Sancho Panza. *One less rival for the job*, I thought as I rose from the chair. It was my turn now. I held my head high, like a bird drinking water, and entered the testing room.

•

AS I SAT by a desk where the polygraph was perched, my palms began to sweat. I felt more like a patient on life support than a pilgrim on a mission. A blood pressure cuff, plump with air, gripped my upper arm like a hall monitor; a couple of rubber tubes, also tightly inflated, hugged my chest and abdomen; and a pair of electrodes pinched two of my fingers like dime store rings. The cuff was to measure my heart rate, the tubes were to record my breathing, and the electrodes were to pick up whatever perspiration my fingers might produce.

I tried to chat with Ichabod, but his focus was on the machine. Clearly, he had no interest in whatever I had to say. "Answer the questions truthfully," he mumbled. "Don't be making stuff up."

Activating the polygraph, he asked me some baseline questions.

"Your name Tom Hemmings?"

"Yes," I replied, and the scrolls began to nod.

"Are you sitting down?"

"Yes," I said.

"Have you got a bachelor's degree?" he inquired.

"I have a master's," I said.

Ichabod shut off the polygraph as though he was swatting a fly. "That's *not* what I asked you, pardner," he muttered. "Stick to yes or no answers."

I felt familiar anger as he turned the machine back on. How many times was I going to be penalized for advancing my education?

"Have you ever stolen from an employer?" he asked.

"No," I sarcastically said.

"Have you ever lied to someone who trusted you?"

"No," I fibbed.

"Have you ever driven a car when you had too much to drink?"

I knew enough about polygraph tests to know that these were control questions. Who hasn't taken a pen from work, lied to a friend, or driven a car after having a sip too many? I was expected to lie on these questions, which would provide a comparative response. If the scrolls fluttered less on the relevant questions, that meant I would pass the test.

"Ever committed a sex crime?" he asked.

"No," I proudly replied.

"Ever been addicted to drugs or alcohol."

"No," I triumphantly chirped.

"Ever stolen an automobile?"

"No," I crowed with glee.

The questioning continued for another minute then he turned the polygraph off.

"How'd I do?"

He scratched his jaw. "The results are inconclusive."

"What does inconclusive mean?"

He sighed. "Shall we try it again?"

He asked another series of questions, this time intermingling the control questions with the relevant ones. Whenever I was asked about job theft or drunk driving, I dug my fingernails into the palm of my free hand. If I spiked on the control questions, I reasoned, I would surely pass this damn test.

When the questioning was done, he turned off the machine and gave me the final verdict. "*Deceptive*," he snapped.

I looked at him incredulously; I felt as though I had been slugged. "Just where was I deceptive?" I asked.

"Alcoholism, drug addiction, sex crimes, and car theft."

"You're kidding," I stammered. "I've done all that? When would I have found time to go to work?"

He folded his arms then stared at me like a grand inquisitor. "Ya may as well come clean, Tom Hemmings. Whaddya trying to hide?"

"Nothing," I snapped.

"Horse turds," he answered. "Whaddya trying to hide?"

I knew my anger was showing when he opened the drawer to the desk. The drawer contained a handgun and several ammo clips. As I looked at the gun, he pushed the drawer shut; he was only warning me to calm down. But the sight of the weapon did not dissuade me from taking a shot of my own.

"Ask me if I killed John Kennedy," I said. "I'd like to see the result."

He looked at me so piously that I felt like a Salem witch. "Whaddya trying to hide?" he repeated. "Whaddya trying to hide?"

Arguing was useless; his mind was as closed as a tomb. *What have I done to deserve this?* I wondered. *What is my unavowed crime?* Whatever the sin, I would never forget that unforgiving gaze.

I unhooked myself from the tubes and wires. "Have a good day," I said. I could feel his eyes boring into my back as I walked out of the room.

Only when I stood in the hallway did I feel the full weight of my anger. I had a crime coming to me, I reasoned, and vandalism would do.

I whipped out my number two pencil as though I were drawing a sword. And I scrawled a single word on the door to Room 101.

Deceptive

° ° °

Spooks Alive

"NOT ALL THOSE who wander are lost." This heartening phrase from *The Fellowship of the Rings* may be taken one step further: "Some who wander thrive." As a young man void of substance, I dropped out of a Midwestern college, caught a freighter to Australia, and spent seven years roaming the continent. Too restless for study, too lazy for love, I found less to annoy me on the cattle stations of the Northern Territory, the barge runs to New Guinea, and the fishing boats on the Tasman Sea. Like the Happy Wanderer of song, my romps were no means to an end—rather they were an end in themselves. How delicious to cast off norms, to rove like a swagman, to see the towns vanish behind me like ships fading into the night. Since my soul was that of a drifter, it was all but inevitable that I would one day join a traveling carnival.

I latched onto the carnival in Cairns after working a few weeks in a Queensland sugar mill. Strolling the midway, checking out the tent shows, I felt an instinctual quickening of the pulse, the kind of thrill a tramp might feel upon finding a ten-dollar bill. Who was I to resist such eclectic attractions as Vanessa the Undresser, The Two-headed Dog Boy from Borneo, and Jimmy Sharman's Boxing Troupe? Most garish of all was The Princess Atasha, an African goddess who metamorphosed nightly into a ferocious ape. Determined to join these masquerades, I scoured the grounds for a job. Minutes later, I was hired as a roustabout on The Ghost Train.

The Ghost Train consisted of a whiplash monorail, half a dozen crash doors, and several gruesome masks lit up by fluorescent lights. The banners facing the midway displayed hunchbacks carrying off buxom women, and a mournful organ solo droned through the crackling speakers.

On the opposite side of the midway stood the fabulous Princess Atasha, a dark-skinned woman with upturned breasts and a cape that draped down to her feet. Perched heroically upon a catwalk, she resembled Wonder Woman. *Will she sleep with a bespectacled drifter?* I wondered as I watched her wave to a crowd. Maybe not, but I vowed to hit on her even though she was partly an ape.

It was not until the carnival reached Tully that I had a chance to meet her. She was sitting alone in a local pub, sipping a glass of beer. She seemed deaf to the third-rate band belting out "Paint It Black," and the dance floor, crowded with locals, did not even merit her glance.

I approached her and bowed like a courtier, hoping to draw a smile. "How rude of that witchdoctor to hex you," I said. "Perhaps I might break the curse."

She looked at me with tired eyes and kept on sipping her beer. "Tom Hemmings—that's my name," I boasted. "And casting off roles is my game."

"Yank, I know who you are," she said finally. "You're that bloke who runs the spook train and never stops perving on me."

"You're not the only one under a spell."

She yawned and crossed her legs. "No need to talk like a tall poppy, Yank—not when you're running a bleedin' spook train. For a bloke who's throwing off roles, as you put it, you have a ways to go."

"Will you give me a chance?" I said.

She shrugged. "A chance to do what? Jabber on like a poof? If a fuck is all you're after, luv, you just have to buy me a beer."

Disappointed, I sat down beside her and ordered a pitcher of lager. Were she less alluring, I'd have saved my money and left her sitting there. But her sailor's mouth did not blunt her appeal: a beauty so animalistic that she looked like a pagan queen. "I wish you would let me work for it," I said as I filled her glass. "Seduction has its stages, you know."

She chugged her beer. "I'm easy, luv. Ask anyone on the fairgrounds— they'll tell you I'm easy as sin."

"I don't want my sins to be easy," I said. "I'd rather anticipate them."

She covered her mouth as though guarding a smile. "So you want me story first," she murmured. "All right, Yank, I'll tell you me story."

Her story was such a downer that I forced myself to listen. She was a Maori girl from New Zealand's North Island, her stepfather raped her when she was thirteen, she had left The Land of the Long White Cloud to escape a brutal husband. After working as a stripper in Sydney's King's Cross, she joined the carnival, and had spent the last two years as one of the midway attractions. "I wanted to see me a bit of the country, and I wanted to stay on the move. Anything else you want to know, luv, before you bugger me."

"Have another beer," I said. "I'm not ready to bugger you yet."

She rolled her eyes and passed me her glass. "If you get me soused, I'll get into a fight. I always start a bleedin' row whenever I get soused."

My trepidation mounted as I filled her glass again. "I'd rather defend your honor myself."

She cracked her knuckles and belched. "Fighting gets me horny, luv. You ought to be happy for that."

"I'd be happier to be your rock," I said.

"Me rock?" she scoffed. "What I need is a ghost. A bloke to shag me proper then disappear before morning."

"That's no way to treat a princess," I stammered.

Pushing her chair from the table, she sighed. "You're running a ghost house, aren't you? You might want to have a go."

She rose from the chair—"I'm off to the loo"—and melted into the crowd. When she came back twenty minutes later, her hair was disheveled, her blouse was torn, and she was breathing heavily. "*Sorry* to disappoint you," she huffed, "but I don't want my honor defended."

"How did you start the brawl?" I asked.

"Same way I always do, luv. I told some rowdy tart to get stuffed, and then the fight was on."

Thirsty from her donnybrook, she drank a final beer. "Hurry up, luvvy," she said. "Time to shag." She gripped my hand as though clutching a tote bag, and we walked towards the fairground.

"Should we get more acquainted first?" I said as the Ferris wheel loomed into sight.

"Can you chat up a sheila then dump her? That's all I want to know."

"Let's chat over coffee."

"Let's not," she replied. "That's how the shit gets started." She looked at me suspiciously. "You sure you can get it up?"

Hoping to raise her standards, I kissed the back of her hand. "I bow to the Princess Atasha," I said.

"Me name is Louie," she snapped. "You're not cut out for carny life, are you? You don't know when it's time to fuck off."

She did not say another word until we stood in front of her motorhome. Dropping my hand, she shook her head and patted me on the back. "I've changed me mind, luv. I'm not going to shag you. You'll be wanting to stay for coffee."

As she disappeared into the motorhome, my hesitancy turned to shame. I chastised the untimely etiquette that had kept me from seizing the moment, and I cursed the hustler's instinct with which she had summed me up.

I would have to rid myself of more baggage if I wanted a second chance. I would have to champion the one-night stand. I would have to become a real carny.

•

MY DEVOLVEMENT depended on emulating the dynamics of the midway, on becoming a flashy charlatan, on being all hat and no cowboy. There was nothing inside those tents, after all, but the good old bait-and-switch. Jimmy Sharman's Boxing Troop featured only a few minutes of boxing per crowd, Vanessa the Undresser only stripped to her panties and bra, and the Two-headed Dog Boy was nothing more than a calf fetus in a jar. Even the Princess Atasha show was a wham-bam-thank you-ma'am rip-off: a trick performed with mirrors that lasted for less than a second. *Con the marks out of their money* was the philosophy of the midway. *And hurry them out of the tents before they have time to think.*

Not to be outdone by the professionals, I devised my own repartee. "Banned in Tully! Banned in Proserpine!" I fibbed into the mic. "A witchdoctor rode the train yesterday and came out white as a sheet!" After the marks bought their tickets, I made them wait to get into the cars. Longer lines drew customers like turds attracted flies. I also paid local kids a dollar or two to ride the train for an hour. Their job was to shriek like cockatoos when they burst through the final set of crash doors. *My god*, I thought as the cars filled with riders, *people are just like cattle. How easy it is to herd them.*

The evening the carnival docked in Rockhampton, a meat-processing town on the Fitzroy River, I went looking for my enchantress. I found her again in one of the pubs, drinking all alone. Since I was drawing larger crowds than she was, I felt cocky enough to join her.

"Yank, why don't you give it up?" she muttered as I sat beside her.

"A princess deserves more attention," I said.

"I'm getting *less* attention, luv, thanks to your silly rants. The way you rave on about witchdoctors is pulling me customers away."

"I'm learning the trade," I protested. "I'm chatting the marks up then dumping them like a whore on Saturday night."

"So you think I'm going to shag you now?"

"I'll be gone the moment I shoot."

She drained her beer with several deep chugs then poured herself another. "Listen to what you're saying, Yank. You're still calling me a princess."

"That doesn't mean I won't screw you then leave you."

She wiped her mouth with her sleeve. "Why don't you make a pass at Vanessa the Undresser? There's a bit of lady in her, they tell me. You two should hit it off well."

The thought of Vanessa the fussy undresser did nothing to change my mind. A tall dour woman with too much makeup, she lacked the lure of the jungle. She would probably insist that I pull off my shoes before taking me into her bed.

Louie was eyeing a heavyset woman, leaning on the bar—a meat boner in a slaughterhouse judging from her massive forearms.

"A quid says I can drop her, luv."

"I'm not going to bet against *you*."

"Then at least keep an eye on me purse," she ordered, and she stood up and crossed the room.

The fight erupted with the suddenness of a downpour during the wet season. It started when the woman grabbed Louie's hair and shook her like a rug, and it ended when Louie landed a haymaker right on the point of her jaw. It was a perfect punch, worthy of Muhammed Ali, and the woman dropped like a sack of grain.

Afterwards, Louie helped her to her feet and bought her a glass of beer. But her face was harder than granite when she came back to the table.

"Take me home, luv," she murmured. "The tart wants to get in me pants."

She hugged my arm like an orphan as I walked her back to the fairgrounds. "Everything's spinning, Yank—please don't let go," she said as we stumbled along.

"Some coffee?" I offered.

She poked my side. "That's how the shit gets started, luvvy. Don't make me say it again."

The charity I was showing her seemed a perilous indulgence. How can one pity a predator—a she-wolf on the prowl? But my apprehension in no way affected my desire to take her to bed.

Perhaps if I became an alpha male, I could rise in her estimation. If I joined the ranks of the boxers, would that not rouse the woman in her? I decided to become a member of Jimmy Sharman's troupe.

•

AS A FORMER high school wrestler, I was not unequipped for a scrap. And since the pugilists had a grappler among them—a barrel-chested Thursday Islander billed as The Cannibal—I was able to join their ranks as a shill. Once every evening, I shut down The Ghost Train—let the suckers wait!—and blended into the crowd outside the boxing tent. When the Cannibal stepped onto the catwalk, dangling some shrunken heads, I accepted his boastful challenge that he could lick anyone in the crowd. Our routine consisted of several feigned punches and a couple of well-timed rolls, after which I picked up a breakaway chair and knocked the heathen out. I was a savior of civilization, a defender of church and God, a scourge to soul-sucking savages that crawled from jungle depths. How could a bedeviled sovereign hope to resist me now?

One morning, she invited me into her motorhome and brewed a pot of tea. The motorhome harbored a single cramped room that was about as welcoming as a cage. A huge stuffed gorilla sat on a divan, watching us like a bouncer.

There was nothing inside her gypsy home to hint of royalty. The closets were packed with cheap glittery costumes, the odor of cigarettes thickened the air, and a dozen Harlequin romance novels were stacked on a tiny table. I sat at the table opposite her and blew upon my tea.

"Don't mind Nigel," she said as I glanced her mothy chaperone.

My prowess as a grappler had failed to impress her—"A can of bull" she called it—so I quoted from *Romeo and Juliet* to get her to spread her legs. *Some women are intellect fuckers*, I reasoned. *They'll hump a well-read man.* "'The ape is dead,'" I recited, "'and I must conjure him.'"

"Do you often quote Mercutio?" she said. "He's nothing like you, luv."

"You've read Shakespeare?" I said, incredulously.

"I lasted a year in Auckland University. Does that surprise you a bit?"

"Did you major in stripping and barroom brawls?"

"I was going to study *literature*, but then I gave it up."

This was not something I needed to know, and I hurried to finish my tea. It was too much information; it did not go with pull of the jungle. How could I keep things bestial if she recognized quotes from the Bard?

Relishing my discomfort, she spooned sugar into her tea. "You're more like Romeo, luv," she said.

"A cocksmith and a swain?"

"A wanker whose pants are too tight. When his lover lay still on the slab, did he trot off and fetch her a doctor? No, the silly twit killed himself and that was the end of that."

"He flew the coop after fucking her. You have to admire him for that."

"She was thirteen years old when he buggered her, luvvy. That's the same thing that happened to me."

"It's a made up story," I protested.

"That's just the problem, luv. I made up stories meself whenever me stepdad snuck into me bedroom. Sometimes, I even pretended that he was Father Christmas."

"You should have sicced Nigel on him," I said. "Or was he a baby then?"

Was it my cavalier comment that cast the frown upon her face? She was not in the market for intimacy, so pity was out of the question. Still, she looked at me as though I had morphed into a thief.

Folding her arms across her chest, she drew a labored breath. "Yank, it's time you came in from the rain. Do you really think I'll shag you because you're pretending to wrestle a clown?"

"What can I do that you'll approve of?" I said.

She robotically stirred her tea. "You can take your ass back to the spook house, luv. I don't want any more stories."

•

WHEN THE CARNIVAL arrived in Bundaberg, a new act joined the midway—an act of such authenticity that it made me feel like a bandit. It was billed as The Boy in the Pit of Death, and it became an instant hit. The pit, a ten-by-ten foot pen, snatched my breath away: it was filled with all varieties of poisonous Australian snakes. Taipans, brown snakes, adders, and copperheads slithered behind the partitions while their keeper, a tattooed carny named Liam, sat in the midst of them. Occasionally, he picked up one of the snakes, draped it around his thick neck, and offered a hundred quid to anyone who could prove it wasn't venomous.

Since the snake pit was next to the spook train, Liam's spiel competed with mine. "Snakes alive, snakes galore!" he shouted into his speakers. "Snakes you've never seen before!" he promised the swelling crowds. Such an offer rendered The Ghost Train a laughable pretender, and I stewed as droves of customers lined up to peer into the pit.

I chatted with Liam between demonstrations, and he told me the secret of serpents. "A snake won't bite ya, mate," he said, "unless it's scared of you." Determined to salvage the dregs of my pride, I handled a couple of black snakes. They did not feel slimy or scaly. They felt like basketball leather.

Of course, my friendship with Liam was destined to be brief. I needed to pose as the king of the midway; I needed to keep up my pitch. How else could I assure my siren that I was still the consummate con? So determined was I to seduce her, to lower myself to her terms, that I was willing to stoop to plagiarism to prove myself a fraud. Holding the mic to my mouth like an apple, I uttered nine fateful words: "Spooks alive, spooks galore, spooks you've never seen before!"

In an instant, Liam perched himself on the guardrail in front of the ride. His hands were cupped behind his ears in a mock attempt to listen. "Did I hear ya correct, mate?" he bellowed. "Have ya got no bite of yer own?"

This was not a slapstick challenge, the kind the Cannibal made. This was a fight in the making; this was a test of machismo; this was a chance to declare myself the ultimate cock of the realm. Since the Princess Atasha was eyeing us from the opposite side of the midway, the only way to save face was to puff out my chest as well. "Spooks you've never seen before!" I repeated into the mic.

He hopped over the railing; the battle was on. I snatched off my glasses and pocketed them while squinting to make him out. Without my corrective lenses, I saw only a ghostly blur, but I pushed out my foot defensively, striking him below the belt. "Kick my privates, will you!" he shouted. He climbed back over the railing then disappeared like smoke.

Had I bested him already? Had I proven myself a stud? Had I won the war of the midway with a dubious blow from my foot? I had expected far more from a man who handled serpents for a living.

It was only the blare from Liam's speakers, turned up to double volume, that reminded me of what might have been a clash of juggernauts. "SNAKES ALIVE, SNAKES GALORE, SNAKES YOU'VE NEVER SEEN BEFORE!" His boast rolled through the midway like a hollow cannonade.

Hoping the princess would blow me a kiss, I put my glasses back on. I prayed that my victory was sufficient to fill her eyes with longing. But Louie had left the catwalk to begin another show.

•

IT WAS A SIGN of my deprivation, the drought that had claimed my heart, that I took my consolation from the carny rumor mill. "Don't mess with that big Yank." "That bloke's got feet of iron." "That Yank'll tear yer balls off and make you swallow 'em." This was the caliber of the stories that floated around the midway. One of them even endowed me with the strength of Mighty Joe Young. "He held Liam up with one hand, he did. Lifted him above his head while he slowly took off his specs." At least, I could pose as a primitive, a brute with thundering balls. They clanged with the authority of church bells whenever I strode the grounds.

In spite of these giddy fables, she came to me in Toowoomba. I was falling asleep in the spook train powerhouse, having closed down the ride for the night, when I heard a tapping like raindrops upon the powerhouse door. I opened the door and let her in; she smelled of beer and sweat, but my heart thudded like a drumbeat when she pulled me into my bunk. "Don't say nothing, Yank," she ordered. She tugged off her jeans and panties and got on top of me.

She rode me with such urgency that I felt like an unbroken horse. When it ended, she snaked her panties back on and fell asleep at my side. She was still in my bunk when I stirred the next morning; she was sitting upright beside me, running a brush through her hair. Her breasts, still trapped in her bra, nodded with every stroke.

"Yank, stop perving on me," she snapped.

I grudgingly averted my eyes. "How come the marks get to look," I said, "but I have to turn my head?"

"Marks don't count," she snorted.

"And I do?"

She rose from the bed, slipped on her jeans, and tucked the brush into her pocket. "Liam's good with his fists," she said. "I seen him fight in Townsend once. He'd have cleaned your clock in a second if you hadn't kicked him in the balls."

"So why did you decide to sleep with me?"

She slowly buttoned her blouse. "We had this date from the beginning, luv. We may as well get it behind us."

•

OUR AFFAIR did not survive Brisbane, the site of the Queensland State Fair. We had been on the fairgrounds for only a week when her tent show folded down. In its place was a clown dunk: a water tank with a collapsible platform above it. If you dunked the clown on the platform three times, you could win a stuffed rabbit or bear.

I sat in her motorhome and watched her pack; she seemed to be in a hurry. She told me she had sold the motorhome and was moving to southern Queensland. She was going to marry a sheep farmer—a mark she had met on the midway a couple of days ago. He was going to pick her up in an hour and drive her to Cunnamulla.

My disbelief assailed me like Banquo's grisly ghost. How could I, the king of the midway, have been so easily duped? "A sheep farmer?" I parroted. "What do you see in him?"

She stopped packing and carefully folded a dress, a sheath with purple sequins. The task appeared to require her total concentration. "He has clean fingernails," she said finally. "There's something to be said for that."

What was I hoping to rescue her from when I gave her a piece of advice? Pastoral billabongs, green rolling plains, and eucalyptus groves? "Hang onto your motorhome," I muttered. "You'll be back in a month or two."

She covered my mouth with her fingertips and kissed me on the chin. It was a gesture intended to silence me, but her lips were gentle and soft. "No need to lecture me, luv," she said. "It will last as long as it lasts."

After she left, I went to the clown dunk and tried to win her a bear. I planned to give it to her when she came back to the midway. This was incredible folly for a stud of my repute. I threw the softballs heroically, and not once did I soak the clown.

Despite this impotent display, my reputation survived. I was still the boss of the midway, my balls still boomed when I walked, and Vanessa the Undresser was giving me the eye.

That night, I asserted my dominance by turning up the speakers. The crackle was louder than wildfire, the organ moaned like a haunt, but my voice commanded the midway like a mighty Tarzan yell.

"SPOOKS ALIVE! SPOOKS GALORE! SPOOKS YOU'VE NEVER SEEN BEFORE!"

○ ○ ○

I Am Not a Crook

WHY DO THEY call it death? I have never felt more alive, more vibrant, more sensitive. I have never been more aware. And colors are sensational: they pulse like jellyfish.

Looking around me, I try to take stock of the spot where death has dumped me. The place looks so utterly familiar that I begin to doubt my demise. Redwood trees tower above me, a creek chuckles close to my feet, and black squirrels chase one another about on golden plains of grass. Even the mist is stunning: a silvery, sheltering fog. For all practical purposes, I may as well be in a California state park.

It is all a mirage, of course, and I take some comfort in that. My entire life has been little more than a courtship of illusion. Thank goodness illusion continues with death: I would hate to be held to account.

I am sitting alone beneath a redwood that climbs into the mist. Since I have no sense of location, I decide I had better stay put. I do see a narrow hiking trail on the near side of the creek, and I suspect a welcoming committee will soon come down this path. But the hours pass like tortoises and nobody appears. I begin to feel weary—incredibly weary. I close my eyes and sleep.

•

I AWAKE. I am dead. I am wholly alive. Sunlight is leaking through the trees: it is either dawn or dusk. Still, nobody comes to greet me, and perhaps that is for the best. Were my passing to trigger a fanfare of angels, I would feel like a total imposter. Yes, I had roamed Australia as a young man; yes, I had written five books; and yes, I had lasted thirty-four years as a San Francisco probation officer. But heroics come too easily to me: I am unfit for anything else. And the bullet that took my life was the result of my own carelessness. Had I remembered to load my Glock, had I worn my Second Chance vest, had I made my home searches earlier in the morning—a time when the addicts are usually asleep—I would never have stumbled onto a drug buy. I would never have been shot in the chest. No, I'm more deserving of a walk of shame than a ticker tape parade, but even so petty a justice does not seem imminent. Perhaps it is enough to know that I am sixty years old and dead.

Despite the seductions of limbo, there is still some unquiet in me—enough to prompt me to rise to my feet and do a little exploring. Since I have no celestial sea legs, each step is like walking in quicksand, and, although I have never been more sober, I teeter like a drunk.

By the time I have gone fifty steps, my legs are cramped and shaky, but my pitiful excursion is sufficient to give me the lay of the land. I am not as isolated as I had believed: there are other souls sitting underneath trees, and they seem to be in a stupor. This sight is no consolation: I now feel inconsequential. My vanity had actually let me believe this place was my province alone. Depleted and demoralized, I stagger back to my tree. Fatigue hits me like a tsunami. I once again fall asleep.

.

ANOTHER DAY DAWNS and nobody comes. I take a longer walk. I probably should be hungry by now, but I have no appetite. Occasionally, strangers breeze past me along the hiking trail. The strangers take no notice of me; their eyes are gentle but distant as though fixed on some insular mission. The inventory of my life is of no importance to them.

The fog has dissipated a bit, and I am able to see things more clearly. Sometimes, a soul abandons its tree accompanied by one of the strangers. Occasionally, I spot larger animals: wild pigs and wallabies. These animals move rather stiffly and watch me with unfriendly eyes. Their incongruity seems odd until I realize what they are. These are the animals I shot in Australia: creatures I had picked off from the boot of a Land Rover with a .22 Magnum. How sporting it had been to shoot them at the time. How haunting they seem to me now.

Discouraged, I stumble back to my tree and curl up in a ball. Clearly, I'm not a candidate for heaven: I truly deserve to be flogged. The best that I can hope for now is a benevolent purgatory. It can only be symbolic when the light begins to die. Until my guide spirit fetches me, I will have to remain in the dark. I bury my head in my folded arms and wait for sleep to come.

.

THIRTY DAYS pass: days that I measure by the presence and absence of light. I watch the sunlight bleed through the trees; I watch it disappear. Since nobody shows up to fetch me, I take even longer excursions. My celestial legs grow stronger—I am able to roam at will—but the terrain remains so changeless that exploring it seems a waste. Everywhere, redwood trees tower above me, everywhere souls sit under the trees, and everywhere pigs and wallabies watch me with uncharitable eyes. Each day, when I've done my exploring, I return to my allotted tree. I wonder, *Will this be the day when my guide spirit picks me up?*

One day, while I sit beneath my tree, a dog trots down the trail. Noticing me, it perks its ears and it bounds in my direction. It covers my face with undeserved kisses before curling up in my lap. I stroke the dog behind its ears then pat it on the rump. It is Corky, my French bulldog who preceded me in death. A seizure took her life when she was only six years old.

After a while, Corky jumps from my lap and bolts back up the trail. I call her name, but she does not come back. Her snub is disconcerting; she always obeyed when I called.

Overcome with nostalgia, I close my eyes and nap. I awake when I hear Corky growling; she is crouching by my side. Her eyes are locked on a potato-face man who is ambling down the trail. The man is of medium height, and he is wearing a dark blue suit. His arms stretch out from his shoulders as though he is nailed to a cross. Instinctually, I know I am on his agenda. I stagger to my feet.

Corky bursts into frenzied barking when the man stops in front of me. Although he is not a stranger, he surely deserves her reproach. His five o'clock stubble has never been darker; his scowl has never been deeper. And his eyes are shifting so rapidly that they look like tumbling dice. It is as though he searching for a log with which to cave in my skull.

My god, I think, *things are worse than I thought. My guide is Richard Nixon.*

•

NIXON POSES before me like a gunfighter about to draw. He then fishes a handkerchief from his jacket and blots his sweat-beaded brow. "Harumph," he says. "The least you could do is muzzle that shitass dog."

And what is the most I can do? I wonder, a purely rhetorical question. Kicking his ass is the most I can do—a chore I would deeply enjoy. No bounty from heaven would satisfy me more than kicking this despot's ass.

Instead, I stroke Corky behind her ears; she whimpers happily. "Shouldn't you be in hell?" I ask Nixon.

He raises both hands above his head in a double victory salute. Smiling like a possum with gas he says, "Ayyy am not a crook."

Maybe hell has paroled him, I muse, a thought that I quickly dismiss. His darting eyes and plastic grin do not imply self-renewal.

Reading my mind, Nixon lowers his hands. "They let me out for a few days every year."

"How do I know that you haven't escaped?"

Nixon chortles, shakes his head; his jowls wobble as he replies. "If you want to know the truth," he says, "I kinda prefer it in hell."

"I'd kinda prefer you there too," I reply.

Corky sniffs Nixon's leg then starts barking again.

"Will you call off that shitty dog?" Nixon snaps.

I shrug. "She no longer obeys me."

Nixon rocks back on his heels and glares. "Well, she's acting like I'm gonna rob you or something. Ayyy am not a crook."

I pick up a stick and toss it. Corky dashes after the stick.

No, I decide. *Nixon isn't transformed. Not even his tag phrase has changed.* "I wasn't expecting an angel," I say, "but why have they sent me *you*?"

Nixon dances a soft-shoe then takes a deep bow. His mood has mercurially lightened. "How should I know?" he laughs. "I'm a tour guide, not a sage."

I watch Corky vanish into the forest. She has run off with the stick.

•

"SHALL WE GET on with it?" Nixon says.

I abandon my tree reluctantly. We walk along the trail.

"You're getting the VIP tour," Nixon says.

"What the fuck does that mean?" I say.

"Writers get special treatment—even the half-assed ones."

I feel as though I've been struck with a hammer. "My books are read *here*?"

Nixon throws up his hands. "Why wouldn't they be?—there's plenty of time. Hell, I've read a couple myself. I read like a fiend, you know."

"Thanks for the praise," I say. I feel as though I have been bribed.

"That's not a compliment," Nixon snaps. "Your writing is godless drivel. Your books should have bombed long ago. All you did was pollute the country, soften it up for the communists."

"You're lecturing *me* about bombing?" I sputter.

Nixon squints and his eyes turn red—redder than cherry tomatoes. "Get your ass back in ranks!" he bellows. He is not talking to me but a presence he has spotted among the trees.

I look. I see nothing. I hazard a guess. "An eighteen-year-old kid you sent to the fray?"

81

"You'd think he'd be proud to have died for his flag. Proud that his name's on the Wall. But no, that little fucker would rather pester me."

"I'll bet you get pestered a lot."

Nixon sighs and again mops his brow. "They won't stay in ranks, what the shit can I do? I was bowling the other day, you know—we bowl a lot in hell. Well, I was six frames away from a perfect game when one of them gave me the finger. That fucked up my concentration and I threw a gutter ball."

Corky comes running towards us. She is holding a bird in her mouth. She drops the bird and snarls at Nixon. I watch the bird fly away.

•

WE TRUDGE UP a hill; the light is retreating. I barely see Corky scrambling before us, sniffing the trees and the grass.

Nixon is now aglow with a vomity greenish hue. Noticing my astonishment, he pats me on the back. "It's my aura," he says. "You'll soon have one too. Mine used to be the color of pus, but its mellowed up a bit."

"How did you pull that off?" I ask.

Nixon snorts as we climb the hill. He is huffing like a horse. "I've never stepped out on my wife, for one. And there's plenty of pussy in hell."

"Why would she care where you stick your pecker?"

"Beats me," Nixon says, "but for some reason it matters. I see her every now and then when they let me out of hell. She isn't wearing her wedding ring—nobody wears one here. But she always blows me a little kiss, asks if I'm wearing my galoshes. She gave me a pair of galoshes because hell is kinda swampy."

A couple of strangers pass us. They pause and glance our way. In the gloaming, they shine like acetylene torches. Corky barks at the strangers as aggressively as she barked at Richard Nixon.

"Give your dog a treat," says Nixon. "She drove those assholes off."

I watch the strangers as they continue along the hiking trail. Their light seems colder than foxfire. I'm relieved to watch them go.

"Angels!" scoffs Nixon. "They're worse than the Mormons. Always soliciting folks to get them to check out heaven. If you give those fuckers an inch, they'll bend your ear all day."

"Do they recruit very many?"

Nixon hawks and spits. "They'll draft an occasional priest if he hasn't screwed any kids. Sometimes they'll land an old woman or maybe a celibate monk. But no one with any hair on his crotch wants to go off with them."

The hill grows steeper. The darkness expands. In a while my eyes adjust to it—it looks like a velvet shroud.

•

WE COME TO a gate. A guard signals us through. My eyes have adjusted so well to the gloaming that I can see we are in a park. When we come to a complex of tennis courts, I spot a familiar man. He is standing on one of the courts, dressed for tennis, and he is practicing his serve. His eyes are fixed on his ball toss, and he does not see us approach him.

Noticing my hesitation, Nixon elbows me in the ribs. "Don't waste too much time here," he says. "This is only the first of our stops."

"That's my father," I say.

"What of it?" says Nixon. "You're older than he is, you know."

I look once again at the man on the court. Although he is my father, he looks ridiculously young. I recall that my father was forty years old when a blood clot took his life.

Leaving Nixon behind me, I stroll onto the tennis court. The man pauses in his service motion and looks at me incuriously. His eyes suggest that he wants to get back to working on his serve.

"You there," he shouts, "you need to wear whites if you're gonna come onto a court!" His voice is deep and resonates with the self-absorption of youth.

Do I have to remind him that I am his son? I cannot shake this thought from my head. "Call me *Tom*," I stammer. "Thanks for siring me."

"Did I?" he says. He bounces a ball. "Well, as long as you're here, let me give you some pointers. Tom never could serve worth a shit."

He lobs the ball above his head and snaps off a killer serve. "After your toss, keep your hand in the air. Pronate your wrist when you hit the ball. Strike the ball at two o'clock—that'll put some mustard on it."

He fires off half a dozen more serves before looking in my direction. "I see you drew Richard Nixon," he says.

"He's a bowler," I pipe, "so we have to move on." I realize how silly I sound, but it's all I can think of to say.

"Don't keep him waiting," my father replies. "I hear he gives a pretty good tour. I got stuck with Bobby Riggs, and he wasn't worth a damn."

I feel as though I am trespassing, I leave the tennis court.

"Why the sour face?" Nixon asks.

"I was hoping for something else."

"Did you see the kick on that serve? You ought to be happy for him."

"So what's the lesson here?" I ask him. "That souls dry up, that nothing lasts, that the afterlife doesn't mean shit?"

Nixon reaches into the pocket of his jacket and takes out an electric razor. He turns it on with a flick of his thumb. It hums like a bumblebee.

"You goddamn newbies are all alike," he says as he strokes his jowls. "Always expecting me to expound like some sage on a mountaintop."

"I assumed that's what you're here for," I say.

Nixon finishes removing his stubble then flings the razor away. "I'd rather be bowling," he mutters, "but they got me here giving a tour. They drag my ass out of hell every year to give these goddamn tours."

"Maybe you *should* be a guru by now."

Nixon folds his arms. "The only thing I know for sure is that you wanna kick my ass."

He sits down in a lotus position. His face is sweaty and flushed. "Well, that's already happened," Nixon says. "You've come along too late. I gave them a sword. They sliced off my nuts. You can't slice 'em off again."

Nixon closes his eyes and sits for several minutes. When his meditation is over, he rises to his feet. His gaze is as hard as marble when he looks at me again. "You want a lesson, I'll give you a lesson," he says with a weary shrug. "Don't go onto a tennis court if you aren't wearing whites."

·

WE CONTINUE OUR CLIMB until we come to a motionless body of water. We stand on a beach that is tideless: no wavelets comb the shore. Fog blankets the water so heavily I could write my name in it.

A chill electrifies my spine. I look at my chaperone. "Is this the River Styx?" I ask him. My palms are as damp as a tomb.

"How should I know what they call it?" growls Nixon.

"It has to have a name?"

"Fine," says Nixon. "I'll dub it Lake Liddy. Is that enough for you?"

Holding my breath, I look out on the water. The water is black as slate. No sunlight touches its surface, no ripples whiten its skin, not even the splash of a sea bird dimples its soundless expanse. I feel as though I am standing beside an enormous inkwell.

"Hurry it up," says Nixon. "The boat leaves in ten minutes."

"The boat?" I say. "The boat to where?"

"How should I know?" he replies.

We walk for another minute and come to an empty dock. A towering luxury liner is fastened to a piling. The ship does not sway in the water or strain on its mooring lines. It looks like a painted craft upon a painted lake.

I try to count the numerous decks, but they stretch into the fog.

"Where is that thing going to take us?" I ask.

"Just get aboard," Nixon mutters.

Corky hangs behind us. She does not want to board the ship. As we walk toward the gangplank, she barks then scampers away.

•

I FOLLOW NIXON up the gangplank. A steward waves us aboard. A promenade deck is packed with people who pay no attention to us. Scattered conversations fill the air like dead ash from a windblown fire, and a piped-in music system is playing "My Heart Will Go On."

Nobody seems to notice when the ship pulls away from the dock. Not even the drone of the ship horn interrupts the arid chatter. I clutch the deck railing and watch the dock recede into the haze. In a matter of seconds, it vanishes as though it has been devoured.

I look at the hundreds of passengers crammed upon the deck. Some are chatting in groups, some are texting on cell phones, others are walking around with no apparent destination. Although we are sharing a voyage, no one looks back at me.

I stare over the water. I see only fog. The ship horn groans again. "Where are we going?" I ask my guide.

"We'll both know when we get there," says Nixon. "C'mon, I'll show you the boat?"

"If this is the VIP tour," I reply, "I would hate to go tourist class."

Nixon chuckles. "I lied about that. Sorry to have built up your hopes."

We enter a giant foyer that is lit up like a mall. The foyer is a hub to dozens of suites whose doors are open wide. The suites are filled with people who come and go at will. Some of the suites are chapels, others are casinos, others are barrooms that relinquish the roar of televised football games.

The acoustics of the foyer are powerful; I hear conversations more clearly. "Don't call yourself a golfer," a voice says. "'Cause you're three-putting every green." Another voice says, "The Dave Clark Five had nothing on the Beatles." A third voice cries, "I'll tell you who shot him. It hadda be Jack Ruby!"

I follow Nixon up a long spiral staircase. We climb from deck to deck. Each of the decks is brightly lit and a home to dozens of suites. I see a stock exchange, a bowling ally, and an adult entertainment store. I see a beauty salon, a disco, and even a Chinese restaurant.

"Some Peking duck?" Nixon asks me.

I shrug.

Nixon steps into the restaurant and comes back with two takeout containers. He hands me one. "I ordered it spicy. You can't get it spicy in hell."

Although I don't feel hungry, I bite into a breast. It stings my mouth like a scorpion. I toss it into a trash bin.

Nixon pockets his takeout box—"I'm saving it for hell"—and we continue to mount the staircase. We pass decks with bingo parlors, decks with dog grooming salons, decks where blazing angels are passing out literature. When we come to a deck with a Disneyland logo, Nixon pauses to catch his breath. The deck contains dozens of shops, all of them Disney stores. The shops are packed with customers who are buying memorabilia.

"Good ol' Walt," Nixon mutters. "I could always count on him."

"Count on him for what?" I say.

"You're a writer," says Nixon. "Figure it out.'"

The answer seems redundant, but I answer anyway. "His corny movies kept people from thinking."

"A nicer way to put it," says Nixon, "is that he kept them from thinking too much."

"So what's the lesson here?"

Nixon yawns. "What lesson do you want to hear?"

"That your tripe went over too easily. Walt Disney did most of the work."

Nixon scowls. "You goddamn writers—always wanting a lesson. Well, I don't have a lesson to give you, and you're starting to piss me off."

"Am I here for your approval?" I say.

"No, you're here for a goddamn tour." Nixon reaches into his jacket and removes a bottle of throat spray. After lathering his tonsils, he takes a labored breath. "All right, here's a lesson. You can write it down or shove it up your ass. Check for a fortune cookie when you order Peking duck."

•

THE STAIRWAY ENDS at a sundeck, and we step into the night air. The sky is starless, the fog is like soup, the deck is slick with dew.

"Is this boat bound for purgatory?" I ask Nixon.

"How the hell should I know?"

"So where are we going?"

"Stop asking me that! Where the fuck do you wanna go?"

Remembering Dante's *Inferno*, I say, "How about the circle of Limbo? I hear the ancient poets live there, and they have it pretty good. They get to stroll in a meadow and philosophize all day."

Nixon slaps his forehead. "You want to go *there*? Those gasbags will bore you to death."

"I'm dead already," I say. "What have I got to lose?"

"You'll lose your *mind* in the circle of Limbo. Those cocksuckers talk in riddles."

"This whole damn ship is a riddle," I snap.

"It's only a riddle to you," Nixon laughs. "That comes from thinking too much."

"The circle of Limbo," I repeat, and I feel like a pompous fool. Since I don't know the ship's destination, I can hardly make demands.

"Well, think it over first," Nixon says. "I gotta go for now."

"You going to check our course?" I ask.

"No, I gotta take a piss."

•

NIXON DISAPPEARS down the stairwell; I stand alone on the deck. The fog is relentless; the air is so damp it clings to my skin like a suit. The piped-in music system is playing "The Girl from the North Country."

A woman's voice says, "Tom, you'll catch your death of cold."

The fog is so thick that I barely see her loitering beside the stairwell. Despite this benevolent haze, I see more than I want to see. She is no longer a girl of twenty but a woman past menopause. Her hair is white and disheveled; her eyes no longer sparkle. She is wearing a yellowed caftan, and love beads droop from her neck.

I close my eyes and will her away. When I open them she is still there. What a sticky thing one's first love is even when thrown away. I had loved her when we were in college; I had loved my adventuring more. When my letters from Australia no longer sustained her, she wisely discarded me.

She remains by the stairwell; she does not walk toward me. She nibbles her underlip. "Why am I still caring for you?" she puzzles. Her voice is honeyed with sentiment; her tenderness touches me still.

I choose my words as though they are jewels. "I should think you'd have lost the habit."

"I did," she replies. "But when heart failure took me, I wanted to see you once more."

Why has illusion abandoned me? I think as I look at her. My memory of her—which I treasure—is a memory nurtured by distance. Her presence is like a wax statue. I want her to go away.

"I have something for you," she murmurs.

"Galoshes?" I ask. My skin starts to prickle.

"Will a snapshot do instead?" she asks.

She shuffles toward me, hands me a photo, then goes back and waits by the stairwell. In the photo we are a couple. In the photo she looks more alive. We pose in her dormitory, arm-in-arm. The flashbulb reddens our eyes.

I slip the photo into my pocket. It gives me a paper cut. "Why did you bring me this?" I ask.

She replaces a loose strand of hair. "I've always been fond of collectibles, Tom. I just hate to throw them away."

"Thank you," I say.

"I must go," she replies. "Bingo starts in ten minutes."

She hurries down the stairwell. Her footsteps patter like rain. I am looking at the photo when Nixon returns to the deck.

•

"GUESS WHO I saw?" I tell Nixon.

"Your college squeeze," he replies. "I hope you don't wanna marry her."

"I wanted her to go away."

"Atta boy," says Nixon. "Way to go with the flow." Nixon lifts his bottle of throat spray and once again coats his tonsils. Borrowing from Thomas Wolfe, he quotes, "'You can't go home again.'"

Do I only merit clichés? I wonder. I am sick of this fool of a man. Feeling contentious, I shake my head and try to outdo his quote. "'Like bubbles on the sea of matter borne, they rise, they break, and to that sea return.'"

"The fuck are you trying to say?" Nixon says.

"That you've shown me nothing of substance."

"So you're reciting Alexander Pope?"

"If it helps me make sense of all this—yes."

"All right," Nixon says. "Let's do literary quotes. I read three books a day, you know." Nixon fills his mouth with chewing tobacco then spits the wad into a lifeboat. He then dances a jig and grins like a jackal. "How about something from The Book of Revelation?—that's always good for a laugh. 'Since you are neither hot nor cold, I will spew thee from my mouth.'"

I concede to Nixon that he has won. "That explains this vapid boat."

Nixon pirouettes and laughs. "You eggheads are so easy to fuck with," he crows.

"I'm trying to rise like a phoenix," I say. "I want my celestial wings."

"Yeah, but you're more like a baby bird. All beak and fulla shit."

"So where are we going?"

"Come with me to hell—you can chase those damn soldiers away. If I can get some more spin from my follow through, I'll bowl that perfect game."

The ship horn drones like a trumpet.

"We're arriving," Nixon says.

A shoreline is creeping toward us. I can make out a shadowy dock. It takes me a moment to realize it's the exact same place we embarked from. Corky is sitting on the dock. She barks as the ship approaches.

•

SOME ANGELS trail us like pickpockets as we take our leave of the ship. Corky bares her teeth at them. Nixon waves them off.

"Go to hell," he snaps. They bow and walk away. I wait until the fog swallows them before I speak to Nixon.

"Is that how you talk to heavenly hosts?"

Nixon spits a tobacco-stained loogie. "I wasn't trying to be rude," he says. "I just told them where they should go. Those fuckers will pluck more souls in hell than they will on that goddamn boat."

"You should have let them recruit you," I joke.

"They've tried," he replies. "Half a dozen times. When heaven lands a big-time sinner, it's great publicity."

"They're persistent if nothing else," I say.

Nixon gives me the Boy Scout salute. "Persistence pays," he recites. "Shit, I might just let 'em recruit me once I've bowled my perfect game."

Amused by the look on my face, Nixon laughs like a donkey. "Hadja going," he brays. "Damn, it's fun to mess with your head. How'd you become a writer if you're this damn easy to fool?"

We walk for an hour. Neither of us speaks. We come to a carnival. I see an endless midway that is packed with thousands of people.

The racing lights of the midway barely penetrate the darkness, but the many sights and sounds are distracting nonetheless. A roller coaster rattles above us; a Ferris wheel spins like a giant roulette wheel; a barker from a break-a-plate booth stuffs a softball into my hands. "Hurry, hurry, hurry!" he hollers. "Hurry, hurry, hurry! Smash three in a row and pick your prize. A Kewpie doll or heaven."

Annoyed, I toss the softball away. Corky bolts after it, fetches it back. I throw it away a second time, and she vanishes into the crowd.

"Is this our destination?" I ask.

"Damned if I know," Nixon says. "But I wouldn't mind some cotton candy. You can't get that in hell."

We come to a booth where a dozen people are playing Russian roulette. They sit in a circle, awaiting their turn as a pistol is passed around. A crowd lingers around the booth, egging the contestants on. Bookies move among the crowd, giving odds and collecting bets.

Among the contestants, I spot Spiro Agnew, Lyndon Johnson, and Andrew Jackson. They sit like stuffed monkeys, their hands on their knees, while the pistol makes its rounds. Each contestant spins the cylinder and puts the gun to his temple. When one of them blows his brains out, the crowd erupts in a cheer.

As the bodies are dragged from the booth, the bookies settle the bets. A concert band plays a few bars from "Happiness is a Warm Gun."

Nixon points to a scar on his temple and sighs like a dog in a cage. "I lost in my very first round," he says. "Hell, I coulda been a contender."

"Take another shot at it," I say dryly.

"Fuck it, I'd rather be knocking down pins. That goddamn game is rigged."

We continue to walk down the midway. The darkness tightens around us. Although I stroll among droves of people, I feel no connections at all. It seems like they are devolving on their way to oblivion.

•

THE TOUR CONTINUES for three whole months. I see many incalculable sights. I see hordes of angels shepherding children who are shrieking for their mothers. I see mummified church people holding up signs that say, Christianity Saves. I see gangs of Hare Krishnas swiping apples from a mart. Although the sights are myriad, the effect is always the same. I feel like I'm watching a movie that has no storyline.

"So whaddya think?" Nixon asks me one day.

We are standing on top of a snow-capped mountain. The fog below us rolls. An aura is starting to light me up, but I can't tell what color it is.

"What do you want me to think?" I say. "You've taught me nothing at all."

Nixon pantomimes a golf swing then squints as though watching the ball. "If you want to be enlightened," he says, "go chat with a fucking angel."

"They're a little too hard on the eyes," I say. I look down at the infinite fog. Random lights peak through it like a scattering of fireflies.

"Yeah," Nixon says. "And they lay it on thick. You'd think they were selling used cars."

Nixon unzips his pants and pees a smoky stream. After yellowing the snow, he wags his penis, shaking the last drops loose. "A guru might give you the scoop," he says as he tugs his fly back up. "But me, I'm just a tour guide and I wanna get back to hell."

"Just tell me what comes next," I say.

"Fucked if I know," Nixon says. "Go sit under another tree—I'm done with his goddamn tour."

"Any parting words?" I ask as he starts to walk away.

"Plenty," he says, "but none of 'em matter. Except for one damn thing." He spreads his arms like an eagle in flight. "Ayyy am not a crook."

o o o

The Phoenix Climbs

THE DAWN OF MATURITY—that critical moment when a boy becomes a man—varies. Taking over the family farm might qualify; going off to war would suffice; and slaying Goliath with a single stone would certainly do the trick. But one's passage to manhood need not be severe: there is too great a shortage of nine-foot giants or the temerity to go out and slay one. So consider instead the term "rising manhood," a phrase I found in the porno books I snuck from my dad's bedroom closet. That an epiphany can come from a smut book is an irony best disregarded, but the flower of revelation should not be crushed when it springs from fetid soil. As I read through those well-fingered, slightly stained books, a light as profound as a burning bush seared itself into my soul. One's ascension to manhood need not entail more than a generous debut: the instant one's eyes first linger upon a beautiful, naked woman.

My rite of passage did not take place until well after I turned sixteen. Admittedly, this is a little bit late to claim one's rise to manhood. But there is much to be said for late bloomers: a seed I might have wasted in the back of a car—in some tacky lover's lane—had ripened within me until it became a pungent, glowing flower. When it came to the worship of fannies and breasts, Hugh Hefner had nothing on me.

It happened in the summer of '64, during our annual family foray to Delaware's Rehoboth Beach. I spotted her while strolling the boardwalk, and instantly fell in love. She was as lean as an eel, as brown as a penny; her long dark hair hung in braids. And her tiny bikini clung to her as though it had been painted on.

She was standing alone at one of those spin art booths, squirting dye onto a whirling paper square. Absorbed in this casual pastime, she did not see me approach her. A mole the size of a thumbprint lay under one of her cheekbones, and I hoped that she considered it a blot upon her beauty. It was that heavy mole, that proverbial damn spot, that gave me the courage to speak.

I almost said, "Gee, you're pretty," but I caught myself in time. I did not wish to sound like what I was: a gangly horny kid. So I put my hands on my hips and deepened my voice. "Tommy Hemmings at your disposal," I said in my best James Bond imitation.

She was clutching four tubes of dye, so my intrusion was not untimely. But she looked at me noncommittally before handing me three of the tubes. I resisted the urge to squeeze dye onto my fingers and decorate her face. With her prominent cheekbones and shoulder-length braids, she looked like an Indian maiden.

"Don't drop 'em, kid," she said, and she smiled when I blushed like a berry. Her teeth were white and even, like the keys on a brand new piano.

She squirted the paper several more times then handed me the final tube. "Whaddya think I should call it?" she said, plucking the paper from the wheel.

As I studied the concentric circles, my heart pounded in my ears. The pattern suggested a whirlpool that might pull me to uncharted depths. "*A Siren's Seduction*," I offered.

She giggled and patted my cheek. "You're quite the romantic, aren't you, kiddo? I think I'll call it *Paint*."

"Can I have it?" I asked her.

"Kid," she said. "Your mother know what you're doing?"

"I'm a spin art collector."

She laughed. "Don't feed me that line of crap. You're trying to pick me up, aren'tcha, sonny?"

Stung by her candor, I reverted to form. "G-gee, you're pretty," I stammered.

She handed me the painting and shrugged. "And you're pretty lamo," she said. "Guys hit on me all the time, ya know, so you're going to need some game. A spin art collector—that's gotta be the most pitiful come-on I've heard."

I folded her artwork meticulously and tucked it into my bathing trunks. "If it's pity you're offering, I'll take it. I'm a pretty needy case."

"Is that why ya talk like an out-of-work actor? That's really, like, freaky, ya know?"

At least, I had her attention, so I decided to toss her some Shakespeare. I'm extremely well-read for a sixteen-year-old kid. At Jefferson High, where I go to school, they put me in a college-level English class. I'm also in the drama club, and I played Prospero in *The Tempest*.

Looking into her smoke-grey eyes, I gave her a dose of the Bard. "The weight of your kind gaze I must obey." Damn, if I didn't sound like a Renaissance man, all I needed was a sword and a cape.

She looked at me like I was a bug, so I paused for further affect. I then bowed like a reed in the wind and hit her with another line. "I never saw true beauty 'til this day."

When she feigned a yawn and clucked her tongue, my cock shrank to the size of a bean sprout. Had she noticed that I had mixed up Shakespeare's quotes? I prayed she wasn't a critic.

"Keep that crap for the stage," she said. "You sound like a total dork."

"If all the world be a stage," I replied, "you must be my Juliet."

She laughed so hard tears dampened her cheeks. "What a loada shit."

I slapped my chest as though wounded. "I hope it will nourish a rose."

Her laughter had barely subsided when she gripped my hand in hers. "C'mon," she said. "Let's dodge a few waves. You need some cooling off."

•

IF *FINNEGANS WAKE* is the most challenging of books, I had much to bring to it. Because I spent that entire summer in Cleo's magnificent wake. With her, the beach and the boardwalk became as magical as a Joycean rant. Tossing bean bags into baskets was like piercing the Cyclops' eye; returning the surfer boys' envious stares was like slaying Penelope's suitors; and rubbing lotion into her back was like yielding to Circe's spell. Not that turning men into pigs was a challenge in my case. As my hand roamed between her warm shoulder blades, it was all I could do not to grunt.

Of course, she had a boyfriend; he was in the Army somewhere. Why else would she spend time with the likes of me: a cock-flogging adolescent? Clearly, she regarded me as safe, not sexy—fun yet conveniently harmless. I was suitable only to carry her beach umbrella and rinse off her boogie board. But I accepted my role as her servant with the deepest of gratitude: a reverence befitting a drowning sailor whom a mermaid had plucked from the sea. As we bicycled along the boardwalk, as we bounced among the breakers, a maudlin line from a country tune bespoiled my literary brain. *Yes, if I can't have all of you, just give me what you think is fair.*

Although I treated her like a princess, she did not have a regal soul. The entertainment magazines she tucked in her beach bag filled the horizon of her mind; top ten songs, like "Ring of Fire," blared from her portable radio; and clichés like "dork" and "lamo" peppered her conversation. She had no interest in going to college although she'd been offered a gymnastic scholarship. Instead, she planned to attend beauty school and work in a salon.

I told her I was going to major in literature, but I didn't want to teach it. Instead, I wanted to be like Jack London and take off on adventures. I wanted to pen novels about diving for pearls and sailing the South China Sea. I wanted to be like Hemingway and write about giant marlins.

"So why are you reading *Paradise Lost*? Ain't that a little bit lamo?"

She was lying face down on her beach towel, digging her toes into the sand. Even so, she had noticed that dog-eared paperback that I read whenever she napped. Since we were only a passing liaison, the stuff of midsummer dreams, the title of Milton's worn classic did not seem out of place.

"I like the Devil in it," I said. "He's an independent guy."

"What are ya tryin' to tell me, kid?"

"That I'm gonna be my own man."

"Is that why you're lugging my bag around and rubbing lotion on my back?"

I shrugged and tickled the arch of her foot. She pushed me away with her toes. "Buy me a hot dog, Satan," she said. "Go easy on the relish this time."

Her sense of entitlement was remarkable, but who was I to object? Were she more than a self-absorbed vixen, what use would she have for me? Yes, I was only her lackey, her fawning pitiful page, but the wages of my debasement were as rare as pirated gold.

When I returned with her hot dog, she was lying on her back leafing through *Paradise Lost*. Her leg was propped on her bended knee, her foot swung like a pendulum. Her eyes did not stray from the book as I handed her the hot dog. Instead, she wrinkled her nose and waved me away from her. Oh, how I envied that lucky frank as she slipped it between her lips.

After another minute, she tossed the book into the sand. "So that's what gets you off," she said. "Snakes and fallen angels."

"Isn't that kind of obvious?" I said.

"I s'ppose it is," she replied. She devoured the rest of her hot dog like a seagull gulping a fish. She then rolled back onto her stomach and rested her chin on her forearms. "So many times have ya jacked off to my image, Mister Beelzebub?"

I poured sand onto her ankles and pretended not to hear her. The count was probably forty, but she did not need that much information. "I jack by the book," I said finally, once again parodying Shakespeare.

"The fuck you saying?" she said.

"Your image is not yet complete, my queen—it barely rivals a sex book. I won't do you so great an honor 'til I see you in the flesh."

"'Til I contribute to the delinquency of a minor, you mean. Kiddo, I'm not *that* depraved."

"Corrupt me," I begged her. "All it would take is the innocence of Eve."

She laughed and rubbed my thigh with her foot. "That's all your gonna get. Now be a good little buccaneer and fetch me a Royal Crown Cola."

•

PARTING IS SUGARY SORROW, if I can borrow from Shakespeare once more. But humor can fan dying embers and make sunsets brilliant again. Yes, my time with Cleo was dwindling, but why sour it with gloom? It was in this spirit of lively rebellion that I came up with our little game.

I planted my copy of *Paradise Lost* whenever she wasn't looking. I slipped it into her beach bag, I rolled it up in her towel, I even tucked it under her feet whenever she was napping. On discovering that mothy paperback, she flung it away like a frisbee. "Tommy, don't force me to read that," she'd cry, and we both dissolved into laughter. She got pretty good a flinging the book: her record was thirty feet.

"Why won't you read it?" I asked her one day. We were sitting on our beach towels, having finished a jaunt on our boogie boards, and we were dipping into a box of animal crackers she had bought at a 7-Eleven.

"Kiddo," she said as she bit the head off a hippo, "I don't want smoke in my eyes."

Her willful insularity was becoming a little bit tiresome. So when I answered her, I did not try to disguise my irritation. "I revere you like Pygmalion. I live to give you a soul."

"Waddaya talkin' about, kiddo?"

"This guy carved a woman out of ivory then fell deeply in love with her. One day, Aphrodite took pity on him and brought the statue to life."

"You're crazier than Lucy Ricardo," she said. "And you live in Tommy Land."

I should have been more amused; I should have kept eating my cookies. What else could I expect from someone who read nothing but *The Hollywood Reporter*? I felt like a prince whom fortune had doomed to wait upon a goat herder.

"Maybe it's time you *sampled* a little forbidden fruit."

"Like Eve in that goddamn book of yours? You see where she ended up?"

"The Land of Nod," I said, and I gave her a sporting grin.

Was it the sugar in the animal crackers that animated her scowl? Or were her eyes too muddied by *I Love Lucy* reruns to handle a bite of culture? Whichever the case, our relationship changed when she threw a giraffe at my head. "Whenever you look at me, Mister Pig Malion, all you see is a pair of tits."

"What else do you have to offer?" I snapped.

96

"How about a view of my ass?"

When she packed up her beach bag and strode towards the boardwalk, I should have been heartbroken. But as I looked at her elegant backside, I felt the phoenix rise. No, it wasn't because of the oil on her thighs or the wiggle in her butt. It was because she had lost her temper. We had actually had our first fight.

•

RECONCILIATION IS easy when you're grateful to be a flunky, when beach umbrellas and boogie boards are more than your heart throb will tote. And since she was staying at a flat next to my family's beach house, a reunion was all but assured. The following morning, she knocked on my door and I practically fell at her feet.

"Tommy," she said matter-of-factly. "I'm givin' you one last chance."

It was one last chance to carry the beach bag that hung from her slender hand. It was one final chance to haul the umbrella that sheltered her face from the sun. But gone was my independence, forgotten my reckless pride. Laden like a pack mule, I followed her back to the beach.

It was after I put up the beach umbrella, fetched her a taco, and rubbed Coppertone onto her back, that she broke the news to me. She told me her boyfriend was on leave from the Army, and that he would show up tomorrow morning. She said they were going to get married in the fall, and he had bought her a diamond engagement ring. After an enormous wedding, which two hundred people would attend, they would honeymoon on a Caribbean cruise and dance to a ballroom band. She was especially looking forward to the smorgasbords because she loved ice sculptures and cold salmon.

I was not upset that our summer was ending; I had long been prepared for that. But the thought of Cleo as an Army wife was something I could not endure. A vampire, yes, a dominatrix for sure, but not a Military spouse.

"I'll give your marriage a week," I said. "The honeymoon will probably last longer."

Removing her sunglasses, she looked at me stonily. "Did I ask for advice from the king of the dreamers?"

"I think you've done me one better."

"Pig Malion," she said, sitting up on her towel, "that's a helluva thing to say."

"You're my island witch, my Circe. You *turned* me into a pig. Yet you're selling yourself to servitude for the sake of a cut-rate cruise."

"Maybe," she shrugged. "But don't lecture me, kid. I bought you much cheaper than that."

I cleared my throat dramatically then opened up my heart. Balling my fists and fighting back tears, I dared to raise my voice. "Cleo," I said, "you make me feel like a goddamn teaser stallion."

"The hell is that?" she muttered.

"A runt horse that hangs around breeding farms and never gets any ass. The breeders use him to excite the mare before they bring in the stud."

She sighed and rolled onto her stomach. "Seabiscuit," she muttered, "you'd better go take a swim."

Later, after I walked her home, she gave me a peck on the mouth. Her lips were chapped, not velvety; her breath smelled of garlic, not spice. Was this to be the blossoming of my cherished ivory girl?

"Kiddo, it's been real," she joked as she disappeared into the house.

•

WHEN CLEO TRANSFORMED ME into a pig, I was not without concessions. Pigs have remarkable hearing; pigs have noses like radar; pigs have a talent to scour and sniff out forbidden fruits.

Did I mention the beach house she stayed in was adjacent to our own? Did I mention that house had an outdoor shower that I could see from my second-story bedroom? It took only the sound of water running to draw me to the bedroom window, to pull my gaze to the courtyard below and spot Cleo showering nude.

I stood like Romeo scorning the east because Juliet was the sun. I stood like Odysseus lashed to the mainmast and drinking the sea maidens' song. Since the slings of fickle fortune had brought me to this moment, I was ready to pardon Olympus the capriciousness of its ways.

As I watched the spray pucker her nipples, the rivulets caress her brown skin, the shampoo stream from her cascading hair, I managed a stiff salute. But I wished I could erect something more than my willie—it hardly did her justice. Why not the string of my bathing suit or the towel that lay limp on my bed? Why not the hose in the courtyard below or the very hairs on my head?

She showered for only a minute before vanishing into the house, and I thanked Aphrodite for giving me no more that I could handle. Who was I to ponder Nirvana, to fathom its hillocks and swamps? Who was I to stare into a vision as fiery as the dawn? If I could turn back time to that glorious minute, I would hesitate to do so. I fear such an indiscretion would turn me into stone.

•

THE MEMORY OF CLEO haunts me like the Ghost of Christmas Past. Thirty years later, I commissioned a painting and hung it in my den. So stark was my recollection of her, so potent my memory, that I described her to the artist as though she were standing before my eyes. She hangs behind my writing desk, a glowing ocean sprite, the spray from the shower forever anointing her shoulders and upturned breasts. "What's that?" my wife asked when I hung the painting.

"A passing," I said. "The pyre of my childhood. The day I became a man."

"The day you became a perve," she sniffed, and she walked out of the room. She had spoken like an ingrate, she had desecrated a shrine. But I swallowed my indignation and forgave her her callous reply.

And where was I in that painting? I was peeping from a window like the Kilroy caricature. That ubiquitous voyeur, that phantomish stray, that mooch at the banquet of life. No, her beauty could not be done justice by the specter at the feast—she deserved a gift as epic as the one she had given me.

I placed a worthier tribute on the corner of my desk. A plaque with a cherry red finish that read: *The Phoenix Climbs.*

° ° °

The World Baseball League

1

Songs of Ourselves

THE WORLD BASEBALL LEAGUE was born in the basement of our suburban home in Arlington, Virginia. My kid brother and I invented it on a sweltering Fourth of July. It was a heroic invention—a vehicle by which two avowed nerds might wear the colors of champions. Armed with dice, meticulously drawn charts, and a cardboard baseball diamond, Robbie and I commanded the destinies of twenty baseball teams. We played daily throughout the long hot summer—up to six games a day—and we tweaked team standings and player averages after every game. So absorbed were we in horsehide heroics that we rendered the summer neither long nor hot.

Our rosters consisted of four hundred individual players, each represented by a 2" by 2" square of cardboard. Batting averages, fielding percentages, slugging potential, and base running speed were recorded on each of these squares along with the name and number of the player. To avoid the stigma of nepotism, we recruited our players liberally. Politicians, demagogues, movie stars, and literary characters were listed among the players—each with his respective stats. Hitler, for example, was a .224 hitter with a .142 slugging percentage and better than average base running speed. Our rosters also included caricatures we made up to lend comic relief to an otherwise serious pursuit. My favorite was Percy the Balladeer, a switch-hitting fop who recited Elizabethan poetry every time he came to bat. Of course, we knew nothing about Elizabethan poetry, so Percy's recitals amounted to the merest of doggerel. An example:

Hi diddle de diddle de di.
What a marvelous player am I.
My swing is as keen
As a ripe tangerine.
Hi diddle de diddle de dee.

To pad the standings of our stronger teams, we created several doormat teams that we allowed John, our toddler sibling, to manage. The lowliest of them all we named Happy Hill after the little fellow's daycare center. Its players consisted of the hapless Peanuts characters who almost always struck out on three quick pitches. But Happy Hill did have one good player, Snoopy, whom I eventually acquired from John in exchange for a coloring book and a Hershey bar. I inserted Snoopy as shortstop on my strongest squad, The Neutralists, and it immediately rose to the top of its division.

Baseball is arguably our national recreation, but The World Baseball League was hardly a pastime. It was more a vocation, a proclivity, a life obsession to be celebrated in legend and song. And so we composed the most vitriolic of anthems, which one of us sang whenever blessed with victory. Polemics, after all, is the privilege of the winner no matter how dubious the enterprise. "This land is your land!" thundered the Lord, giving the Israelites unimpeachable license to wipe out indigenous people. "Manifest Destiny," our nation cried, allowing our Union Civil War generals, the champions of emancipation, an exemption to enslave aboriginals. "Remember the Alamo," cried swarthy Sam Houston as his crew of assassins slew Mexican soldiers who were taking an ill-timed siesta. It was in this spirit of hubris that we composed our personal anthem: a litany of ninety-three verses, which we sang to the tune of "Auld Lang Syne." A sampling:

I win again, I win again,
I win again, I win.
So raise the flags, strike up the band,
For I have won again.

It was during our first World Series, our ultimate struggle for bragging rights, that our anthem reached fever pitch. After edging Robbie's Potomac Patriots three games to two, with just one game left to play, I sat back in my chair, grinned like a ghoul, and belted out a brand new verse. My voice was so clear, so booming and proud, that it echoed throughout the county.

I am a champion of old.
I never ever lose.
I'll beat your pants off anytime
At anything you choose.

Not to be outdone, Robbie beefed up his lineup by giving contracts to several free agents. Dipping into his cash reserves, he recruited George Wallace, a hard- hitting right fielder, Holden Caulfield, a formidable catcher, and Ulysses Grant, a third baseman who specialized in long belts. After winning the penultimate contest, and tying the series at three games apiece, Robbie chanted his favorite verse.

Ten thousand souls will sing my praise.
Their hearts will pound with glee.
So don't despair if I should win.
It's only destiny.

And so the die was cast for a seventh and decisive game—a clash that would endow the winner with the peerless ranking of a god. Robbie's pitcher was Richard Nixon, a junk hurler with one of the best changeups in the league, so I countered by saturating my lineup with batters adept at hitting off-speed balls. I also put Che Guevara on the mound, a left-handed knuckleballer fresh from three hours rest. The contest was an epic pitching duel. Idi Amin, Mao Zedong, and Vlad the Impaler—my most consistent hitters—all failed to reach second base while Barry Goldwater, Aaron Burr, and John Hancock—the meat of Robbie's order—did not even get a hit. Entering the top of the ninth, the score was knotted at 0-0 with the bottom of my order scheduled to bat. But how could I tip the scales with such feckless hitters as Adolf Hitler, Joan of Arc, and Richard the Third?

To my sweet surprise, Adolf, after taking two strikes, was brushed by a high inside pitch and awarded a trip to first. I immediately signaled Joan to lay down a sacrifice bunt. Obeying my signal, she tapped a dribbler down the third base line and took off for first. Amazingly, she beat out the throw after sprinting like her pants were on fire. As Richard the Third shuffled up to home plate, muttering about his winter of discontent, I had two ducks on the pond and nobody out.

When a dropped ball allowed Hitler to slide into third—scoring position!—my heart began to race. But Richard the Third was my poorest batsman. A compulsive chaser of bad pitches, he had not smacked the ball out of the infield all year. I gambled on an infield hit and signaled for a delayed swing. Robbie's second baseman, somber John Hancock, was notoriously slow on his release, so there was a better than average chance that Hitler could make it home.

While Richard was fiddling around at the plate, adjusting his helmet and calling for a horse, Nixon tossed a slider down the middle. Startled by the pitch, Richard swung like a girl. *Crack!* A hopper went bouncing towards second base—a perfect triple play ball. *Whump!* John Hancock sealed the out at first. *Whump!* Lyndon Johnson, a strong-armed first baseman, beat Joan's slide at second. *Whump!* Hancock's throw to the plate thundered into Caulfield's glove. As I watched the dust at home plate settle, the roar of the crowd told me what had happened. Hitler had beaten the throw by a whisker. We were ahead 1-0.

In the bottom of the ninth, I substituted flame-throwing Adolf Eichmann for a tiring Che Guevara. Three pop ups later, The Neutralists were champions of the world. It was the trashiest of wins; it was the cleverest of triumphs. But my victory would not be complete without outdoing the verse Robbie had crooned. As I watched Robbie sit there, fighting back tears, it came to me in a flash. Heroically, irresistibly, I began to sing.

> *The angels will call out my name.*
> *Their harps will keep in time.*
> *That one like me should walk the earth,*
> *A boon to all mankind.*

I sang it to Gabriel's trumpet; I sang it to Pan's lilting pipes. So rich was my voice that sirens rejoiced and the garlands of heaven were mine. Later, mobbed by reporters in the locker room, I waited for the president's call.

2

The Vegas Differential

"YOU TWO LIVE IN NERDVILLE," Dad snapped. "Why doncha play baseball for *real* steada sitting at that table all day, rolling those goddamn dice?" He was referring to the World Baseball League, that marvelous horsehide fantasy game that I played with my kid brother, Robbie, throughout every summer day. A game we invented to fill the void after Dad banned our video games. Dad was laboring under the illusion that we could actually play real baseball. But my hand-eye coordination was dismal, I flinched when a ball bounced my way, and Robbie, a scrawny runt of a kid, could barely lift a bat.

"Have you ever *seen* Nerdville?" I said. The question, of course, was redundant; all our dad saw were two kids in the basement, forever checking hand-drawn charts while rolling a pair of dice. He did not see what we saw: the massive cheering crowds, the twenty colorful teams, the stats of the four hundred players our 2" by 2" cardboard squares represented. Nor did he see how destiny hinged upon every toss of the dice. The higher a player's batting average, the more likely it was that a fling of the cubes would favor him with a hit. But the odds of a hit would fluctuate with the pitcher's earned run average.

So enthralled were we by the World Baseball League that it had become a hallowed ground. Everything else—sleeping, eating, jacking off—were nagging distractions we had to fulfill to return to our field of dreams.

Dad placed his hands on his hips like a cop. "Don't wanna know about the crap in yer heads cuz that game is destroying yer minds. What I *do* know is it's time you got out of the house and hit a baseball for real."

"First thing Saturday," I remarked, and I gave him a big thumbs-up. What I was actually saying was, "Fuck that shit." I was using a code Robbie and I had devised for talking back to Dad. A code that allowed us to be insolent without consequence.

"First thing Saturday," Robbie chimed in, and he gave Dad a possum grin. "After I brush my teeth," he added, which meant "Go fuck yourself."

Of course, we had no intention of hitting a baseball for real. We had lineups to seed, stats to adjust, endorsements to consider. We had players to coach, pennants to win, and anthems to compose. With the playoffs only a few games away, there was no time for vulgar pursuits. Our hearts, our minds, our very souls were pledged to the World Baseball League.

•

ALTHOUGH WE HAD no use for Philistines, we were not averse to converts. And so that summer, we opened the League up to one of the neighborhood boys. A tall rangy kid with a budding moustache and a Stetson hat on his head. As a high school senior, he was one year older than me, six years older than Robbie, but he looked upon the two of us with an air of a veteran gambler. He insisted we dispense with his name—Chad Sylvester—and call him the Vegas Fox.

The Fox made frequent player trades to beef up his stable of teams. Deals he promoted by tapping the table, sitting back in his chair, and drawing a dramatic breath. "Tell you what I'm gonna do," he would say as he chewed an unlit cigar. And then he might offer up Willie Mays for Mickey Mantle or Roger Maris.

Through a series of clever and well-timed trades, the Fox built one of his teams, the Gatlinburg Ghostbusters, into a playoff contender. In juggernaut fashion, this team swept through the playoffs and stormed into the World Series. There, it faced the Potomac Patriots, a team I had purchased from Robbie for eight million dollars, six farm teams, and an advertising contract with Gatorade. But the Patriots had suffered badly in their march to the Fall Classic. Depleted by injuries, hitting slumps, and player suspensions for steroid use, they were a very poor match for the Gatlinburg Ghostbusters.

Sensing my desperation, the Fox stroked his thin moustache. "Tell you what I'm gonna do," he announced in his best used car salesman drawl. "I'll give you Babe Ruth, Ty Cobb, and Cy Young if you'll part with Jimmy Piersall."

I could not believe what I was hearing. Babe Ruth, Ty Cobb, Cy Young—the tallest legends of baseball—all for Jimmy Piersall, a volatile self-promoter with a .272 lifetime batting average? As a ballplayer, Jimmy Piersall was the very definition of ordinary.

Stunned by the offer, I struggled to speak. "H-h-how did you get those p-p-players?" I stammered.

"Brought 'em back from the grave," laughed the Fox. "That ain't hard to do when you're a ghostbuster."

I made the deal immediately and he handed me three cardboard squares. I fingered the squares as though they were jewels. I could not believe what I held in my hands: Babe Ruth, a .342 hitter with a .690 slugging percentage, Ty Cobb, a .366 hitter with a .433 on-base percentage, and Cy Young, a backstop-busting fastballer with a 2.62 earned run average. The Fox must have lost his mind to have made such a stupid deal.

Since the trade had not yet been announced to the press, I phoned my bookie in Atlantic City to get the spread on the Series. The line was even money that the Patriots would lose in five games or less. I quickly cashed out my liquid assets and auctioned off my franchise with Coca-Cola. Altogether, I raised ten million dollars, which I bet on my revamped team. My entire bankroll was on the line, but I didn't give a shit. With the legends of yore in my lineup, I was making a no risk bet.

•

THE SERIES began on a glorious Sunday. After the Marine Band played the National Anthem and the Blue Angel jets roared over the stadium, I handed my lineup card to the home plate umpire. Ty Cobb, of course, was leading off, the Babe was batting cleanup. And Cy Young was perched on the pitcher's mound, taking his warm-up tosses. I figured ol' Cy was good for five games—hell, in the prime of his career he used to pitch double-headers.

As the umpire shouted, "*Play Ball,*" the crowd gave an ear-splitting cheer. At that moment, the Fox leaned across the table and handed me a chart.

"The fuck is this?" I asked him.

He grinned and chomped his cigar. "That," he said condescendingly, "is the Vegas Differential. Every time ya throw the dice, ya gotta consult this chart."

Annoyed, I tossed the chart aside. "I'll read it later," I muttered. "After I brush my teeth."

The Fox produced a toothpick and used it to groom his nails. "Ty Cobb was a shrimp," he said. "He weighed just a hundred and seventy-five pounds. And he never faced the kinda heat that pitchers throw today. As for Cy Young, he had it easy. He got to stand on a built-up pitcher's mound and throw the ball just fifty feet. Hell, he never even developed a change-up 'til halfway through his career." The Fox finished cleaning his fingernails then handed me back the chart. "If you're gonna be lettin' those dinosaurs play, that shit's gotta factor in."

"What about the Sultan of Swat?" I sputtered.

"The Babe," laughed the Fox. "He was outta shape, dude. He ate too many hotdogs, chugged too many beers. And he fucked so many women he could hardly swing a bat. They shoulda called him the Sultan of Twat."

"He *still* hit a ton of home runs," I protested.

"That's easy in Yankee Stadium—it was *built* for left-handed hitters. If they hadn't shortened the distance to the right field fence, he'd have flied out most of the time."

My team had not yet taken the field, and the fans were getting restless. But I sat there for fifteen minutes, studying that goddamn chart.

"C'mon," said the Fox. "Ya gonna play ball? Ya act like you've seen a ghost."

•

THE PATRIOTS dropped the Series opener by a score of 8-0. Ty Cobb did not hit the ball out of the infield, Babe Ruth got picked off at first base, and Cy Young could not hurl the ball sixty feet without hanging it over the plate. Unimpressed by Cy's heat, Jimmy Piersall stepped back and walloped three home runs. *Blowout*, the evening *Tribune* read. *Patriots Give Up the Ghost*. We took such a brutal shellacking that Robbie went and hid in his room.

I tossed the *Tribune* aside. "Those men were legends," I muttered.

"Legends are crap," said the Fox as he penciled in his line-up for the second game of the Series. "Since you live your life in la-la land, you oughta have figured that out."

"Your *chart* is crap," I countered.

The Fox yawned and shook his head. "Ya gotta allow for time and tide if this game's gonna be realistic."

Was that charity I saw in his eyes as he eased himself back in his chair? Or was the Fox just smelling blood and readying himself for the kill?

"Tellllll ya what I'll do," he said. "I'm gonna give you a chance. I'll give you Mel Ott, Honus Wagner, and Walter Johnson in exchange for Roger Maris."

The offer looked like a setup, but the Fox may have run out of luck. Roger Maris was riding a terrible slump—he was batting just .209 for the year and had only hit three home runs. I had nothing to lose by trading him, so I quickly agreed to the deal.

The Fox blew an imaginary smoke ring and handed me three more squares: Mel Ott, a .304 hitter with a .414 on-base percentage, Honus Wagner, a .329 hitter with 722 stolen bases, Walter Johnson, a fastballer with 2.17 earned run average and 110 shutouts to his credit. Not even the Vegas Differential could neutralize icons like these.

But the second game was worse than the first. Mel Ott was too small for the World Baseball League and could only hit lazy fly balls. Honus Wagner reached first base a couple of times then got thrown out trying to steal second. Walter Johnson pitched well for several innings, slinging the ball from his hip, but when the batters got used to his sidearm delivery, they stung him for nine home runs. Even Roger Maris, in the throes of his slump, belted four balls out of the park. We lost the game 16-0, a record Series defeat.

Patriots Choke Like Chickens the morning *Tribune* read. And *The New York Times* and *The Boston Globe* accused me of fixing the Series. *When a manager is blessed with the team of the ages, The New York Times* article read, *he has no excuse for losing. If he can't even keep the games close, there is something going on.* As I finished reading the article, I prayed the rumor would stick. I would rather be accused of racketeering than managing such feckless defeats.

The Fox sat back in his chair and gave me a sleepy wink. "Tell ya what," he announced. "I'm feelin' kinda generous. I'll give ya Joe Jackson, Lou Gehrig, and Jimmy Fox if you'll let Marv Throneberry go."

"No more trades!" I spat, and I pushed the table away. It was time to prove the naysayers wrong, time to seize the day, time to reclaim bygone glory and walk amongst the gods.

My heart pounded like a hammer as I stormed into the clubhouse. And while the players puffed on cheroots, I delivered the speech of my life. "Play for each other!" I bellowed. "Play for the history books! Play for motherhood, apple pie, and the good ol' red, white, and blue!"

The players looked at me curiously as though I were some kind of freak. But then Ty Cobb threw away his cigar and slowly began to clap. It was not an applause but a cadence, like a war drum coming to life. And it swept throughout the clubhouse with the force of an avalanche. *Clap, clap, clap. CLAP, CLAP, CLAP. CLAP! CLAP! CLAP!*

I sank to my knees and wept like a child—every player was pounding his palms. I was witnessing divine resurrection. I was witnessing herculean pluck—a selfless suspension of ego like in the Charge of the Light Brigade.

With a mighty "*Hurrah,*" the team dashed down the tunnel and exploded onto the field. Fifty thousand fans arose as one and gave a thundering cheer. So loud were the fans, so frantic the play, that I watched as though lost in a dream. I barely noticed the final score.

We lost the game 13 to zip.

•

I COACHED the fourth and final game in a fog of utter despair. I groaned as I chose my lineups, I cringed as my team took the field, and when I shook the dice in my trembling palm, they rattled like ancient bones.

We lost the last game 7-1, a consolation of sorts. Babe Ruth, in the bottom of the ninth, hit our only homerun of the Series. It was a lingering fly ball to center field that should probably have been caught at the warning track. But it somehow sailed over the eight-foot fence. I think the wind must have grabbed it.

3

The Fix

"AGAIN WITH THOSE GODDAMN DICE!" Dad cried. "I thought you were gonna play baseball for real steada sittin' there scramblin' yer minds!"

We had been at it for six hours—Robbie and me—throwing our dice, cross-checking our charts, and pushing our 2" by 2" paper squares, each representing a ballplayer, around our cardboard ballfield. We were seeking banished glory; we were chasing dying light. A flush that had paled like a sinking sun when the Fox stole our innocence away. And so, like Jay Gatsby, we hunched in our boat, straining against the tide. *Row harder, dip deeper, stretch further,* we swore, *and we would once again embrace the glow.*

"First thing Saturday," I replied, but this time my words were empty. How could I defend a pastime that had failed us so completely? My best team, the Potomac Patriots, had been totally routed; my soul, once trusting and eager, was crippled with doubt. All I had now was stifling debt and a mounting pile of bills. And Robbie, who had bought back a third of the team, was a broken, beaten kid. Our sole consolation was that the Fox had pulled himself out of the League. "I don't belong in la-la land," he muttered before leaving our basement for good.

"First thing Saturday," Robbie repeated as he attempted a jack-o-lantern grin. But his eyes were glazed, his brow was damp, his hands were trembling like rabbits. For every practical purpose, his ten-year-old life was over.

Once Dad had left the basement, I gazed at my little brother. Was it not my duty to protect and guide this skinny, freckled-face kid? Instead, I had brought him to ruin; instead, I had broken his heart. The League was in shambles, attendance was down, and the ghost of destitution was knocking at our door.

I spoke the inevitable, shaking my head. "We can't go on like this."

"We gonna play baseball for real?" Robbie gasped. He was sweating like a martyr on a rack.

But the wings of Icarus were still on my back; a phoenix still stirred in my breast. And the heroic cries of the Light Brigade were peppering my ears. "We're gonna play *hardball*," I told him. "We're gonna take back the League."

He looked at me, and his eyes said it all. Could we rise from the ashes? Could we turn back time? Could we once again harness the cheering throngs and walk amongst the gods? "How we gonna do that?" he whispered.

I rose from my chair as Lazarus must have risen from his coffin. "It's time," I announced.

"Time for w-w-what?" Robbie stammered. He looked as though someone had stolen his bike, but his eyes were beginning to shine.

"Time for an owners' meeting," I said. "We're gonna be great once again."

•

AFTER CONSULTING with our attorneys and financial advisers, Robbie and I sat at the kitchen table, sipping root beer floats through straws. We were determined to put together a plan: a plan that would curb our expenses, a plan that would spark our players, a plan that would again pack our stadium with hordes of screaming fans.

The first thing to consider was player salaries. Our standard player contract was for a million dollars a year. But our debt had robbed us of our marquee performers—the Hank Aarons and Derek Jeters. We had auctioned off every one of our stars to the leagues in Japan and Canada. All we had left were dullards—uninspiring journeymen like Marvelous Marvin Throneberry. Players that were not worth a third of what we were paying them.

"Let's do this," I suggested. "Let's pay those bums just three hundred grand a year. And we'll offer 'em performance bonuses?"

Holding his straw between his lips, Robbie blew bubbles into his root beer float. "Won't the player unions get pissed?" he said finally. He was a nice enough kid, but I wondered about him. He was utterly lacking in vision, and he certainly had no balls.

"It'll work like this," I went on. "If a player hits sixty homeruns in a season, we'll double his salary. If he hits eighty, he'll get his million bucks. The unions need to know we don't reward slackers—that we're paying those duds to produce."

Ever the doubter, Robbie shook his head. "Nobody's *ever* hit eighty homers. Not even Barry Bonds."

"There's never been this much incentive," I said. "And we'll do the same for the pitchers. If a pitcher throws fifteen no-hitters in a season—*that's* when we'll pay him a million."

"The unions are gonna get *maaad*," Robbie said. "The players are gonna *striiike*."

"*Divide et impera*," I quoted because I knew the unions weren't shit. The players were represented by three feuding guilds: the Teamsters, the Steelworkers, and Laborers' International. And I had enough spies in each of these guilds to spread more dissent among them. All that was needed to hold off the unions was to keep them at each other's throats.

"Divide and rule," I explained, and I gave Robbie a Roman salute. If such tactics served Julius Caesar, they would certainly do for us.

•

ONCE OUR LAWYERS had drawn up new player contracts, which included our performance incentives, we turned our attention to another matter. We were currently insuring our players for seventy percent of their contracts. That meant if a player got too injured to play, we were forced to shell out the difference. This, of course, would have to change. We could no longer waste our payroll on nonproductive players.

"How about this?" I said to Robbie. "If a player is on the disabled list, our team doctor will give him a physical. Any pre-existing condition, any hint of steroid use, even a trace of venereal disease will render his contract void. I don't want unscrupulous players representing the World Baseball League."

"We only want Christians," yelped Robbie, and he clapped his hands with glee.

"As for the pitchers," I said, "let's do this. We'll no longer insure their arms. The insurance for pitchers is out of this world 'cause their arms almost always give out. We'll only insure them for broken bones—that'll cut the premiums in half."

"Hurrah!" Robbie cried. "If we save enough cash I can buy me a Schwinn Mountain Bike."

We drafted an owner's agreement, and I had Robbie initial each clause. I then phoned our team physician and finance officer and updated them on the plan. We had fifty-one players on the disabled list; it was high time we checked them out.

I looked at Robbie and grinned like a ghoul; we were practically out of the woods. "Now," I said, "lets discuss player pensions. *Another* big expense."

•

I SPENT the next two hours reviewing our financial spreadsheet. And my eyes nearly leapt from their sockets. We had ninety-eight players on pensions averaging two hundred grand a year. That meant we were paying almost twenty million dollars annually to jocks whose heydays were over. There was no way we could ever recover with that kind of drain on our cash flow.

"Here's how it's gonna be," I told Robbie. "As long as we're paying those slackers, we may as well put 'em to work. There's plenty of jobs we can have 'em do: keeping the grounds, cleaning out urinals, sweeping up litter after the games. Let's fire our custodians and groundskeeping crews and replace 'em with goldbricking players."

"Could you have 'em clean up my room?" Robbie asked. "Cleaning my room sucks."

"Give me your vote on this matter," I said, "and I think that might be arranged."

"And get 'em to mow our *lawn*. Dad makes me mow the lawn every Saturday. With a *push* mower."

"If a player gives us lip, I'll make him push that mower. After he picks up the snails."

I emailed our League secretary and had her draft a letter to our retirees. A letter instructing them to report to the stadium for sixty home games a year. Our mascot, Dumbo the Elephant, would assign each one a job.

•

THE VERY NEXT DAY, the unions announced that the players were going on strike. We were also the butt of a class action lawsuit, accusing us of breach of contract. I laughed after reading the lawsuit and forwarded it to our attorneys. With three law firms on retainer, we could drag it out for years.

But the ballgames would have to go on if we were to stay out of bankruptcy court. So I contacted the Mexican Baseball League and recruited four hundred out of work players. Destitute players whose teams had folded because of franchise disputes. I gave each of these players a contract for ten grand a year. That and all the hotdogs he could eat.

"Is that with mustard and relish?" asked Robbie.

I assured him the hotdogs would be fully dressed and had him endorse the contracts.

That evening, a Fox News broadcaster accused us of importing drug dealers. But I had anticipated some negative press, and I had prepped my media shills. In a matter of hours, a chivalrous column appeared in *The New York Times*:

Saving the Tempest-Tossed

Let it never be said that corporate wealth is the edge of an iron heel. In an unprecedented move, the World Baseball League has raised Mexico's huddled masses. Thanks to the vision of the World Baseball League, impoverished ballplayers chasing their goats can now chase the American Dream.

Never has our world community been stronger. Never has liberty's torch burned so bright. Hats off to the World Baseball League.

"We're kosher!" Robbie shouted, and I gave him a big high five. But I also phoned the Pinkerton Agency and hired an army of goons. Already, a hostile crowd was collecting on the street outside our stadium office. Players demanding their contracts back, trade unionists cursing NAFTA, and border guards with drug-sniffing dogs straining at their leashes. Below our office window, the Pinkerton agents gathered. Wearing helmets and body armor, they looked like Roman legionnaires.

When the buses with the Mexican ballplayers arrived, the crowd wouldn't let them pass. "Scabs!" voices shouted. "Losers." As demonstrators pelted the buses with hotdogs, our thugs hurled tear gas grenades. The grenades floated like hanging curveballs when demonstrators threw them back.

Our office window exploded; the din of the crowd stung our ears. A baseball with a note taped to it bounced across the rug. *No point sharing the death threats*, I thought, and I kicked the ball under a couch.

"Batten the hatches," I shouted. "Keelhaul the mutineers." This was utter nonsense, of course, but Robbie was *fishbelly pale*. If I could convince him we were just playing pirates, it might keep him from crapping his pants.

Our hammers boomed like thunderclaps as we boarded the window shut. Our file cabinets shrieked like elephants when we dragged them in front of the door. Determined to hold the fort at all costs, I racked the slide of my Glock.

"Remember the Alamo," I bellowed. "Don't let 'em take us alive."

•

"AUUGH!" Dad bellowed. "Sonuvabitch! Why have you trashed the basement, and how did you find my gun?"

I hung my head and fought back tears—what a terrible day this was. Our sacred ground was smoldering; barbarians were at our gates. "It's that goddamn game," Dad muttered. "It's finally fried your brains."

Words could not save us and so I said nothing. I stood as though hogtied as Dad gathered our charts up and burned them in the outside barbecue pit. My lips remained sealed as he seized our dice and shattered them with a hammer. I did not even speak when he grabbed Robbie by the collar and frog-marched him out to the car. "Yer gonna play live baseball!" he shouted. "Yer going to the Little League park."

"*No, no, noooo!*" Robbie shrieked, but I abandoned him to his fate. His cries died as though the wind had snatched them when the car pulled out of the drive.

Feeling like a Jonah, I watched Dad drive away. But at least I could salvage a timber or two from the shipwreck my life had become. At least, I could hold my head up as I entered the heart of the storm. So I rummaged about in my closet and found my old baseball glove. And I put on a pair of Nike Mid-cuts and clumped to the local park.

Like Daniel facing the lions, I joined a drop-in ballgame. My first turn at bat, I flinched as though slapped—the ball nearly struck my head. But I dug in my cleats, choked up on my bat, and stared the pitcher down. It was time I hit a baseball for real.

∘ ∘ ∘

Little Darling

WHEN I SAW the ghost sitting on my living room couch, I blindly overreacted. My palms dampened, my breathing grew shallow, my skin crawled as though covered with ants. The ghost, a dark-haired woman in her thirties, did not really merit dramatics. Her stature was small, her skin was parlor pale, and her hair was drawn up in a neat unobtrusive bun. She was pretty, in her black hooped dress, but her sunless demeanor and lack of makeup suggested that she was a lonely spinster.

For a moment, I wondered if she were really a ghost. She was not transparent, as I imagined ghosts to be, and her face wore a shy intelligence— not the insularity of an earthbound soul. But she clearly was not of this century, so she had to be a phantom. She looked like a governess from Victorian England, a governess with a tale of pathos.

She stared at me and gaped, as though I—not she—were the intruder in my home. She then covered her mouth with her hand, blocking a silent scream. The sight of me terrified her—why, I wasn't sure. Was I following in the footsteps of Dorian Gray, that classic rogue whose monsterdom was discernable only on an esoteric plain? The terror in her face suggested this was so. Hiking her dress above her ankles, she scurried from the room. I could hear the soles of her laced boots tap-tapping as she trotted down the hallway.

I chose not to follow her—I had a more pressing concern. What was it about my appearance that had caused her to dash from the room? Had I grown fangs and horns, had my skin become scaly? Given the extent of her terror, this notion did not seem far-fetched.

I stepped into my bathroom, hit the light switch, and studied my reflection in the mirror. It was the face of a sensual man of forty—a face that was rather attractive in a Hugh Hefner sort of way. But, unlike Hugh, I had my limits. I had not built a shrine to hedonism nor did I view women as disposable pleasures. Rather, it was they who disposed of me, citing my self-absorption as sufficient reason to cast me adrift. And I mourned the end of every affair as though I were attending a wake.

No, I did not have the face of a predator. My eyes were not cruel but exacting, as though straining the world through that rose-colored hue that had roused the romantic scribes. Had I been born in the nineteenth century, I would have surely been a Byronesque poet. The life of Lord Byron would have suited me well: slapdash affairs, mercenary adventures, lavish living on borrowed wealth. "Where the bee sucks, there suck I." Ponder this quote from Shakespeare before deeming me a rogue.

Were it not for that flowery filter, how cloying the world would be. How crushing the darkness that stalks us, how scentless the poppies and trees. Better to suck like the bee sucks and let it go at that.

•

I LIVE IN a midwestern city where I work as a music promoter. And on Saturday, I go to the singles dance at the local Holiday Inn. But the ghost, whom I shall call Little Darling, had distracted me from this sport. I wanted to plead my case to her and wean her from her fears. But, if her terror was any indication, I may never see her again. I thought things over for three entire days. In the end, I decided to go to the dance. When the great-beyond leaks into your life, there is consolation in old habits.

As I entered the ballroom of the Holiday Inn, I drew a consoling breath. Dim lighting, soft rock tunes, and cocktails—these are the things that endure. Even the most draining of unions begins with a honeymoon. And a honeymoon is ever available for the price of a couple of drinks.

I ordered a Tequila Sunrise at the bar then surveyed the half-empty room. Whatever my deficiencies, I *did* have a remarkable line. "Madam," I would quip, upon choosing a prospect. "Might you share a dance with this ignoble Caliban?" If she gasped and rolled her eyes, I knew I had saved precious time. A woman with no sense of humor would too soon prove a tiresome commodity. But if she laughed and accepted my offer, my heart would race like a sprinter's. Only a true adventuress can cope with a Renaissance man.

Perching myself on a barstool, I continued to scan the room. I had picked out my target—a tall leggy blonde—when I spotted Little Darling. She was sitting alone at one of the tables, still wearing that black floor-length dress. She was weeping uncontrollably, her face buried in her hands.

I wanted to keep my distance; I wanted to dash to my car. I have no use for histrionics and hate a woman's tears. But since we had struck up an acquaintance of sorts, I could not abandon her. An unfamiliar chivalry was stirring within my soul.

She wiped her eyes as I approached her then folded her hands neatly in her lap. *What took you so long?* her face seemed to say as though I had stood her up. Although she had deemed me a monster, she was not without expectations.

Hoping that no one would notice, I sat in the chair beside her. "Miss, might I be of assistance?" I offered. She looked at me coolly, shrugged, and touched my cheek with her hand. Stymied by this gesture, I could only revert to form. "Would you spare this ignoble brute a dance?" I muttered, charitably.

Her smile was wry and dismissive. *Is that the best you can do?* it said. Sadly, it was, so I said nothing more. I just gave her a plastic grin.

Although I had tried to be generous, the charity was hers. Had I escorted a specter onto the dance floor, I'd have seemed like a consummate narcissist—a man so self-protective he was content to dance with himself. Thank god, she had not blown my cover. Thank god, she saw fit to be kind.

As she rose from the table, she wrinkled her nose, a gesture both cute and disarming. Had I forgotten to wear my deodorant? Was she trying to stifle a sneeze? Was she perking up like a rabbit about to bolt from a wolf?

She looked at me, her face now flushed, and I felt an untimely arousal. What an ingrate I was—what a barbarous hound. The spirit world was hardly a sheath for the hard-on in my pants.

Hoping to gain her forgiveness, I bowed my head like a servant. But my rod was as tall as a sentinel as I watched her leave the room.

•

THERE IS NOTHING like a whiff of mortality to give a man pause to reflect. By what designation of karma had this shade come into my world? Was she kin to Jacob Marley—a self-righteous prig contemptuous of all who do not lead sanctimonious lives? Or was she the pariah and was I haunting her? The notion did not seem absurd.

Not eager for a third encounter, I stopped going to the singles dance. I did not wish to seek common ground with her whatever the heavens decreed. But I started to cruise the nightclubs and bars where my charms might yet prove productive. "Gather ye rosebuds while ye may" had never sounded truer.

I also decided to get some religion. Not a lethal dose but enough to make me repellant to lonely haunts. The Catholic church in my neighborhood seemed perfect for my salvation. I had only to endure a prepackaged sermon, then drop a few bills into a collection plate, to buy myself a spiritual shield that would thwart less hallowed souls. There was even the chance I might qualify for a little divine intervention. *Sow your wild oats on Saturday night*, I reflected. *On Sunday, go to church and pray for crop failure.*

Six months passed and my romp with religion appeared to have done the job. I saw not the slightest sign of her. My line scored plenty of ass. And I felt so elated that one Sunday morning I joined in singing a hymn. *"Eternal Father strong to saaave whose arm has bound the restless waaave, who biddeth the mighty ocean deep its own appointed limits keeep."* My voice boomed like a foghorn as I belted out these lines.

A woman kneeling in front of me turned around and stared. *I had almost given up waiting for you*, her expression seemed to say. She was holding a tiny gold cross in her hand, and she pressed the cross to her lips. When she hung the cross around her neck, it glowed like a firefly.

I could practically feel the heat from the cross, and I cringed like Count Dracula. But by deigning to become a vampire, I had cleansed her of her fear. Are vampires not the most humane of monsters? Handsome, well-spoken, and vulnerable, don't they belong in a class of their own? As I looked at Little Darling, I knew I had risen in her esteem.

Her eyes were not fearful but bold. Her mouth had a trace of a smile. She knew a few drops of holy water would turn me into dust. And so the hymn now mocked me as it thundered throughout the church. *"Hear us when we cry to thee for those in peril on the sea."*

As though rushing back to my coffin, I hurried down the aisle. Behind me, I heard her footsteps tap-tapping like a hammer burying a stake. As I pushed through the chapel doorway, her hand slipped into mine. It was as cold and smooth as a mackerel. *"This time remember the wine,"* she purred. Her voice was as chilling as frost.

I clutched her hand and looked at her. I now noticed her clear blue eyes, her high sculptured forehead, the hint of blush on her cheeks. I also appraised her long slim neck and the rose tucked in her hair. She looked like a Renoir portrait that had somehow come to life.

What did she mean by *Remember the wine?* Did she want me to take communion? Did she want to me to sample her blood? Or did she want us to have a picnic lunch beneath a sheltering bough?

Her hand squeezed mine like a reptile as I walked her to my car. Her face was as tense as that of an adulteress about to be placed in the stocks. When I let go of her hand and groped for my car keys, her agitation grew. Her head jerked up like the skull of a marionette, and she closed her eyes tightly.

"Take it," she hissed. *"Take it now."* With her head held high, she resembled a blackbird drinking from a pond.

•

WE DROVE in silence. My hands clutched the steering wheel as though it were a life preserver. Although not a word passed between us, an intimacy bound us together. It was not the closeness of lovers, but something more elemental, like the bond of a pair of cave dwellers huddling from a storm.

I stopped at a convenience store to buy a bottle of wine. I decided to pick up some Falcon Ridge Chardonnay, a label that suited her aura. Hunched in a corner of the passenger seat, taking ragged breaths, she made me think of a bandit bird that had washed up on a beach. I rolled down a window to give her some air and went into the store for the wine.

When I returned to the car and saw that she was gone, I did not breathe a sigh of relief. There was unfinished business between us, which I had hoped to get out of the way. Now my anticipation would linger like a crow upon a fence. Unless, of course, I could come up with a plan that would turn her off completely.

I decided on self-parody. Religion had not worked. Compassion had not worked. But if I turned myself into a genuine pig, perhaps that would do the job. After all, it is only the conscience-stricken that specters choose to haunt. If one is content to wallow in muck, the spooks will leave him alone.

I bought myself a dick mobile: a cherry red Mustang convertible with leather bucket seats. I put a license plate on the car that said, Ibrake4ass. And I fitted my bedroom with ceiling mirrors and a well-stocked mini-bar. Since my image was now that of an aging rake, I was unlikely to score much tail. But I was willing to make the sacrifice if it kept Little Darling away.

Was I doing this for her sake? I wondered. *If she saw me as the means of her ravagement, was I hoping to spare her the ordeal?* I suspected that this was probably so, and I knew she had touched me too deeply. In the stately glacier of my soul, a dangerous spring was bubbling.

But streams that begin in heaven end up in the vilest of swamps. The thought that my valor would soon dissipate curbed my uneasiness. *Does she really need a hero?* I wondered. *Does she really need lofty intentions? Had she not spoken desperately when she told me to take it now?* No, I would not be a hero to her—not if she wanted a beast. The cruelest encroachments of all are founded on noble intentions.

Although our coupling seemed imminent, I still wanted to be a pig. I wanted no magnanimous guilt to contaminate the act. So I continued to drive my dick mobile, I continued to brake for ass, and I started to hit on chicks with lines like, "Oy, baby, your place or mine?"

I think Little Darling must have known that my debasement was not yet complete. A month went by then another, and she failed to reappear.

•

THE CRUX OF SEDUCTION is timing—finding the perfect moment. But time had no meaning to Little Darling; she was content to leave me bereft. Wasn't I pig enough for her? Wasn't I shallow and gross? Hadn't I rivaled Hugh Hefner in trivializing my lust? I finally grew weary of waiting for her, and I chose to take a vacation. If I could not ravage her, why not outrun her?—it would not be that hard. Ghosts are territorial, after all, creatures too earthbound for flight.

I took the most vulgar of holidays: a Carnival Cruise to the Bahamas. No museums in Paris for me. No Great Wall of China for me. Nothing to cultivate my soul and make me a person of merit. When she came to me— if ever she did—I wanted to be a brute. I wanted to make our coupling so base it would free her from this earth. So I contented myself with dozing in deckchairs and being force-fed six times a day. And I sat by a poolside so crowded with bodies I could barely draw a breath. For all cultural purposes, I may as well have been a boar on a factory farm.

One evening, when I returned to my stateroom, a woman was lying in my bed. She was wearing a long black nightgown that barely hid her breasts. She looked at me reproachfully, like a heretic tied to a stake.

Not wishing to break the silence, I did not say a word. I just hung my clothes in the closet then slipped into the bed beside her. Unwilling to stir, I lay like a log; the first move would have to be hers.

She leaned on an elbow and gazed at me, her face a mask of despair. Her hair was undone and it tickled my chest as she wearily shook her head. *"You're all I have,"* she whispered. *"You're all I'll ever have."*

I felt a deep pity for her when she kissed me on the mouth. The kiss was not tender but tentative, as though she were sampling a meal. Her breath was cool, musty, and hinted of the grave.

When she mounted me she mewed like a kitten. Her eyes were like sinking stones. She clung to me as though fighting a current. She slipped her tongue into my ear.

We climaxed together. She wept like a child then snuggled into my arms. As though guarding a statue of infinite worth, I held her through the night.

•

HUGH HEFNER has nothing on me when it comes to exalting lust. I had actually thought that by sleeping with her I would free her of this world. I had truly believed she might walk among angels when her carnality was spent. Maybe if I had remembered the wine, my scheme would actually have worked.

She comes to see me regularly now—once or twice a year. And although I instinctually dread her, I ache for her as well. I have never felt such a tenderness, I have never felt so alone.

Our couplings are quick, like summer storms, and afterwards she weeps. "*You're all I have*," she tells me each time. "*You're all I will ever have.*"

o o o

Sam the Poontang Man

SAMUEL MAZZETTI needed a hustle. He was homeless, broke, and out of options. Nobody wanted to buy his paintings, and his disability claim with the Veterans Administration had been stalled for over three years. *Why isn't anything coming my way?* he wondered. Perhaps it was because he looked like what he was: a burned out Iraqi War vet. With his crooked teeth and piercing eyes, he also resembled a troll on the prowl. So he sang Bob Dylan's "Clean Cut Kid" when he panhandled for change on the sidewalks of San Francisco. "*I was a clean-cut kiiiiid*," he sang, "*an' they made a killer outta me, that's what they did.*"

But Samuel had never been a clean-cut kid. After dropping out of junior college in Fresno, he had stolen from Walmart, boozed with the Hells Angels, and peddled meth outside high schools. After selling several caps to an undercover cop, he had found himself faced with a typical Hobson's choice: he could serve three years in the Military—help Uncle Sam fight its wars—or put in the same amount of time behind bars. A risk taker by temperament, Samuel had opted for the Army, and was sent to Iraq as a member of the 43rd Combat Engineers. A year later, suffering from hypervigilance and a chronic case of the shakes, he was given a medical discharge.

"You been smokin' too much weed," his counselor at Swords to Ploughshares told him. "A dude who thinks he can squeeze the government ain't livin' in the real world. Now I can get you a place to flop, I can get you methadone, I can even hustle up food stamps for you. But I can't help you stick no VA claim. If the country took *care* of its veterans, it'd be too broke to fight its wars."

Convinced that his case was hopeless, Samuel gave up on his VA claim and began to look seriously for a hustle. He tried pimping for the whores on Polk Street, but his scraggly hair, unkempt beard, and haunted stare only discouraged prospective Johns. He strummed his guitar in Civic Center Plaza, but his voice was so hoarse from nerve agents that no one put money in his tip jar. He even took classes at City College, hoping to improve his

121

painting, but his work was too embryonic to provide him an income as a street artist. "You *do* have ability," an instructor told him, "but it'll probably take you another five years to develop any kind of style."

Unfortunately, Samuel did not have the cash to bring his art to fruition. His biweekly General Assistance checks, amounting to $400 a month, were barely enough to keep him self-medicated on pot. His only option was panhandling.

One afternoon, while Samuel was sitting outside an adult video shop on Sixth Street, a sketchbook in his lap and a Nehi soda in his hand, he was struck with the germ of inspiration. It did not come in the form of a bountiful muse, hovering lovingly over his head, but a randy gentleman of fifty in a pinstripe suit. Glancing at Samuel before entering the shop, the gentleman rolled his eyes. "If my wife pulled down my fly now and then," he complained, "I wouldn't be coming here all the time."

Samuel began to draw as the gentleman entered the store. His hand roamed of its own accord, and a sketch leapt to life on his pad. In a matter of minutes, he drew a buxom woman on a bearskin rug, her legs obscenely spread. He printed beneath the picture, *A BROAD ON THE FLY WILL LAY DOWN FOR HER GUY.*

As the gentleman came out of the store, a dozen DVDs in his hand, Samuel handed him the sketch and winked. He then held up the bottle of soda. "Spiked," he grinned. "Just fifty clams, man."

"Highway robbery," the gentleman snapped, but he forked over a Grant for the bottle of soda.

"Put an ounce in her morning coffee," said Samuel. "She'll be balling your brains out by noon."

*

FLUSHED WITH INSPIRATION, Samuel scrounged up some wooden boards and built a peddler's stand. He then drew a dozen more sketches. Sketches of waitresses, milkmaids, and nurses—all on their backs with their legs lewdly spread. *FLY ME TO THE MOON*, the captions read. *JUST FIFTY DOLLARS A FLASK.* By the end of the day, he had sold a dozen more bottles of Nehi. The drawings he gave away free of charge since advertising pays.

Of course, some of his customers came back to him, accusing him of fraud. "You call this Spanish Fly?" they griped. "She didn't do nothing but burp."

But Samuel, a born merchandiser, knew how to spin a setback. "The effect is cumulative, maaan," he drawled. "Ya gotta break down her resistance. Slip her a dose every day for a month, and she'll gush like a garden hose." Then he sang "Gonna Fly Now," the theme song from *Rocky 1*, and handed them another sketch. Inspired by that infectious ditty, those customers wanting their money back doubled their investments.

Soon, precariously soon, Samuel became a one-man corporation. He took out an ad on Craig's list, he put a website on his iPad, and he e-mailed dozens of sketches to adult online magazines. Sketches of housewives, schoolmarms, and meter maids—all of them spreading their pussies and spouting like Moby Dick. *TO OIL UP YOUR CHICK, COME TO HOWARD AND SIXTH* he wrote beneath the sketches. Horny patrons came flocking to him, and he sold hundreds of gallons of Nehi, which he displayed in nondescript bottles. In a matter of weeks, he was driving a Lexus, living at the Marriott, and dining on oysters and quail. And he changed his name from Samuel Mazzetti to Sam the Poontang Man.

•

ONLY IN AMERICA, Sam thought as he sat at the corner of Howard and Sixth and lit a Habano Cigar. Only in America—the land of the quick fix—can a tramp with delusions of grandeur become a celebrated doctor of love. Only in America can a street bum aspire to the ruse of the politician. *If one doesn't get hung up on scruples,* he mused, *the American Dream ain't dead. And to think I wanted to hang around Paris—learn how to doodle like Dali. Bummer, man.*

Opening his box of charcoals, he drew another sketch. It was a sketch of the Statue of Liberty, holding up a bottle of pop. *GIVE ME YOUR PRUNE TWATS AND FRIGID,* he wrote. *I'LL SOON HAVE THEM HUMPING LIKE WEASELS.*

A day after he posted this message online, a band of women descended on him. Women with a bone to pick. They were carrying placards displaying Sam's sketches with Xs drawn through the middle. "No easels for weasels," they chanted as they paraded in front of his stand.

A natural politician, Sam rose to his feet and held out his hands like Jesus. "Ladies, ladies, ladies," he cooed in a voice as gentle as down. "A broad on the fly will do well by her guy. He'll treat you just like a queen." He then grinned like a grape-eating possum and danced a little jig. And he sang them a song he had been working on to expand his customer base. A jaunty little ditty, which he sang to the tune of "My Bonnie Lies Over the Ocean."

> He'll buy you that poodle you're wanting.
> You'll get that vacation in Rome.
> He's gonna be generous and fawning.
> You just gotta grease up his bone.

123

Unimpressed, the women set his stand on fire and smashed every one of his flasks. And Sam was left to realize the vulnerability of a dream. As he watched his stand smolder, sweat beaded his brow and he shook like a morning drunk. *Unless I can handle the fallout*, Sam thought, *I'm gonna be back on the dole.*

But providence was not yet done with Sam. As he scrambled about, snatching his drawings from the flames, a figure emerged through the smoke. A towering man with a barrel chest and arms as sinewy as ropes. His eyes were cold and intuitive, his face was scarred and tattooed, and his head was so bald and shiny that it glittered like a jewel. He looked at Sam the way that a lion might gaze at an antelope.

"The fuck are you?" Sam asked him.

The man grinned broadly, winked like a headlight, then rescued a sketch from the fire.

Sam's heart began to hammer. "Don't mess with my hustle, man."

The stranger blew on the sketch as though cooling a cup of coffee. It burst into a flower of flame. He dropped the sketch to the sidewalk and shook his polished head. When he finally spoke, his voice was so deep it seemed to arise from a well. "You're tryin' to soak pussy that wants to stay dry. Just what kinda hustle is that?"

"Them bitches are gonna be gushing," Sam bawled. "They're gonna be flowing like streams."

"You some kinda rainmaker, son," the man boomed. "You seem to believe yer own jive."

"I'm the Poontang Man," Sam stammered. "I make the rivers rise."

The stranger chortled, a menacing laugh that sounded like rolling thunder. "If I was you, motherfucker, I wouldn't be buildin' no ark."

Sam shook his head. "Dude," he protested, "*you* got no jive at *all*. Yer gonna need more 'an putdowns if ya wanna bid for my soul."

The stranger put his hands on his hips and glared; his eyes reddened like burning coals. "Dog, I ain't makin' no offers. I don't want yer pissant soul. I got a million more just like it, and they ain't worth a pinch of shit."

"So why did ya come here to pick on me, man?"

"Cuz I want you to pick up your game. If ya wanna spread lies and depravity, dog, ya oughta be doin' it right."

·

FACED WITH THE forfeiture of his dream, the collapse of his fortune, the loss of his very identity, Sam decided to collaborate with the stranger. As they sat on a bench in the Yerba Buena Gardens, the stranger suggested a campaign. "My man, you can fix up that soda pop stand, but them ballbusters are gonna return. What choo plannin' to do about that?"

"Give 'em free samples," Sam joked.

The stranger clucked his tongue and glowered. "If you want a hustle, you gotta have muscle. That's elementary, dog." He waved his hand and a mist arose—a cottony, silvery veil. As the mist evaporated, a startling sight replaced it. Sam's peddler's stand was completely rebuilt and surrounded by a pack of feral looking youths. Their red bandanas, loose-fitting sweatshirts, and crooked tattoos denoted their status as Norteños, one of San Francisco's toughest gangs. They were selling Sam's flasks to passersby, raking in hundreds of dollars. And nobody was approaching *them* with complaints.

"They'll take fifty percent of your gross," said the stranger. "But now you got yer *protection*, dog, and now you can make you a *mint*. That poontang oil sells better 'an crack. Sheeit, it ain't even illegal."

As Sam looked at the sight, his heartstrings hummed. He observed himself standing among the Norteños, bathed in a pearly light. A couple of cherubs floated above him, holding a streaming banner. Sam's eyes grew misty as he looked at the banner: it was spangled with stars, alive in the wind, and it bore the profoundest of tidings. *Sam the Poontang Man's his name. Oiling pussy, that's his game.* And the voice of the stranger, accompanied by the peal of trumpets, was singing from on high.

> *It ain't about mom's apple cobbler.*
> *It ain't about freedom of toil.*
> *It ain't about wastin' a dollar.*
> *It's all about reapin' the oil.*

Stunned by the light, Sam covered his eyes. "I-it's beautiful, man. Like a Grateful Dead concert. I've never seen anything like it."

"Sheeit," said the stranger. "That's just lesson one. Now we gotta talk diversity of product." He waved his hand and another mist billowed. When the haze disappeared, Sam's stand was replaced by a giant department store.

The stranger waved his hand yet again, and they were standing inside the store. Sam saw hundreds of bottles aligned upon shelves like troops awaiting inspection. The bottles varied in size according to the degree of titillation they promised. *Trickle, River, Torrent, Monsoon* the different labels read.

As Sam's eyes caressed the bottles, he felt a lump in his throat. "Fantastic, man," he cried. "It's like *Fifty Shades of Gray*."

The stranger laughed. "There ain't nothin' but soda in every one of them bottles. So you gotta keep changing the packaging, dog, if you wanna keep selling that crap."

"What happens if customers figure that out?"

"We'll just point 'em to something else." The stranger gestured to a display case secured with a ratchet lock. The case contained hundreds of eyedropper flasks arranged like a jewelry display. A cheerful sign, placed above the case, testified to the uniqueness of the product: *Give your bitch a single drop, and she'll treat your knob like a lollipop.*

"A knee high lollipop." Sam chuckled at his pun.

"That soda is all they got in 'em," the stranger snorted. "But if we keep them fuckers thinkin' with their cocks, that ain't gonna matter for shit."

"What happens if sales start to peter?" Sam mused.

"Dog, we're ready for that." The stranger pointed to another display case. This one was filled with water pipes, hookahs, and clear plastic pouches crammed with leafy concoctions. The sign boldly proclaimed the thrill that awaited whoever might purchase these items: *When she takes a puff of Poontang Grass, she'll only want it in the ass.*

The stranger folded his arms and grinned like a henhouse fox. "Nehi mixed with oregano—a hundred dollars a baggie. Just keep on changing the staging, and yer gonna stay a rich man."

Sam shook his head. "You're scaring me, dude."

"Watch," the stranger replied. He waved his hand a fourth time, and they were standing outside of the store. This time, Sam could not see the entrance: there were so many patrons mobbing the store that they couldn't all squeeze through the door. Above the store was the cause of the ruckus: an enormous neon vulva pulsating like a heart. *One day sale before we bail*, the racing letters proclaimed. *Six bottles for four hundred dollars. Everything must go.*

"We actually *raised* the price," laughed the stranger. "But them dipshits ain't figured it out."

Overwhelmed, Sam fell to his knees. He clutched the stranger's hands and blubbered like a child. "Thank you, man, thank you," he wept. "I was blind, and now I can see."

The stranger chuckled and patted Sam's head. "Dog, that's just lesson two." He clapped his hands and the mist returned. "Now we gotta talk damage control."

When the veil disappeared, they were standing in an enormous television studio. Technicians were broadcasting videos of bimbos posing in front of Old Faithful; publicists, sitting at tables, were answering dozens of phones. And a loud and buoyant anthem echoed throughout the room.

If your bitch won't baste your ham,
Take a little trip to the Poontang Man.
Don't be flustered. Don't be foiled.
It's your right to get her oiled.

The stranger nodded in time with the anthem then snapped off a sharp salute. "You'll have to become an icon, son, if you wanna keep beating the heat. Like Hershey Bars, Nike, and Coca-Cola. Don't nobody criticize that shit, dog, 'cause it wouldn't be patriotic."

Stunned, Sam looked at the television screens. His heart was so full of wonder and pride, it was all he could do to speak. "Motherhood, baseball, apple pie." He recited these words in a reverent voice, like an infant saying his prayers.

As he looked at the screens, a Fox News broadcast replaced the shots of Old Faithful. A mob of angry women was confronting the National Guard. The troops slowly corralled the women, pushing them backwards, smashing their placards, and hauling them off to meat wagons. And the voice of a Fox News commentator boldly lauded the troops. It was clear from the partisan tone of the spiel that women unwilling to bob for knobs, get screwed in the ass, or otherwise go with the flow were simply un-American.

"Bitchin'," Sam stammered. "Incredible, man. Never in my wildest dreams."

"You're gonna be a household name," said the stranger. "You'll be big as Chevrolet."

Sam felt as though he were floating on air as he stared, transfixed, at the televisions. The Fox News cameras were now focused on hordes of pro-Sam demonstrators. And a commercial sung by the Mormon Tabernacle Choir was shaking the entire the room.

Sam, Sam the Poontang Man.
He's the savior of the land.
If your pecker ain't been christened,
Sam's the one to get it glistenin'.

•

ENTHRALLED BY his newfound celebrity status, Sam began an iconic lifestyle. He joined the Knights of Columbus, he dressed in red, white and blue, and he rented a condominium high upon Nob Hill. And he continued to diversify his product. Soon Poontang Man Kool-Aid and Poontang Man

Mouthwash were common household products. So meteoric was Sam's rise to success, so unremitting his cash flow, that the Republican Party featured him in an infomercial—a hallowed illustration of what rugged individualism might still accomplish. And when the inevitable imitators arose—dirtbags who hawked their brand of fly at a mere ten dollars a flask—Sam's publicists quickly denounced then as charlatans, crooks, and bums. *Sons of Sam*, the spin doctors dubbed them, which shut every one of them down. Deprived of nuisance of competition, Sam lived like the greatest of kings.

But the prickly agenda of fate had another surprise for Sam. One day, a troop of beetle-browed men walked into his department store. They were wearing gray sharkskin suits, and they moved as though they were one. Their eyes were so hollow and sunless, their movements so oily and coiled, they might have been the tentacles of an octopus.

Standing behind a counter, Sam gave them a foxy grin. "Gentlemen, what'll it be?" he purred. "Poontang Man Shampoo or Poontang Man Gel? If you soften her thatch, she'll spread open her snatch."

The beetle-browed men merely looked at him with a hard collective stare. They seemed utterly indifferent to Poontang Man Gel or whatever else Sam might have on sale. Their menacing air and asexual eyes were like an artic chill.

One of them opened a briefcase and handed Sam a document, a hefty ream of legalese that weighed nearly half a pound. As he scanned the pages, Sam's hands started shaking as though he were back in Iraq. These men were attorneys. He was being sued by the American Pharmaceutical Industry.

•

HIS HANDS STILL TREMBLING, Sam locked up his store and fled down Mission Street. Was his dream at an end? Would that pack of goons succeed in shutting him down? He felt the same panic he'd felt in Iraq when an IED laced him with shrapnel.

Determined to hide, Sam commando crawled into Yerba Buena Gardens. But the neatly trimmed trees and manicured grass afforded him no consolation. Only the towering waterfall, pummeling slate-gray rocks, provided him a moment of solace. As he sat on the wall beneath the waterfall, he saw the stranger approach him. The stranger's stride was hurried as though he were late for an appointment.

Making no comment, the man blew his nose then sat on the wall next to Sam.

Sam looked at him with teary eyes. "Do you know what the feds are doin' to me, man?"

The stranger nodded woodenly.

"So you gonna make 'em stop?"

The man sighed like a furnace and looked at his shoes. "No can do, dog," he said firmly. His voice was as heavy as lead.

"How come, dude?"

The stranger bridled. "You really gotta *ask*?"

A revelation popped like a signal flare in Sam's chaotic mind. "You made 'em a deal for their souls," he gasped.

"'Course I did, dog. A long time ago. A contract's a fuckin' contract, my man—I can't go breakin' it now."

Sam puffed out his chest. "Then I'll take 'em on alone. Those pill peddlers ain't closing me down."

The stranger gripped Sam's elbow as though saving him from a fall. "Think 'bout what choo sayin', dog. That's the biggest drug cartel in the world, an' you're treadin' on its turf."

"They ain't no match for the Poontang Man."

"Really?" the stranger replied. "They hook millions of folks on opiates. They fix prices all over the land. They take the last dollar from widows and don't even blink an eye." He looked at Sam with pity and sternness. "So what choo think they're gonna do to you?"

"I'm Sam the Pooner," Sam sputtered. "*Nobody* messes with me."

"No, you ain't, dog," the stranger said. "You're a pissant that just got lucky."

The stranger cracked his knuckles then took a giant breath. "Dog, I don't say this too often, but you got you a bit of talent. Why not *do* somethin' with it and leave the swindlin' to the pros?"

"I ain't no goddamn Picasso," Sam bawled.

"You don't gotta become one, dog. Become a pop artist, maybe, or even a goddamn Norman Rockwell." The stranger chuckled generously and slowly rose to his feet. "Do somethin' else with your pissant soul, and I may just come back and pluck it."

As he watched the stranger walk away, Sam sat as though paralyzed. His eyes were darting like minnows, his brow was soaked with sweat. The stranger's gentle berating had hammered him like a wave.

•

REAL PLUTOCRATS do not heed warnings. They forge ahead incautiously and rule with sightless fists. But Sam, a Renaissance man at heart, was made from a different mold. He longed to stand on the bank of the Seine and sketch the bridges and boats. He longed to practice his brushstrokes while sitting in sidewalk cafés. And he hungered to sell some paintings on the terrace outside of the Louvre.

And so he closed up his department store and emptied his bank account. The bulk of his money he donated to the Wounded Warrior Project. A few weeks later, passport in hand, Sam caught a flight to Paris. It was time he got serious about his art.

° ° °

Like a Motherfucker

NIETZSCHE said it well: "In individuals madness is rare, but in groups it is the rule." But just what facilitates the madness of groups, their cow-like instinct to reject contemplation in favor of a collective cud? Is it the retractability of language, its potential to shrink all thought to the level of a verbal belch? If you cannot articulate, you cannot think—demagogues know this well. And so they appeal to the gut—not the mind. A couple of well-timed slogans, a few jingoistic rhymes—that's all that is needed to sway a crowd and turn it into a herd.

In Orwell's *1984*, language is skillfully dismantled. The architects of Newspeak, a mind-dulling version of English, worked meticulously to eliminate hundreds of troublesome words. They dug like surgeons to rid the tongue of nuance and ambiguity. But are such efforts necessary? Given the drift of the common idiom, this is bound to happen anyway. Verbs will die out, nouns will perish, and we'll have no need of grammar. Eventually, even our similes will fade—all but that cheery, all-purpose phrase: "like a motherfucker."

Think about it. You can be as strong as a motherfucker, as sweet as a motherfucker, even as sexy as one. You can be as smart as a motherfucker, as brave as a motherfucker, also as fast as a motherfucker. If we give this infectious phrase full rein, it could dominate even further. "How did you bowl today, Papa?" I ask. "Like a motherfucker," he replies. "Mama, how was *American Idol*?" I coo. "Bitchin'," she says. "Those contestants sang like motherfuckers."

But why should a motherfucker, a partner in Oedipal incest, have the monopoly of a god? Why should he be *anything* but pitiful, loathsome, and vile? What qualifies him to be sexy, what licenses him to be sweet? How can he even be smart or fast unless he evades the police? That we can grant him Olympian stature is a dismal indictment of what language can become.

The denser the group, the thinner the language—that seems to be the rule. And the thinner the language, the more accessible the psyche to the polemics of excess. Consider a chat I overheard at the Indiana Penal Farm, an overpopulated Midwest prison where I worked as an inmate counselor. The conversation took place among several inmates sitting in the dining hall.

"So what did that officer do to you, Jackson, while you was in the hole?"

"The bitch took away my Cadillac then he put me on report."

"That ain't cool at all, bro. Can you believe that shit?"

"All I was doing was mindin' the store when that bitch got in my face. He been watchin' me like a motherfucker."

"Dog, that's Gestapo shit—know what I mean? What choo gonna do 'bout it?"

"Gonna dust his motherfuckin' ass off is what I'm gonna do."

In this incident of groupspeak, an inmate, aggrieved that an officer confiscated a rope made of towels, plans to knife him. Would this decision have happened without the perversion of language? Calling a rope a "Cadillac" lends it inordinate value. Describing a hit as a "dusting" diminishes its grisly effect. And of course that pet word, motherfucker, spices the whole exchange. Like ketchup poured over sodden fries, it facilitates easy digestion.

After locking Jackson up in the Special Housing Unit, I felt the call of a muse. So I wrote the incident into a script and distributed it to a self-help class: a group of thirty inmates to whom I taught interpersonal skills. I had begun to doubt the value of the course curriculum: the most adept of lawbreakers have excellent interpersonal skills. Unfortunately, they use them to con and, in some cases, seduce children. But the study of rhetoric seemed useful enough since language validates crime. And most of the devices of rhetoric were contained in that simple chat.

I chose several inmates, assigned them roles, and had them perform the incident as a skit. Afterwards, I quizzed the class on how language was misused. A few quick prompts were all I needed to illicit torrential responses.

"Hyperbole?" I asked them.

The class spoke almost in unison, "That's when Jackson's roadie said, 'Can you believe that shit?'"

"That's also a rhetorical question," I said. "Did you notice anything else?"

"When Jackson said he was mindin' the store, he hadda be dealin' drugs. The only use for a Cadillac is to pass contraband between cells. The fucker was *minimizing*."

"He also used a euphemism," I said. "Did you spot any more of those?"

The class paused only a moment before offering a case in point. "Jackson said he was gonna dust the officer off, like maybe the fucker had lint on his shirt. Ain't no dusting about it, he was gonna kill the dude."

"How about false analogies? You notice any of those?"

Hardly a minute passed before the class spoke up again. "Jackson's road dog said the Gestapo was there, but there weren't no Nazis around. Only an officer walkin' the range and tryin' to do his job."

"How about evading the question?" I asked. "Did Jackson dodge the issue when the officer wrote him up?"

The class heaved a collective sigh as though I were trying to be cute. With the certainty of a hanging judge, they spoke up once again. "He said the officer was spyin' on his ass. That ain't what was comin' down. The motherfuckin' issue was that Jackson was hustlin' drugs."

"How about labeling? Any of that?"

"He called the officer a bitch. A bitch *deserves* to be punished, bro, but a strict-ass officer don't."

Finishing the exercise, I placed them in groups and had them do skits of their own. After each skit, we discussed the scenario and reviewed the use of polemics. The quality of the skits was excellent, the observations astute. And when the class was over, the performers all took a bow.

Having witnessed their flexibility of mind, I was somewhat taken aback. Why, I wondered, did they allow themselves to wallow in toxic slang? Why had they been seduced by a jargon that could only sanctify crime? And why did most of them return to prison within five years of release?

Had I done them any good at all? I had no answer for that. My pitch was a proverbial shot in the dark—there was no way to gauge the results. But I remember overhearing an exchange in the yard while I was walking back to my office.

"Who that joker?" an inmate asked as I strode past the basketball courts.

"Our instructor," said another. "He's one cool-ass dude. Makes you think like a motherfucker."

∘ ∘ ∘

Bull Croc

TOM HEMMINGS, a college dropout, had not expected to find romance on a cattle station deep in Australia's Northern Territory. He had come to the Territory to reinvent himself, to cast away commitments, to lose himself in a consoling wilderness—an outland far removed from the lockstep of college and the shadow of the Vietnam War. And so he was better suited to heroic tests than tender moments. Still, he had necked with the head stockman's daughter after running into her on one of his evening strolls.

A scrawny girl with a weak chin, she was not particularly attractive, but her kiss had so aroused him that he had forgotten that he was to keep away from her—that Jim Cooper, the head stockman, usually kept her in his trailer when the drovers were in camp. "Don't go near her," Jim had warned him. "Mad as a hatter, she is. Been that way ever since her mum passed a year ago—poisoned by an ironwood splinter." Thankfully, the girl had tried to talk Tom into accepting Jesus—an offer that had restored him to his senses. Otherwise, he might have screwed her and gotten himself into a *real* entanglement. And, thankfully, he was gone from the homestead the following evening, riding in the boot of the Toyota with Andy, an Aboriginal fencer. *Forget that damn girl*, he told himself as Jim drove the vehicle south.

They were following the east bank of the Daly River, a large silty waterway a quarter mile wide that wound northwestward towards the Timor Sea. Their plan was to hug the shore of the Daly, hauling bogged cattle up its steep embankment as they traveled in the direction of Darkie's Hole, the most distant paddock on the station. In a day or two, when they had saved what stock they could, it would be time to trailer their horses and round up the cattle in Darkie's Hole.

The Toyota jounced aggressively—the trail along the Daly was poorly defined, the land a constant intercession of hummocks and creek beds. Big red boomers and blue-tinted does leapt out of their way, avoiding the bull bar by inches then thud-thud-thudding away to disappear among the hardwoods and cane grass. Occasionally, a village of termite castles—rock-solid pillars the height of a man—loomed in the headlights like ancient ruins, forcing Jim to steer carefully to avoid a collision that would have damaged only the vehicle.

Jim stopped the Toyota at intervals, allowing Tom to jump from the boot, slip-slide down the thirty foot embankment, and hook a winch cable to the horns of stranded cattle. The animals stiffened when Jim activated the winch, their horns plowing ruts in the dirt as they were dragged up the slope, sometimes to clear the top of the bluff, other times to topple back into the river, the top of their skulls popped off like bottle caps. The corpses, sweeping downriver, then vanished in a boil of water, dragged beneath the surface by estuarine crocodiles—salties Jim called them—that were attracted by the blood. "Now those crocs are as timid as lizards," he told Tom, "so you don't need to be worryin' about 'em. Not unless you're a wallaby, you don't." Despite these words, Tom watched the water closely as he hooked up the cattle, often convincing himself that what he saw was the tip of a floating log. He was frequently surprised when the log changed directions and moved against the current.

Late that evening, too tired to haul cattle any longer, they made camp in a grove of tea trees, stocking the fire with scrub wood and dining on a huge barramundi that Andy had caught in the river. The fish was charred and grainy but, being a change from bully beef, it elicited a stream of praise from Jim Cooper, who smacked his lips loudly as he ate.

"This'll put lead in your pencil," Jim said. "Won't have nothing to write on out here though—not unless you want to drive four hours to the nearest reservation. The lubras there will do you for a bottle of plock." Jim laughed and shook his head. "If they haven't found *Jesus*, they will."

Jim tossed a bone onto the fire, watching with interest as it burst into a yellow rose of flame. When the bone had withered to a crisp, he arose, belched, and emptied the rest of his scraps into the fire. He looked at Tom pleasantly before speaking again.

"Adrian went walkabout last night," he said. "She mentioned talking with you. When I asked her what about, she said it was none of me concern. Said the two of ya were lovers now, and there wasn't a bloody thing I could do about it. Likely as not, I'd have believed her if I didn't think she was out to get me goat."

Tom shook his head vigorously. "I was stretching my legs. I ran into her by accident. I didn't feel her up or anything."

"It's a mucker just running into her," Jim said. "She tried to convert ya, I'll bet, though I don't know what kinda sense it would make if she did. If ya want my opinion on the matter, she's a bit too randy to call herself a Jesus freak."

"I can see why you keep her in a trailer."

Chuckling, Jim pressed his tobacco tin. After popping it open, he poured a few brown strands onto a piece of rolling paper, tapping it with his index finger to spread the tobacco evenly. He sealed the cigarette then lit it with a twig from the fire.

"She *tried* to convert me," Tom said. "But all it did was turn me off. No woman is worth getting saved over."

"Good on ya," Jim said. "I don't want her knocked up—crazy as she is. She oughta be in Queensland with her aunt, but I doubt I'll ever get her there. Not with the way she's carrying on. She wants to stay in the Outback, she says. She wants to be close to where her mum died."

Jim blew a thin stream of smoke and watched the fire. When he spoke again, his voice was monotonic as though he were checking for an echo in a well bore.

"It's a rare few who can handle the Never-Never," he said. "Most folks can't for long. Drive 'em troppo, it would, if they didn't find little stories to tell themselves. Yarns are all they amount to, but they call 'em by fancier names. Taming this land—that's a *fine* little yarn. Salvation through Jesus is another. And the Aboriginals like to conjure up their tales about the Dreamtime. But utter rubbish is all it comes down to. The Outback isn't even listening."

"Have you told that to the missionaries?" Tom said.

Jim shrugged. "Bible bashers, I call 'em. They been here for years and they're worse than the clap. It only takes a few of 'em to muck it up for everyone else. Lubras won't have a thing to do with a bloke once they get 'emselves a dose of Jesus. Seen a bunch of lubras in a mission house once. They were bangin' on tambourines, singin' like sin, and there wasn't a *real* bang in the lot of 'em."

Jim tossed the butt. It flashed like a penny before disappearing among the coals but, a hundred feet away, Tom could see a more enduring glow. Perhaps it was the twin embers of a dingo's eyes. Or maybe it was the unblinking gaze of a saltie that had wandered upon dry land.

"Let me tell you something about Jesus," Jim said. "Biggest dust storm I seen started up on a Christmas day in Queensland. Banshee winds that howled for a week an' dust that turned noon into night. Lost a thousand head of sheep before it was over, not to mention a couple of black range riders who had managed to get caught in it. And the buggers had just gotten baptized to boot. Now I wonder what the Bible bashers would make out of something like that?"

Jim snorted without bitterness then stretched himself out upon his swag roll. He had placed his .303 beside him, but the rifle remained in its scabbard. It seemed, for this evening at least, that he would dispense with the ritual of cleaning his gun.

"You never did tell me her name," Tom said.

"Me dead wife?" Jim said. "Leona it was, but that's a bit of a mouthful, isn't it? Helen is what I called her. She wasn't a bad sort as far as sheilas go, but all she could ever talk about was going to live in Sydney. I told her finally she could go there with me blessin', but it looks like the Never-Never had other business with her. Didn't take much for it to spoil her big plans. Just a splinter of wood no bigger than a pin."

A movement on the river caught Tom's eye. When he looked more closely, he could make out a slender trunk moving gradually with the current. It could only be a mangrove tree, or a piece of one, but it still startled him. He had not expected to see floatage this late into the dry season.

"Now I've had better pokes from the lubras," Jim said, "but I won't say I don't miss her now and again. Still, I wish she had just up and left me 'stead of leavin' her flamin' spirit out here. At least it would have gotten that bloody Adrian out of me hair."

"You're stuck with Adrian," Tom said. "She swore that she'll *never* live anywhere else. I think she *likes* that fucking trailer."

Jim laughed. "The Outback took her spirit too. But the only salvation she'll find in it is the lock I'll be puttin' on the door."

The scrubland, as though emboldened by the thinning fire, was more visible now and a few grains of watery starlight appeared upon the river. The twin embers were fading along with the flames and, when they disappeared entirely, Tom thought he could make out the rangy form of a dingo scuttling towards the paperbarks. He looked towards Andy, hoping for reassurance, but the man was unpacking his swag, his face a mask of concentration. Tom's skin was now cold, his stomach was tight, and he felt his scalp prickle. And why was he missing that damn girl?

"That's the *trouble* with yarns," Jim said. "They'll last you for awhile if you're lucky, I guess, but the Outback hasn't got a bit of bloody use for 'em. Now it won't warn ya outright for puttin' your rubbish in front of the land, but if ya listen closely ya oughta hear it laughin' at ya."

Later that evening, as Jim began to snore, Tom sat and watched the river. He now noticed the opaque color of the water, an observation less attributable to the moonless evening than the bleak timber of Jim's words. That Jim could embrace cheerily what seemed to him better disregarded— the lengthening of shadows, the trickery of the dark, even the futility of firelight—was a mystery to him, and he wondered if he had perhaps read too much into Jim's words.

And then it came—just once and then silence—a guttural belch from somewhere on the river although it seemed, in the blackness of the night, to be only a few feet away: an erupting bellow so hollow and cold that only the stars in the vastness of the firmament seemed immune to its summons. Andy, upright upon his swag roll, was aware of it also, but he did not rise from his bed or reveal any other sign of alarm. His face was fading along with the coals and his voice, when he spoke at last, was distant and resigned.

"Bull croc," he said.

° ° °

Busting Willie Sherman

SINCE RETIRING from the San Francisco Probation Department and relocating to Sarasota, Florida, I have been lunching with Roscoe Bennett in a pizzeria on Route 41. We don't go there for the pizza, which tastes like warmed-up cardboard; we go for the happy hour and a generous choice of beers.

Roscoe, a former vice squad detective, is overbearing and loud, qualities I do not admire since I'm a compulsively private person. But we share too common a legacy for our differences to endure. Although Roscoe may be a vulgarian, we both are former cops, and so we are too easily tempted to match each other's war stories. It was in the spirit of comradery, our baptism of born of fire, that Roscoe told me about the time he busted Willie Sherman.

"Yah, it happened right here," said Roscoe in his lazy southern drawl. His voice bore a hint of pride, as though he had collared Al Capone, but Willie Sherman, an androgynous clown, did not seem to merit such swagger. Willie had once hosted a nationally televised children's show, and his mincing walk, staccato laugh, and elastic facial expressions suggested that he was already a captive of his trifling persona. But, when Sheriff detectives arrested him, the media took the bust seriously and plastered his Liliputian mug shot in newspapers across the country.

"So you were the one who brought him to justice," I said in a teasing tone. "I thought that happened at an adult movie theatre."

"It did," said Roscoe, pausing to belch. "The theater was right where we sit. This place was the South Trail Cinema before it became the Mellow Mushroom."

"I hope you allowed him to mellow his mushroom before you slapped him in cuffs."

"I let him finish—yah," said Roscoe. "Whaddya think I am?"

The hardon police, I said to myself, and I felt an uncomfortable anger. Had I been given an order to patrol an adult theatre and bust its sad clientele, I'd have told my chief to go fuck himself and handed him my badge.

"Tell me that wasn't your idea."

Roscoe folded his muscular arms and leaned back in his chair. His face was so broad and jovial that he looked like a tipsy Buddha. "Nah," he said, "but it *was* kind of fun. You know, we actually trained for it. We put pants on first aid dummies and sat them on rows of chairs. And then we tucked hotdogs into their crotches and practiced our arrests."

"You're kidding," I muttered.

"Not a bit," Roscoe said. "We couldn't go in half-cocked. Now if a dummy was holding his hotdog and the dog was still in his pants, we hadda let that go 'cause it didn't add up to indecent exposure. And if a dummy was holding the hotdog of a dummy sitting beside him, we hadda let that go also unless we could see the dog.

"But if a single inch of pooch was exposed, that was a legal pop. And it didn't matter whether the dummy was holding it or not."

"Didn't you feel rather intrusive?" I said.

"Nah, we gotta uphold the law. The sight of an unholstered wiener can traumatize someone for life."

"I doubt if anyone would have been shocked in that darkened movie theater."

"Maybe not," Roscoe said. "But if ya don't set firm standards, things'll get outta hand quick."

"You mean give them an inch and they'll take a mile."

"Exactly," Roscoe said. "Libraries, schools, and churches will never be safe again. Hell, it won't be long 'til the entire country has San Francisco values."

"So tell me how it went," I said, while hating myself for inquiring.

"We trained for two weeks," said Roscoe. "Up to ten hours a day. Ya can't leave nothing to chance when you're busting godless perverts. No telling what them sickos will do when you try to hook 'em up."

"Sounds like a pretty stiff challenge," I deadpanned.

"We rose to the occasion," joked Roscoe. "We dressed in jeans and old sweatshirts 'cause we wanted to look like slobs, and we practiced making arrests in teams so's to keep the odds in our favor. We even practiced buying tickets and popcorn while keeping our eyes half closed. Yer pupils have gotta be big as saucers when ya enter a den fulla perverts. Ya can't be protecting society if yer stumbling around half blind."

Roscoe grinned like a diva embracing an applause—he was clearly enjoying the strained fascination with which I listened to him.

I said, "Tell me about the day that you arrested Willie Sherman."

"We had been making busts for about a week," Roscoe said, "and we had become a well-practiced team. I was the spotter, which meant I sat in the theatre pretending to watch the movie. But all the time, I looked for stray franks outta the corner of my eye. My partner, Martinez, he was the relay—he sat at the back of the theatre. When one of them bums was done bleedin' his dog and shuffled back up the aisle, I signaled to Martinez so he could run out and alert the arrest team. As soon as that scumbag walked out the front door, the arrest team hooked him up, then they tossed him into the meat wagon so he could be hauled downtown for booking."

"And that's how you caught Willie Sherman?" I said.

"Yah, it was a textbook bust. 'Cept, at the time, I didn't know that he was Willie Sherman. He was wearing a beard and a hoodie when he walked into the theatre, and, all the time, he kept looking around like a shoplifter casing a store. I suspected right off that he was a flogger, and I sat down close to him. If we hadn't had to make our quota, we'd have probably called it a night, but we'd only busted three perverts so far and that number was pretty sad."

I said, "I guess you have to expect a slack night now and then."

"Not if the movies are spicy," said Roscoe. "But the movies were bad that night. They was showing a triple feature, and all three of them flicks were duds. We were thinking of asking the management to raise the quality of the flicks. If they were showing *Deep Throat* or *Debbie Does Dallas*, we'd have made our quota like that."

Roscoe snapped his fingers, making a sound like a chestnut popping. He then leisurely chugged a glass of beer and wiped the foam from his mouth.

"Wouldn't that be entrapment?" I said.

"Yah," said Roscoe, "I suppose it would. But I hadda wait thirty minutes while Willie sat there, snacking on quiche. Now I can't even stand the smell of quiche—only commies and perverts eat it. But I sat there, holdin' my nose, in order to save us from 'Frisco values."

"The free world owes you its thanks," I said, dryly.

"Nah, the thanks goes to a flick called *Nurse Nancy*—it wasn't quite as bad as the others. It was while they were showing *Nurse Nancy* that Willie released the hound. Well, I waited 'til he was finished 'cause that's the considerate thing to do, but, after he left his seat, I gave Martinez the signal."

"The poor little squirt," I said. "Did he put up a fight at all?"

"Yah," said Roscoe. "He fought like a ninja and bellowed like an ox. I could hear him out in the parking lot while I was sittin' inside the theatre, so

I pulled my taser outta my pocket and ran out to assist with the bust. Well, it took me and three other detectives to clap the bracelets onto him. From the way he was struggling to get away, you could tell that he had an agenda—that it wouldn't be long 'til he let slip the dog in libraries, churches, and schools."

Roscoe picked up a napkin and used it to blow his nose. He then yawned like a hippo and ordered a waitress to fetch him a pitcher of beer.

"And so you became a hero," I said.

"That ain't exactly what happened," said Roscoe. "But hold that thought for a minute 'cause I gotta take a leak."

•

AFTER HE DRAINED his lizard, Roscoe told me the rest of the story, and his voice took on the sobriety of a martyr facing the rack. It was a voice of noble disparagement, a voice of brave despair, a voice of an unbowed paladin whose toils had come to naught.

"When I got home," said Roscoe, "some shit began hitting the fan. By then everyone in the country knew how Willie Sherman got busted. They even knew he'd been packin' quiche when he moseyed into the theatre. Well, my wife she met me at the door and she looked me right in the eye, and she sez to me, 'Roscoe, tell me the truth. Were you involved in that?' Well, I sez to her, 'Honey, I wasn't involved no more than I hadda be. I wasn't involved no more than was needed to save us from 'Frisco values.' And she sez to me, 'Roscoe, you always think the country is going to hell. I doubt if we'd be dining on little French pies if you'd left that poor man alone.' 'He was defiling the public trust,' I sez. 'He was screaming like a baboon.' 'Oh really,' she sez. 'If that man was so ill-bred, he wouldn't have been eating tarts. And I doubt that he'd have been sitting there having some gentleman's time.'

"I sez, 'What are we gonna do about our libraries, churches, and schools?' And she sez, 'What's your daughter going to do without *The Willie Sherman Hour*?' Well, that's my daughter's favorite show, and I once saw her nibblin' quiche, so it wouldn't have hurt her none to be watchin' *Home Improvement* instead. But my wife she called me a fascist and she said no more nookie for you, so when I went back to that theater to bust some more perves, it was hard not to look at the screen. Hell, I kept getting stiff all the time I was keeping America safe."

"What an unfortunate ending," I said, although I felt little pity for him.

"That was just the *beginning*," said Roscoe. "Soon the public got involved. Folks picketed CBS in droves when it killed Willie Sherman's persona, and the Catholic Church received hundreds of letters asking that Willie be

canonized. And celebrities all over the country spoke out on Willie's behalf—
Zsa Zsa Gabor and Annette Funny Jello and Bill Cosby got involved. 'Course
a bust like that woulda been a step up for a fella like Bill Cosby."

"How sad," I said to Roscoe, and I paid for his pitcher of beer. "How sad
that our culture celebrates icons and leaves its true heroes unsung."

Roscoe topped his glass off. "Celebrate, hell," he said. "The public
worshipped that little fucker like he was the second coming of Christ. Hell,
signs started popping up everywhere like mushrooms after a rain. Signs that
said Free Our Willie, signs that said Willie for Pope, and the fertility clinics
were posting signs that said Willie, Send Us Your Seed. On top of that, a
buncha his fans held a prayer vigil in Bayfront Park, and dozens of mothers
all prayed that their sons would grow up to be just like Willie."

"That's about as bad as it gets," I conceded.

"Nah, it got a whole lot worse. Willie took a plea bargain for ten hours of
community service, so we had him picking up a buncha dead fish that washed
up on Siesta Key Beach. And that's when the American Civil Liberties issued
a proclamation. It said the Thirteenth Amendment abolished slavery over a
hundred years ago, and if we were going to have Willie pick up dead fish, we
oughta pay him for it. Well, I was supervising Willie while he was picking up
them fish, and, when the press came crowding around us, I made a public
statement. I said dead fish smell like pussy and Willie was ogling that, so Willie
oughta be happy to be pickin' up them fish up for nothing."

"So how did that make things worse?" I asked.

Roscoe frowned like a judge. "I was quoted in the *Sarasota Herald-
Tribune*, and I appeared on the local news. And the pervert lovers found
out where I lived, and they decorated my lawn. When I walked out of my
house the next morning, my whole lawn was covered with fish. There was
grouper, kingfish, and snapper. There was tarpon, sheepshead, and trout. It
looked like half the fish in the bay had been dumped on my front lawn.
And my wife came out on our front porch, and she told me this stupid
joke. She sez, 'Roscoe, how do men and fish get in trouble?' I sez to her, 'I
dunno.' And she sez, 'Men and fish get in trouble when they can't keep their
big mouths shut.' And my wife she took my daughter and she drove away in
our car, and the next day she sent me a divorce petition that was wrapped
around a cod."

When I offered to buy Roscoe some artichoke dip, he said, "Lemme
finish my story. We thought we was cleanin' the city up when our task force
snuck into that theatre. We thought we was busting the dregs of society and
getting them outta our hair. But, after a while, it seemed that we was nabbin'
the pillars instead. We arrested a banker and a gynecologist and a high school

principal. We arrested a surgeon, a football coach, and a coupla firemen. Hell, we even arrested a priest from a local Catholic church."

I said, 'What happened afterwards? Did the Knob Squad lose its pull?"

"The mayor shut us down," Roscoe said, "and none of them folks got charged. But we did nail Willie Sherman, and we can be proud about that."

° ° °

The Time Dad Took Me to a Whorehouse

ON THE DAY I turned seventeen, Dad gave me a surprise. We were sittin' in our kitchen and Dad was butterin' toast, and he said to me, 'Toby, today's the day I'm taking you to a whorehouse." I said to him, "Pa, you don't gotta do that. I don't have to pay for pussy." Dad said to me, "You ain't paying for it—I am." I said to him, "Save your money, Pa. I get all the pussy I want." Well, Dad he knows I ain't never had cooze, so he cackled like a hen. "If you're getting all the pussy you want," he said, "I guess you don't want *no* pussy."

Well, I said to him, "Pa, what's it matter to you if I ain't gettin' no snatch?" He said, "Ya been stealing my cock books—that's why. Once ya get a taste of the real thing, Toby, I'm hopin' that shit will stop." I said to him, "Pa, I ain't stealing your cock books. I swear on a stack of Bibles." Dad said, "Toby, I take offense when you use the Lord's name in vain." I said, "But I ain't stole your cock books. I swear on grandmother's grave."

Of course, I been swiping Dad's porno, but I ain't dumb enough to admit it. I figure if I keep on denying it, that'll mean it never happened. Anyhow, if Dad hadn't alphabetized them books, I'd have gotten away with it easy.

Well, Ma she came into the kitchen and heard our library talk. She said to me, "Toby, stop stealing Dad's porn. As long as he's pleasuring himself with those books, he won't be bothering me."

Dad shut up about the whorehouse because he didn't want Ma to know. But later that morning, he loaded me in his pickup and we headed for East Chicago. Dad said all the best whorehouses in the state can be found in East Chicago. "You don't gotta take me there, Pa," I said. "I swear I ain't stolen your books." Dad said, "Toby, if ya keep on lying you ain't gonna get to heaven"

Well, we got on US 231 and headed north to East Chicago, and Dad popped a cassette in the cassette player and we listened to a song. The song was "Another One Bites the Dust" by a group that calls itself Queen. Dad played the song a couple of times then he started to sing along. After singin' a couple of bars he said, "You ready to pop your cherry?"

"I'm ready, Pa," I told him, "if that's what I gotta do. But I'd rather be shootin' rats at the Putnam County dump."

Dad said, "There's a time for everything, Toby—that's what the Good Book preaches. There's a time to plant and a time to reap. A time to shoot rats and a time to go whorin'. There's a time for everything under the sun 'cept maybe stealing God's apple."

"I read the Good Book, Pa," I said. "It don't say nothin' 'bout cherries."

"It don't gotta say nothin' specific," Pa snapped. "It's there between the lines when ya read Ecclesiastes."

"So according to the Bible," I said, "it's time I had some snatch."

"Naw," said Pa. "It's way *past* time. It shoulda happened years ago. Son, if you had taken the matter in hand, we wouldn't be making this trip."

Now I don't think Pa can accuse me of not taking the matter in hand. But it made more sense to change the subject than speak in my defense.

"Hold old was you, Pa," I asked him, "when you did what the Good Book says?"

Dad told me about this cathouse he visited when he was thirteen. He told me how the madam took a liking to him and paid him to give her quickies. He said he bent her over her desk a couple of times every week, and she told him he was the best damn cocksmith she had ever met

"Was the Lord good with that?" I asked Pa.

Dad slipped a bottle out of the glove compartment and had him a swig of whiskey. Then he scratched his head all-thoughtful and talked more Bible talk. "Ain't ya read The Book of Revelation?" he said. "Ain't ya read about epic sin? Ain't ya read about how the Great Harlot spread fornication throughout the land? Well, ya might say I corralled the Great Harlot—the Lord hadda be good with that."

"Did you turn her into a sex slave?" I asked

Dad told me he put a collar around her neck and led her home from the whorehouse. And he kept her in the basement and fed her oysters and Spanish Fly. "But I finally let her go," he said. "I got to feelin' sorry for her. Hell, even the Great Harlot don't deserve to be stuck in no basement."

The thought of Pa taming the Queen of Darkness made me feel kinda ashamed. I felt bad that I stole his cock books, I felt bad that I told a big lie. I guess I have a long way to go before I measure up to Pa.

•

AS WE DROVE through East Chicago, I didn't feel too inspired. The city is full of refineries, adult shops, and subsidized housing projects. Well, we cruised along Euclid Avenue and we crossed some railroad tracks, and we pulled alongside this restaurant called A Taste of Bombay. Pa said to me, "Toby, ya gotta fuel up 'cause I booked you for an hour." I said to him, "Pa, thirty seconds is all I'm gonna need." Well, Pa he slapped his forehead as though he was swatting a wasp. He said, "Toby, you surprise me! Don'tcha wanna make the whore cum? It just ain't Christian to mount a whore and leave her unfulfilled."

Well, I hung my head like an egg-sucking dog that got caught with yoke on his snout. Guess it never even occurred to me that whores need pleasurin' too. "Didja make the Great Harlot cum?" I asked Pa. Pa said, "'Course I did, Toby. But ya don't need as much time for foreplay when you're humpin' the Great Harlot." I said, "How long's it take with a *regular* whore? I don't think I can last for no hour." Pa he patted me on the head and said, "Don't you worry about that. You'll be lustin' like a spring bull when you've had some Kama Sutra food."

Well, we went inside A Taste of Bombay, and Pa ordered me Indian grub. I had some butter chicken, I had some coconut chutney, I had some fried bananas that tasted sweeter than candy. But all that ginger and garlic didn't make me feel like no bull, and I knew I wouldn't do justice to Pa if I didn't put iron in my pud. So when Pa left the table to take a piss and no one was watchin' me, I took some coconut chutney and smeared it on my privates.

When we got back into the pickup, Dad quoted from the Gospels. He said, "'Love thy neighbor as thyself.'" "What's that mean?" I said to Pa. "Do I gotta yank him off too?" Pa said, "It means, when you go to a whorehouse, you act like a gentleman. You call the whore ma'am and you compliment her and you tell her a couple of jokes. I wouldn't be doing my duty, son, if I didn't teach you these things."

Before too long, Dad got us lost and we drove around in circles. We cruised up and down these neighborhoods that were full of weedy sidewalks, and gangs of dangerous looking kids were giving us the eye. I could tell Dad was getting nervous when he quoted from the Book of Psalms. "'Thy rod and thy staff they comfort me,'" he repeated again and again. When we finally spotted the cathouse, all I wanted to do was go home. The building needed a coat of paint, the lawn was burstin' with crabgrass, and that goddamn coconut chutney had glued my dong to my pants.

•

DAD PARKED THE PICKUP deep in the driveway, so no one would swipe our tires. And we climbed this narrow stairway that led to a tiny porch. A sign on the door said, No Solicitors, which kinda flummoxed me. Because Pa and I had come there in the spirit of the Lord.

Pa rapped on the door. The woman who answered it stared at us like we was tramps. She wore a pair of wire rimmed glasses and her hair was done up in a bun, and she asked Pa to pay for that hour before she showed us the girls. She didn't look like no madam—she looked like a high school math teacher.

Pa paid the woman two hundred bucks in twenty-dollar bills, and we followed her through this foyer that smelled like mildew and cats. We came to a parlor with a bunch of sofas and a giant television screen. And a dozen whores were sittin' on the sofas watchin' a rerun of *Cheers*. All of 'em were dressed in lingerie like they were posing for a commercial.

Most of the whores looked older 'an Ma, so I didn't feel too aroused. But there was one of 'em sittin' by herself that kinda caught my eye. She couldn't have been more than eighteen years old, she was thinner than a snake, and she was clutchin' a bottle of nail polish and paintin' her toenails black. When she looked directly at me, I noticed she had a beak nose, but her dark brown hair, hanging down to her waist, made her look sorta like the Madonna.

Well, Pa he slapped me on the back and introduced me to the whores. "This is Toby, my boy," he announced. "He likes it doggie style."

Some of the whores tittered and smiled at me, and one of 'em showed me her tits. But the one who looked like the Madonna acted like I had fleas. "Bow-wow," she said in a tired voice, and she went back to paintin' her toenails.

When the madam asked me to choose my whore, I picked the Madonna chick. The girl looked a little gloomy, like maybe she was bored, so I figured she was ripe for a bit of pleasurin'. After all, Pa had brought me here to share the gifts of the Lord.

The girl put the cap back on her nail polish bottle and tucked it into her bra. Then she held me by the elbow and guided me down this hallway. Although Pa had paid for an hour, she seemed a little impatient. "Hurry up, Toto," she said. "You're not in Kansas anymore."

She took me into the smallest room that I have ever seen. There was nothing in it but a bed, a dresser, and a tiny rusted sink. There were pictures stuck on the dresser mirror, all of them of some kid, and a poster of Brad Pitt was hanging on the wall.

I ain't sure the chick remembered my name 'cause she started calling me Jasper. It was better than calling me Toto, I guess, but not a whole lot better. Her voice was so flat that I almost decided not to make her cum.

"Come on, Jasper, let's get you washed up," she said as she undid my belt. She tugged down my zipper and lowered my jeans, and her eyes grew bigger than doorknobs. "What happened to your junk?" she said. "It smells like a coconut!"

"That's Kama Sutra paste," I said. "It's so I can pleasure you."

She rolled her eyes and laughed out loud, she seemed to be really amused. "I think you're supposed to eat it, Jasper, not smear it on your dick."

She made me stand in front of the sink and she washed my willie with soap, and it weren't but thirty seconds before I shot my load in her hands.

"Hey, Warren Beatty," she said to me. "You're a little bit quick on the draw."

When she saw me blushing and hanging my head, she walked me to the bed. She said I shoulda gone to Hardees instead and ordered myself a slider. She gave me a towel and I dried my dinky, and I pulled my pants back up. As I sat on the bed beside her, she started brushing her hair.

"Would you like some conversation?" she said. "You still have me for fifty-eight minutes."

"I ain't as good at conversing," I said. "I don't know too many jokes."

She brushed her hair 'til it crackled then smiled like Mona Lisa. "You were forced to come here, weren't you?" she said. She picked some loose hairs from the brush. "Let's talk awhile, Jasper, see what happens. Maybe you'll think up some jokes."

She told me her name was Brandi and she had a three-year-old son. She said she was going to community college to become a paralegal. She said she only worked in the whorehouse a couple times a week. The money paid for her tuition and daycare for her son. She said she was gonna stop fucking strangers when she had her associates degree.

Well, she dabbed her eyes with a Kleenex, and my pecker stayed limp as a worm. So I told her I won't be no stranger when we get around to fucking. I said I would drive back to see her once I have my learners' permit. And we could maybe go to a tractor pull before I take her to bed. "Ya look like a dream," I said to her even though she weren't that pretty. But I remembered how Pa told me to compliment a whore.

She thanked me for the compliment and she chucked the Kleenex away. And she gave me a kiss so tender it felt like it came from a virgin. "Dreams are dreams, aren't they, Jasper?" she said as she rose from the bed.

She dug into her dresser and pulled out a checker set, and we played five games of checkers before the hour was up. She won the first four games real quick—her mind was as sharp as a box cutter. I suspect she threw the final game outta Christian charity.

"I'm sure you'll do better next time," she said, and she gave me a little wink. I weren't sure if she was talkin' 'bout checkers or keepin' the juice in my spruce.

"Whatcha gonna tell Pa?" I said when she walked me back up the hallway. She was holding my hand kinda gentle, like maybe she'd caught a bird, but her nostrils flared at the mention of Pa. I think she was irked at him.

"Don't fret about your daddy," she snapped. "I'm going to take care of you."

When we walked into the parlor, she limped like a three-legged cat. She told Pa to pay her more money 'cause I musta bruised something inside her. And Pa, he grinned like a crocodile and hollered, "Praise the Lord!" And he pulled a wad of bills from his pocket and gave her a hundred dollars.

As the madam escorted us through the foyer, I felt like a stud Quarter Horse. She thanked me for my business and she gave me a Jonathan apple, and she looked at me with interest when she opened the front door. Pa gave her fifty dollars more then hurried me back down the stairway. I guess he wanted to get out of there while the tires were still on our truck.

·

WE DROVE outta East Chicago, and Pa kept ravin' like a preacher. He said I had done the family name proud, and I wouldn't need cock books no more. He said I deserved the key to the city, and that he couldn't have done better himself. He said it wouldn't be too long before whores were paying me.

Well, it woulda seemed like blasphemy not to believe my Pa. So I stuck out my chest like a gamecock, I said the Great Harlot had better watch out, and I told him Warren Beatty didn't have nothin' on me.

As we merged onto US 231, Pa popped the cassette back in the player. And all the way home we sang "Another One Bites the Dust."

∘ ∘ ∘

Busting Yu Yan

RETIREMENT HAS COMPENSATIONS, yet it's much like a haunted house. After leaving the San Francisco Probation Department and relocating to Sarasota, Florida, I've had dreams about the thirty years I spent mitigating crime: dreams where I wrestle bad guys, dreams where I stop a bullet, dreams where a waspish defense attorney vilifies me in court. And so I am eager to seek the company of other retired cops—perhaps too eager because I have lunch every day with Roscoe Bennett. Were he not a former vice squad detective, I would have nothing to do with him: he is boastful and unprincipled, he repeats himself all the time, and he's in the habit of salting his beer, which I find to be annoying. But we still lunch almost daily in Mello Mushroom Pizzeria, a building that replaced an adult movie theatre where Roscoe once worked undercover.

Roscoe often reminisces about combing adult theatres and bringing its patrons to justice, a debatable use of police power although one of his favorite duties. But a week ago he began a story he had never told me before. This time his target was not some poor joker abusing his fist in a theatre, but a woman who spared her clients the bother of performing that chore for themselves. Roscoe's voice, which blares like a trumpet, grew softer as he spoke, and his face wore the feckless composure of a phantom at a feast.

"Her name was Yu Yan," said Roscoe, as he folded his tree-trunk arms. "I caught her in a sting. While posing as a customer in an Asian spa, I got her to touch my cock."

"If you persuaded *her*," I said, "that sounds like a case of entrapment."

Roscoe ordered a pitcher of beer then filled up both our glasses. "Ya may be right," he conceded, "but that still didn't make the bust *easy*. I visited the parlor every night for a week before she crossed the line."

"Every night for a week?" I repeated. "Could you find nothing better to do?"

Roscoe shrugged. "This town doesn't *have* a better class of vice. And the mayor kept insisting he wanted the sex spas shut down. He said tourists need an environment as cheery as Walt Disney World, and them parlors were about as inviting as turds in a swimming pool."

I said, "Those whack-off lounges are pretty much closed already. Their lights are off, their blinds are pulled down, and I doubt that they're registered."

"They still offend some of the tourists," Roscoe said.

"You sure about that?" I replied. "I'll bet the only ones offended were the women you hauled off to jail."

Roscoe's face grew red—he does not like to be interrupted. "Ya wanna hear the story or not?" he snapped.

"All right," I said. "So tell me about the time that you busted Yu Yan."

•

ROSCOE DRAINED his glass of beer then quickly poured another. Foam crept over the rim of the glass as he continued to talk. "I have no use for them joints," he said, "and I'm gonna tell ya why. My dad caught the clap in one of 'em back when I was a kid. Hell, I heard him moanin' and groanin' every time he took a piss."

"He should have sued the place," I joked.

"He did sue," Roscoe said. "But the mama-san skipped town with the girls after the sheriff served the subpoena."

"Sounds like your dad got jerked around."

"Will ya stop with the puns," Roscoe said. "I guess he shouldn't have gone there, but he didn't deserve the clap. So when I got picked for the mayor's task force, I knew it was payback time."

"Sounds like payback was pretty slow coming."

"I toldja to stop with the puns. Now if ya don't wanna hear this story, we can talk about somethin' else."

"No, tell me the story," I said. "I want to know how you busted Yu Yan."

"Only five detectives got chosen," said Roscoe. "We each were assigned a big wad of cash and a parlor that needed bustin'. Mine was a joint called Hands of Gold—it used to be down on Gulf Gate Avenue among all them bars. I'd been hanging around there anyhow, ever since my last divorce, so it wasn't no inconvenience for me to work undercover there. Well, I put an audio device in my pocket to record the conversation, and I headed to the Hands of Gold parlor to bust me a prostitute.

"Now I wanted to look like a snowbird, so I wore an Orioles' cap. That made it appear like I'd come from up north so's to attend spring training. At eight o'clock in the evening, I knocked on the door of that place, and this mama-san, about eighty years old, let me into this tiny foyer. There wasn't nothin' in it but a few plastic chairs, a dusty desk, and a television set on a mount. The television was showing *Leave it to Beaver*, which I thought was kinda funny.

"The mama-san looked at me kinda suspicious, and she said to me, 'You a cop?' and I told her I'd just come there to cop myself a massage. I told her I'd driven down from Ohio, and my shoulders were tight as a banjo. Well, the mama-san called the girls in, and there was three of them. Two of them turned me off—their eyes were dull and tired-looking, and they hadda be in their fifties. But the third one looked about thirty years old, and she caught my eye right away. She wasn't exactly beautiful—her nose was hooked, her teeth were uneven, and she was as skinny as an otter—but she had a real pleasant manner about her, and that got me interested. Hell, she gazed at me with these big doe eyes and she gave me a little wink, and she blushed when I told the mama-san that she was the one I wanted. The mama-san made me cough up a fifty-dollar house fee, and she told me tips were accepted if I was pleased with my massage. 'You get only massage,' she told me. 'You no get a happy ending.' I suppose she hadda to say that in case she ended up in court.

"Well, I followed the dame I'd picked to this room that was smaller than even the foyer, and there was this portable massage table in it that looked yellower 'an a corpse. She introduced herself as Yu Yan and she gently shook my hand, and I was glad her grip was gentle 'cause her hand felt hard as stone. She asked me what my name was, and I said it was Roscoe Bennett. Yeah, I was there to bust her—stop grinning at me like that. I just didn't see no reason to lie about my name.

"Now the broad asked me if I was a cop, so I told her I was a snowbird, and she smiled and said, 'Roscoe Bennett, does that mean that you can't be a cop?'

"I stood there feelin' foolish 'cause I'd just put my foot in my mouth, and I was kinda relieved when she asked me to strip to my underpants. I yanked my shirt and pants off and I hung 'em on this rack, and I straightened my pants real careful so the recording device wouldn't fall out. After that, I lay down on the table and let her massage my back, and her fingers were stronger than whale's breath and my muscles started to howl. I heard her laugh as she worked on me, and her laughter was gentle as rain. 'Roscoe Bennett,' she said, 'I believe you are a cop.'

"'What makes ya say that, honey?' I said.

"'Your muscles are very tense,' she said. 'You are not relaxed, Roscoe Bennett. Is that because you came here to put poor me in jail?'

"'Honey,' I said, 'I'm a fertilizer salesman, and I'm here to watch some baseball.'

"'I hope that is true, Mister Bennett,' she said. 'A cop should not be so nervous.'

"She massaged my back and legs for an hour, and we chatted about this and that, and I had a king-sized hard-on when I finally rolled onto my back. She draped a sheet over it, and she patted me on the shoulder and said, 'Thank, you, Roscoe Bennett, for letting me work on you.'

"I asked her if I could come back tomorrow, and she said, 'Come anytime. You're a very nice man, I believe, even though I think you're a cop.'

"Now I didn't wanna to blow my cover until she crossed the line, so I shelled out an extra-large tip, the kind a rich tourist might give her. She giggled and said, 'Roscoe Bennett, this must be my lucky day.' And she tucked the money into her bra and blew me a little kiss."

"And was it?" I asked.

"Was it what?" Roscoe said.

"Was it her lucky day?"

"Naw," Roscoe said. "But I did kinda like her, and I wanted to know her better. I wasn't in too big a hurry for her to stroke my Johnson."

"How did you stretch things out?"

Roscoe groaned. "Will ya *please* stop with them puns? This is something I'm touchy about, and you're turning it into a joke."

"All right, I'll rephrase the question," I said. "How did you keep it up?"

"I went back to see her every night for a week, and, at first, she did most of the talking. I guess she was pretty lonely and was glad to have someone to talk to. She said she came from Beijing and she missed her family a lot, but she hadda come to Florida to keep house for her grandmother. She said her grandmother was very strict and scolded her like a peacock, but she kept house for her anyway because elders deserve respect.

"She also said she worked at this nail salon in downtown Sarasota, and that if I ever wanted a pedicure I could go and see her there. She said not to give her too big a tip if I went to the nail salon. 'You would make the owner *very jealous*,' she said. 'I do not wish to lose that job.'

"After a few days, she said, 'Oh Roscoe, I'm such a selfish woman. I have done so much yapping that you, my best customer, have had no chance to speak. Will you tell me about yourself, Roscoe Bennett, and forgive me for talking so much?'

"I was hopin' she wouldn't ask no questions 'cause my cover wasn't that great. And, also, her voice got hollow, like she was expectin' to hear bad news. I don't think she ever quite believed I wasn't no cop.

"Well, I told her about my three divorces, and I confessed I was an alcoholic, 'cause ya don't wanna lie more than ya hafta when you're trying

154

not to blow yer cover. But I don't know shit about fertilizer so I made a joke about that. I told her I was an *entremanure* and that's how I made a buck."

"Let me get this straight," I said. "This was a woman you were starting to like, and she was warming up to you. But the moment she offered to jerk you off, it was all going to come to an end."

"Yah," said Roscoe matter-of-factly. "That was it in a fucking nutshell. But I was hopin' she wouldn't offer 'cause I was liking her more and more. Ya know, I took her out on a date before I hadda cuff her up."

"A date," I said incredulously. "Where the hell did you go?"

"The Longhorn Steakhouse on Route 41, my favorite restaurant. I had a ten-ounce T-bone and she had chicken tenders. And I said to her 'Honey, I wish ya wouldn't keep workin' in that dump.'"

"Did you say that to sound like a tourist?" I said.

"Naw, I meant it," Roscoe said. "I really didn't want her to be a hooker no more.

"Well, she looked at me kinda angrily, like she'd heard that line too many times, and she said, 'Do not try to save me, Roscoe. I do not want to be saved.' Now she didn't come out and say it but I think she had this notion that, if I was going to save someone, I oughta start with myself.

"When we finished dinner, I asked her if she would like to go for a drive, and she suggested we go to the beach because the sun was about to set. So I drove her to Turtle Beach and we sat down on the sand, and we watched a fleet of pelicans go driftin' across the sky. She dug her toes into the sand like she was searchin' for gold doubloons, and she said to me, 'Roscoe, it makes me sad to watch the sun go down.'"

"So how did you manage to bust her," I asked, "if she was suspicious of you?"

"I hadda force things a little," said Roscoe. "The police were raiding massage parlors all over Sarasota—that's 'cause the rest of the task force was doin' its job better 'an me. And the sheriff called me into his office and asked why I was lagging behind. He said any detective worth his badge would have made a collar by now. Well, I told him I was workin' on it, and he said that I was too late. He said he already had enough evidence to raid the Hands of Gold."

"From another reluctant witness?" I guessed.

Roscoe nodded and sipped his beer. "Some john agreed to testify that he'd got a handjob there. Probably a repeat offender who was lookin' at prison time."

"So why did you need to bust her yourself?"

"I hadda save face! Whaddya think? I ain't no half-assed cop. Besides, I thought it'd be easier on her if she was arrested by me.

"So I begged the sheriff for one last chance to make a bust on my own. I guess he felt kinda sorry for me 'cause I was practically on my knees. He said he would give me one hour, and that was all I was gonna get.

"Well, I hurried on down to the Hands of Gold, and I musta looked a wreck. The mama-san stared at me like I was sick and asked if I'd like some tea, and she said she would waive the house fee since I seemed to be in a bad way. And when Yu Yan saw me, she gasped and said, 'What is the matter, Roscoe?' and I gave her a hundred dollar tip so she would hurry and cross the line. But when I was laying on the table and she was massaging my chest, I couldn't even get a hard-on. I was that upset.

"Well, her fingers brushed my willy a coupla times while she was workin' on my hips—it wasn't exactly a handjob, but it was gonna hafta do. So I pushed her away and got off the table and put my clothes back on, then I fished my handcuffs outta my pants and said she was under arrest. When I ordered her to turn around and put her hands behind her back, I didn't see no surprise on her face—she just looked kinda sad. It was how she looked on Turtle Beach when we was watchin' the sun go down."

•

ROSCOE EXCUSED himself from the table to grab a smoke outside, and I felt a sudden impatience for his story to come to an end. I was feeling a nagging compassion for him, and that would never do—not when he had every intention of remaining a rabid cop. So when Roscoe returned to the table, smelling like a chimney, I asked him to finish his story and stop beating around the bush.

Roscoe ordered another pitcher of beer and refilled both our glasses. Despite my gnawing impatience, he was determined to take his time. He sat for several minutes without offering a word, and when he spoke his voice was flat, like he was reading a traffic report.

"Well, I herded Yu Yan outta that joint and I put her in my car, and while we was sittin' next to each other, she finally spoke to me. She said, 'My wrists hurt, Roscoe, and I feel so sorry for you.' I said to her, 'Babe, I'm just doing my duty,' and that's when all hell broke loose. Two police sedans and a paddy wagon pulled up in front of the place, and their lights were racing like greyhounds and their sirens were squalling like cats, and half a dozen deputies scrambled outta the cars, and they barged into the parlor like they was stormin' the Alamo. While they was marching out the women and a coupla customers, Yu Yan said, 'Roscoe Bennett, what kind of duty is this?'

"I said I needed to know where she lived and she sat there biting her lip, then she gave me the address of her grandmother's house, which was up in Bradenton. Well, I drove her to her grandmother's place and it didn't look too invitin'—it was nothing but a broken-down bungalow that the city shoulda condemned. We sat in the car for a while then I took the cuffs offa her, and Yu Yan started rubbing her wrists 'cause I put 'em on a bit tight. She said, 'Roscoe, I told you already that I do not want to be saved.' 'Honey, it ain't you I'm savin',' I said, and I let her out of the car."

•

NOT WANTING to improve my opinion of him, I asked Roscoe, "Is there more?" My thirty years as a peace officer had inured me to sentimentality, so I was not going to cut him slack because of a single charitable deed.

"Yah, there's more," said Roscoe, and he slowly finished his beer. "Did I tell you she'd overstayed her visa and there was a warrant out on her, and that some of them girls we rounded up got deported back to China?"

"So you both overstayed your welcome," I said.

"Naw, that ain't exactly what happened. What happened is I married her steada handing her to the feds."

I sat as though I'd been tied to the chair—this was not something I wanted to know. My only consolation was the thought that he had acted selfishly.

"I did her no favor," Roscoe admitted. "She'd have been happier back in Beijing. But the marriage was good while it lasted—I gotta admit to that."

"What ended it?" I asked him.

"She kept workin' in them goddamn parlors," Roscoe said, "and I couldn't handle that. And she didn't like my boozing and hanging around the bars. But we lasted a year before splitting up, and it was a pretty good year."

"Would you call it a happy ending?" I asked.

Roscoe salted his beer. "It was happy enough," he said, "when ya consider the situation. She fell in love with a cop's cover, I fell in love with a whore. How much longer do you suppose something like that could last?"

∘ ∘ ∘

Shackles

Author's Note: Terminal Island is man-made. Home to a federal penitentiary, it is located between Long Beach and San Pedro.

THE HOLDING CELLS sat unobtrusively behind the booking counter of the San Francisco County Jail. They were small—eight by ten feet—with stone partitions hiding the toilets. The floors of the cells were freshly-mopped and glittered from the iridescent ceiling lights. The metal sinks had also been cleaned, but the light did not linger upon them.

The cells were all empty except one in which a drunk was napping. He had been picked up an hour ago by a cop on a morning patrol. The drunk lay prone on one of the benches attached to the wall of his cell. His ragged snores filled the booking area from behind the security glass.

Footsteps sounded, remote and then louder. The door to the main jail rolled open. A small cloud of men walked into the booking area and crowded around the counter. Two of the men were federal marshals wearing Second Chance vests. The other two men were bound by chains and dressed in cheap woolen suits. The marshals held their elbows, protecting them from a fall.

The group waited at the booking counter to pick up certificates of release. While a deputy sheriff completed this paperwork, the men stood patiently. The men in restraints, both federal prisoners, were in transit to Terminal Island. They had been sentenced a few days ago in District Court and were no longer wards of the county.

The marshals pocketed the certificates of release, and the group filed past the counter. There would be an unexplained delay until they were on the road. In the meantime, the two prisoners would be housed temporarily in one of the holding cells.

One of prisoners was blonde and thin. His hands, slim and feminine, peeked from his coat sleeves, fingering his waist chain as he tripped towards the cells. His companion, a black, walked tactfully behind him. A plump,

158

gray-haired man with a cheerful face, he looked as though he could have been a cab driver.

The men paused in front of an empty cell while the marshals removed their restraints. They unshackled the blonde man first, undoing his handcuffs and waist chain. He stood as still as a statue until his leg irons were also removed.

A circuit hummed, the glass door crept sideways. The blonde man walked into the cell. The door remained open while the marshals removed the plump man's chains and cuffs. After the plump man strode into the cell, the door slid home, setting the lock.

The plump man sighed like a kettle then stepped behind the toilet partition. The sound of his urine filled the cell as it peppered the toilet bowl. Zipping his fly up, he crossed the floor and rinsed his hands at the sink. He then sat beside the blonde man who was perched on one of the benches.

"Hey!" said the plump man.

The blonde man looked at him as though noticing him for the first time.

"Are we going by car?" the plump man asked.

As though pondering a matter of epic importance, the other stroked his jaw. "How should I know?" he said finally. "They never tell you these things."

"I hope they're taking us by car. I always puke on planes."

The blonde man yawned; he seemed bored with the topic. "They woke us up early," he groused.

"They want us gone," his cellmate said. "The police are cleaning the streets up for Christmas. The jail is gonna need our beds."

Frowning, the blonde man kept rubbing his wrists. "I didn't get any breakfast."

"Don't worry about that," the other man said.

The blonde man shrugged and kept stroking his wrists. "I guess it's worth missing a meal or two to get out of this goddamn jail."

"For sure," said the plump man. "We'll eat on the road. We might even stop at a Denny's." As he spoke, he reached into his jacket pocket and produced a pack of Camels. He placed a cigarette between his lips then slowly struck a match. Cupping the flame as though trapping a moth, he lit the cigarette.

He extended the pack to the blonde man who eyed it warily.

The plump man said, "Fuck it. We're leaving this shit hole. They can't put us on report."

The pack of Camels was contraband, and the blonde man hesitated. He finally selected a cigarette as though it were crawling with ants. He placed the butt between his lips; the plump man struck another match. The flame nodded like a puppet as the blonde man accepted the light.

The men smoked for a while in silence. Their ashes littered the floor. The blonde man pinched out his cigarette and looked at his companion.

"No need to save it," the plump man said. "The marshals can buy you more. You're allowed to smoke on the road."

The blonde man tossed the butt on the floor. "Will they buy me razor blades?" he said. "I'm gonna miss today's call-out for commissary. I'm flat out of razor blades."

"Don't be trippin' about that," said the other. "When we arrive, we'll go straight to the fish dorm. The fish dorm lets you go to the commissary every single night."

"You been to Terminal Island before?"

"Once. I did five years there for mail fraud. I'm going back on another nickel 'cause I pulled that same hustle again."

The blonde man rubbed his temples. "A nickel for mail fraud, Jesus? They gave me a goddamn dime just for passing counterfeit cash. But they mighta given me a nickel if I had chosen to plead out the case."

The plump man bowed his head like a mourner. "Ten years for passing fake money ain't right. It ain't like someone got hurt."

"No one got screwed but me," said the blonde man. "But I'm not blaming it on the judge. I should never have taken the case to trial with a goddamn public defender."

His companion frowned then clucked his tongue. "Unless you can post an appeal bond, you just got fucked in the ass."

"I'm going to petition for one," said the blonde man. "How's the law library there?"

"It's up-to-date and the law clerks are smart. But you better stock up on cigarettes because they'll charge you an arm and a leg."

The blonde man waved his hand as though shooing away a fly. "I'm not relying on jailhouse lawyers. I'll write that petition myself."

"If you want to prepare your own brief," said the other, "make sure the prison don't give you a job."

"How do I do that?"

The plump man dropped his butt, crushing it under his heel. "When you go in front of the classification board, tell 'em you're too sick to work. That way you can spend all day with the lawbooks working on your case."

The blonde man smiled. "That'll do me just fine. There were plenty of legal issues that my public defender never brought up."

"An appeal bond sounds like a long shot," said the other. "But if you get one, pay with a cashier's check. Don't give the court none of that funny money or you'll end up back in the slammer."

The two men laughed as though this remark were the funniest thing in the world. They did not at once notice that the marshals had returned with another traveler in restraints. Only when they heard the traveler's voice did they stop their conversation.

The traveler was lanky with a neat black moustache. He wore a stylish maroon suit that hugged his lean frame like a glove. Although he had a sunken chest, his voice boomed throughout the jail. He was deeply upset with the deputy sheriff behind the booking counter.

After a minute, the marshals walked the loud prisoner to the cell where the men were housed. The prisoner's legs were unchained, and he walked with an exaggerated limp. While the marshals removed his restraints, he stood on one leg like a stork.

The door to the cell lurched sideways. The man hopped into the cell. He collapsed on one of the benches as the door crawled back into place.

The blonde man looked at him nervously. "Are you Tom Bunker?" he asked.

"No, I'm not!" the lean man snapped. "Why the fuck did you ask me that?"

"The newspapers say he's the next John Dillinger. You look kinda like him, you know."

The lean man said nothing. He eased his hip sideways then lifted his injured leg onto the bench. It was plain he would need some time to adjust before making the effort to converse.

The blonde man said, "He was sentenced last week while we were in the federal courthouse. The halls were so crammed with reporters we could hardly get out of there."

The lean man still did not answer. He slapped his thigh like a parent disciplining an unruly child. When the force of his blow knocked his leg from the bench, he muttered an angry oath. He raised his head and stared at the blonde man.

"Why all this talk about Bunker?" he snapped. "He's just some crackhead from Oakland who robbed a couple of banks. Just 'cause he got his name in the paper don't make him our concern."

"I feel kinda sorry for him—that's all. They gave him fifty years."

"If anyone's dumb enough to hit banks, he deserves every day he gets. There's been too many bank jobs pulled lately—the public is tired of that."

"Even for banks that's a pretty long sentence."

"Fuck him," the lean man said. "This is a damn good state if you lay off the banks. It can stick you with three felonies and free you in half that time."

"What got you nabbed?"

The lean man coughed—he seemed to be embarrassed. "My buddy and I stuck up a mail carrier," he said in a voice that could pickle fruit. "We scared him is all and just heisted his truck. We just wanted to score some shit we could pawn and maybe some checks we could alter."

"If you don't mind my saying," the plump man said, "that sounds a little reckless."

The man hung his head, avoiding the other's gaze. "We *would* have gotten away with it, but there was a stalled vehicle blocking Highway 101. The road was congested and we got stuck in the slow lane. We got in a three-car pileup before the cops put us in handcuffs."

The plump man spoke as though calming an infant. "Guess it wasn't your fault you got caught."

"Well, this cop car rammed us from behind—*that's* what caused the pileup. But no one was hurt and I caught just one slug. We had already tossed our guns away, so the pig didn't need to shoot me."

"Did you cop a plea?"

"Didn't have much choice. You can't go in front of a jury on public endangerment charges."

"How much time did you cop to?"

The man grimaced and stroked his injured leg. "A quarter," he spat—he spoke like a man who had been swindled at poker. "I got twenty-five years on the robbery charge and a nickel for stealing the truck. But at least the judge didn't run 'em wild. I pretended to tremble when he sentenced me, so he ran the nickel concurrent."

"Are they taking you to San Quentin?"

"Naw, they gave me federal time. According to them marshals, I'm going to Terminal Island."

"How come a hothead like you is going to Terminal Island?"

"The judge said the maximum security prisons are too overcrowded to take me."

"Guess you'll be traveling with us," said the plump man.

"I heard there was gonna be three."

"Do you know if we're going by car?"

The lean man shrugged. "Those rent-a-cop marshals didn't tell me nothin' else."

The blonde man broke in. "Did they say when we're leaving?"

"I hope it's gonna be soon," griped the plump man, "We got an all-day drive."

"You been there?" asked the lean man.

"Once."

"Is it hard to get phone calls? I'm calling my lawyer. I'm kinda pissed at the bitch."

"When we get there, you're set. Just ask for that phone the moment you get to the fish dorm."

"How often they let you use the phone?"

"You can sign up for the phone every day, and you can talk for up to ten minutes. And mail goes out twice a week if you want to post a letter instead."

"How many letters can you send out a week?"

"Three personal letters are all you're allowed—they gotta check 'em for contraband. But if you make friends with the chaplain, he'll mail all the letters you want."

The lean man cracked his knuckles. "How long 'til they give you a job?"

"Not long if you're able to work," said the other.

"I'll work when my leg is fit. Maybe as a butcher. I hear you earn good time for learning a trade."

The plump man shrugged. "A few months maybe—you're gonna serve most of that quarter. But the food service jobs pay good money."

"How much?"

"Up to thirty dollars a month."

"Is that enough cash to buy crack and booze?"

"Thirty dollars will buy you whatever you want. Coke, speed, homemade hooch—it's all available cheap."

"Is that right?" said the lean man.

The plump man chuckled. "Even blow jobs are cheap. There's trannies who will suck you off for a dollar, and some of 'em look just like women."

"Is that right?"

The plump man nodded and blew his nose, making a sound like a trumpet. "When you draw your pay, go to the commissary first and spend a few dollars there. That way the guards won't wonder if you're buying contraband."

The lean man stretched. "How's the gambling?"

"Great. And there's no better way to kill time. The bookies there are honest and won't shank you if you win big."

"Where's the best action?"

"The softball games. Providin' you watch the teams carefully and make sure you get decent odds."

"Are they good?" asked the lean man.

"Most of them are—they play every day. They keep the same teams so they gotta be good."

The man flexed his leg. "Is there a weight pile?" he said. "I gotta strengthen my leg."

"They got weights in the gym."

"Can you make use of them?"

"There's usually a crowd at the weight pile—forty or fifty men. But if you give them a couple of cigarettes, I'm sure they'll work you in."

There was movement outside their cell. The men paused in their conversation. Through the transparent door, they could see a trustee pushing a lunch cart in their direction. Framed by the cell door, the trustee looked at them then passed from their view like a ghost. His voice could be heard at a neighboring cell; he was offering the drunk some lunch.

They heard a cell door roll open then slide back to lock once again. Seconds later, they saw the trustee pushing the cart away.

"Seems we missed another meal," said the blonde man.

The plump man patted him on the arm. "That means the marshals are coming to get us. They can't hold us here past lunch."

The lean man snorted. "It's high time they fetched us. I didn't cop to that goddamn plea just to sit in jail all day."

The plump man said, "Where was you housed you before you took that plea? I don't remember seeing you on the main range."

"They put me in segregation."

"How long was you there?"

"Three months."

The plump man whistled. "Sheeit, the hole ain't no way to do time."

The lean man spoke as though chastised. "It wasn't so bad in the hole. I got to go to the gym every day, and the trustees snuck me porn."

"How come you was put in the hole in the first place?"

"I beat up a tranny. The bitch made me hit her. She tried to charge me ten bucks for a handjob. Fuck that kind of shit."

"How come you didn't talk her price down?"

The lean man glared and again rubbed his leg. "I come from South San Francisco—that's why. A man don't put up with swindlers if he comes from South San Francisco."

The plump man rolled his eyes and drew a labored breath. His voice was soft and protective when he spoke to the lean man again. "Think about what you're sayin', son. You went to the hole over the price of a handjob, and you could have done it yourself."

"Staying out of the hole ain't worth it if I gotta take crap from trannies."

"Maybe and maybe not," said the plump man. "Now what's true for South San Francisco ain't true for Terminal Island."

"I don't mind paying a buck for a blow job. That doesn't insult me none."

"Well, you don't gotta beat up hustlers, son—you just gotta agree on a price. Keep pulling that kind of bullshit, and you'll get shipped to a *hard-ass* prison."

"I've been to San Quintin," the lean man bragged. "I didn't take crap there either."

"At Terminal Island," the plump man said, "there ain't that much shit to take. Just be on your bunk three times a day, so the guards can take the count. The rest of the time, you can work at a job or go to programs or recreation."

"How are the programs?"

"The programs are fun. There's drama clubs, college courses, public speaking classes. And they don't watch you too close in them classrooms—it's easy to score liquor and drugs."

"Where did they assign you when you were there last?"

"I collected trash—now that's a good job. It gave me the run of the place, so I hope I can get it back. I hid cigarettes, pot, and porn in the trash bins and ran a traveling store."

"Is that right?" the lean man repeated. He seemed to be deeply impressed. "I might just run a store of my own if you don't mind competition."

The plump man grinned. "That won't bother me none. They got a free market there."

"I sold some meth when I was at Quintin—hid it in my butt-crack. How hard do the guards ride your ass at the Isle?"

"The guards ain't gonna strip-search you unless someone snitches you out. Just watch out who you do business with and be on your bunk for the counts. Except for being counted three times a day, you'll forget that you're in prison."

"How long do they take for those counts?"

"They usually take twenty minutes unless the count doesn't clear. If a count doesn't clear, it may take the guards half the day to get it right."

Shaking his head, the lean man spoke as though his pocket had just been picked. "I didn't cop to that goddamn plea to sit on a bunk all day."

"Just take a nap," the plump man said, "or maybe read a book. It ain't gonna cost you your hustle to let 'em have their count."

The three of them laughed at this curious conclusion. The lean man sat forward and peered through the glass door. The marshals were back in the booking bay. They were sorting out the shackles.

"They come to fetch us," the lean man said.

"They took their sweet time," the blonde man replied.

The plump man scowled. "They took our time also. We're done with this shithole and due at the Isle."

"How long 'til we get there?" the lean man inquired.

"A while," said the plump man. "Six hours if it's by car. But that ain't no worry. It's well worth the journey. We're gonna forget we been locked up at all."

o o o

Acknowledgements

Foremost, I would like to thank my father, Clyde James Hanna, for instilling in me the love of reading. To him, I have dedicated this book. I would also like to thank my wife, Mary, for supporting my ambition to become a published writer. And a big thanks goes to my mother, Catherine, for helping me get myself born.

I am grateful to the following members of my California critique group for their input: Lisa, Chris, Bardi, and Ann. And a big thank you goes to my Florida critique group: Robert, Marisa, Teri, Pam, Shirley, Elizabeth, and Teresa.

Kudos to the open mic programs where many of these stories were first read to an audience: Reach and Teach in Redwood City and Wordier than Thou in Sarasota. And a tip of the hat to the many readers who helped bring these stories alive.

Again, special thanks goes to Tory Hartmann, my publisher, friend, and chief editor. Without her, this book would not have been possible.

Thank you for reading *Shackles and More Gripping Tales*. If you enjoyed it, please consider telling your friends or posting a short customer review on Amazon. Word of mouth is an author's best friend and much appreciated.

About James Hanna

JAMES HANNA roamed Australia for seven years before settling on a career in criminal justice. He spent twenty years as a counselor in the Indiana Department of Corrections, and recently retired from the San Francisco Probation Department where he was assigned to a domestic violence and stalking unit.

James' familiarity with the criminal element has provided fodder for much of his writing. His debute novel, *The Siege*, depicts a hostage standoff in a penal facility. Rob Slavens, Top 100 Reviewer, writes: "This is the raw, gritty, and complex reality of life in prison, and the best of its genre that I have ever come across."

Call Me Pomeroy, James' second novel, chronicles the madcap tales of a street musician on parole who joins Occupy Oakland and its spinoff movements in England and France. He does not join for political reasons but to get on television, attract an agent, and land a million dollar recording contract. The first chapter, appearing in *Empty Sink Publishing*, was deemed Editor's Choice for that issue.

James' short stories are written in many genres, including science fiction. His tales are published in those journals that like stories written in blood. Stories that deal with unvarnished truth over political correctness. *Red Savina Review*, *The Literary Review*, *Crack the Spine*, and *Sixfold* have all published James' stories. Many of James' stories appear in *A Second, Less Capable Head and Other Rogue Stories*, his third book.

James' books received two gold medals and a bronze from Readers' Favorite International Awards and a silver medal from Independent Press Awards. Three of his short stories were nominated for the Pushcart Prize.